Looks Real Good Now

DETROIT PANTHERS 1

SOPHIE THOMAS

Book Cover: Ink and Laurel

Editing: Hummingbird Editing

Proofreading: Glitter Penned Edits

First edition 2024

<h1 style="text-align:center">Author's Note</h1>

Hi, Hey, Hello!

Thank you so much for picking up my little Christmas romance story. A couple of things before you get started; firstly, despite being set in New York, this book is written in British English because nothing will make me give up those 'u's'. Secondly this book contains explicit sexual content and swearing.

Dicktionary
The below chapters contain sexual content
Chapter 15
Chapter 23
Chapter 24
Chapter 27
Chapter 28
Chapter 34
Chapter 36
Chapter 40
Chapter 45

Playlist

1 champagne problems – Taylor Swift
2 'tis the damn season – Taylor Swift
3 Love Again – Dua Lipa
4 So My Darling – Rachel Chinouriri
5 everything – John K
6 Nervous – John Legend
7 This Love (Taylor's Version) – Taylor Swift
8 II MOST WANTED – Beyoncé & Miley Cyrus
9 Forever and a Day – Benson Boone
10 Lost My Mind – FINNEAS
11 Sweet Nothing – Taylor Swift
12 Think I'm In Love With You – Chris Stapleton
13 The Idea of You – Nicholas Galitzine & Anne-Marie
14 Freakum Dress – Beyoncé
15 Church – Chase Atlantic
16 Sideways – Carly Rae Jepsen
17 So Hot that it Hurts – VOILÁ
18 Heaven's Gate – Fall Out Boy
19 I Surrender – Celine Dion

20 Nobody – OneRepublic
21 Easy Distraction – James Bay
22 That You Are – Hozier & Bedouine
23 You Are In Love (Taylor's Version) – Taylor Swift

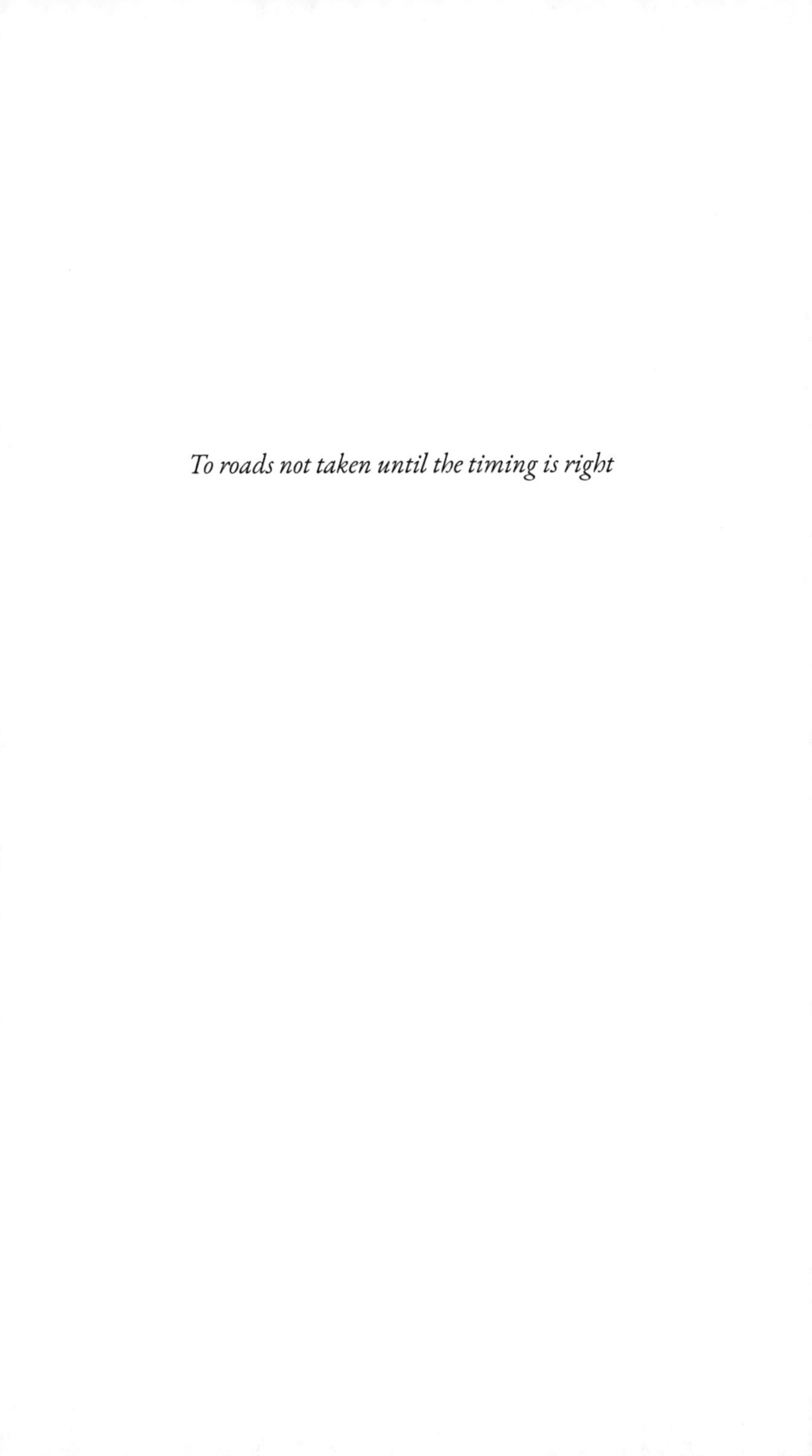

To roads not taken until the timing is right

One

LIAM

The last time I saw Alana Fitzpatrick was the morning of our high school prom.

Before I could muster up the courage to ask her to be my date, Teddy informed me that I would be going with one of the cheerleader twins. Lenny hadn't been all that bothered by the whole thing when I told her, so I assumed she was fine with the idea of going to the prom on her own. She wouldn't have been on *her own* because even though we were saying we had dates, we would have all hung out in a big group. But she also wouldn't have an official date, and I didn't want her to be caught off guard by it.

Her indifference to the whole thing made much more sense when I discovered that by the morning of our prom, she knew she was leaving the state before we officially finished senior year.

How she managed to get out of a graduation ceremony where she was our year's valedictorian, I never found out. But she managed it, and so, with no warning, I had to spend the last few weeks of my high school career explaining that no, I didn't know where my best friend had gone and pretend that I wasn't dying inside.

I'd had a mostly great high school career. My senior year was the cherry on top of that particular sundae, but whenever I thought back to those years, I could only remember two things: one, was how good it felt to put a trophy in the high school trophy cabinet, and the second was the look of surprise on Lenny's mom, Stassie's, face when I'd called to check on her after prom had finished and she realised she was going to be the one to tell me that Alana had already gone to Michigan for college.

Michigan.

I hadn't even realised that she had applied to UoM, let alone been accepted and chosen to go.

Suddenly, the future that I had planned was a blank page and I had to figure out how to be a person without Lenny doing life right by my side.

Twelve years ago, I said 'See you later' to my best friend not knowing that I wouldn't see her again. A feat that was especially impressive because I moved to the same city she'd fled to four years ago. I had put a lot of work into avoiding running into a woman who had cut herself cleanly out of her own life. I could only assume that she put equal effort into avoiding me because my arrival in Detroit wasn't exactly a secret.

I wouldn't have thought it to be true, given how much time had passed, but it turned out that I could still pick her out in a crowd. I still knew the exact slope of her shoulders, the cut of her jaw, and the way it led into her long neck. That one curl at the nape that never stayed tied up after she singed it off when we were thirteen because she thought having straight hair would make her less of a target to the taunts of teenage girls. I could spot the silver ring she started wearing on her thumb when we were fifteen from a mile off because she was always losing it, and I was always finding it. I couldn't help but wonder if she was still doing the former and who was now doing the latter.

I hadn't seen my best friend for twelve years and now we were both standing there, facing each other, in Detroit Metropolitan Airport two weeks before Christmas.

Two

ALANA

It's one of those rare yes or no questions that has a right and wrong answer, and the right answer is always 'yes'.

If you had asked me this time last year if I would say yes when my boyfriend of eight years, Kai, asked me to marry him, I would have said, *"Of course I would."* Heck, if you asked me the morning he proposed, I would have said the same. We had already built a life together, so marriage was the natural next step.

It never would have occurred to me to say no. Or, more accurately, to not say anything at all. But an awkward silence is just as much of an answer as an outright 'no'.

It had been two months since that night, and I kept seeing Kai's face. The love, joy, and hope shining in his eyes as he dropped onto one knee and opened the small, velvet box. The glance he gave the ring, the perfect ring if I was being honest, before he cast those hopeful eyes back at me. The choked-up way he had asked the question.

"Alana Fitzpatrick, will you do me the honour of becoming my wife?"

I could still hear the collective inhale from his family and our friends that they held in preparation to let out a cheer. A celebration. But I was a touch too slow. The silence went on a fraction too long.

The collective breath was released slowly, instead. The hopeful look in Kai's eyes died a slow death. I tried to claw it back. I tried to say something, *anything*, but I couldn't find the words. The box snapped shut. Kai pushed back up to his feet and for the first time in a long time, I felt small.

It should have been the easiest yes of my life and yet it wasn't even close. I have a lot of regrets about that night, but not saying yes isn't one of them.

Which is why I now found myself at Metropolitan Airport waiting for a flight to New York. My initial plans had been to spend two weeks in Aspen with Kai's family, which died the moment I left him high and dry on one knee. So, I was faced with a choice. I could either spend the holidays alone or I could go home. I chose home.

"Lenny?"

I had been so in my head that I zoned out of my surroundings, but that voice pulled me back. The grinding of beans and the buzz of conversation around me came back into focus. I knew that voice. I knew that name too. It was mine, but only to one person. Someone I had done a very good job of physically avoiding for over twelve years.

But when I turned around and set my eyes on him, standing there looking larger than life against the red airport cafe backdrop, I couldn't quite remember why I left Liam Mulligan behind.

Three

ALANA

"Muller." The old nickname rolled off my tongue like it was second nature. Once upon a time, it was. I saw his eyes brighten and then I noticed him holding the coffee with 'Alana' written on the side. I hadn't heard the barista call my name.

"I believe this is yours." He handed me the coffee and I took a greedy sip.

"Thanks," I sighed as the drink ran a heated path down my throat.

"You going home for the holidays?" he asked slowly. Awkwardly.

"Yeah, you?"

"Yeah, surprisingly I've missed Christmas in New York and now that I don't have to think about work, I can really go and make the most of it."

"Oh yeah, I saw that you retired. Sent quite the shockwave through the sporting world." The universe works in funny ways and so, although I tried to cut myself off from Liam completely, the universe gave me a boyfriend who was deeply invested in the professional career of one Liam 'Gunner' Mulligan. Christmas came early when Liam transferred to Kai's home team, the Detroit Panthers.

I knew way more about Liam than I had ever intended.

I pretended that I didn't care about any of it, but I stored everything Kai told me about Liam away in a special corner of my brain. When Kai found out that Liam was retiring, he had reacted in such a way that I thought something terrible had happened. When he told me what he was freaking out about, I felt relief on two levels. One, that everything was okay, and two, that Liam was getting out before he could do himself some real damage.

"Everyone has to retire at some point," he said. It sounded rehearsed. And tired.

"Yeah, but why then?" I'd heard a lot of opinions. The consensus was that he had still time left in him, and he was throwing it all away by retiring when he was in his prime.

"I got slammed into the boards and did something to my shoulder again. I was sitting in the PT's office, and they started talking about all the ways I could rehab it so that I was ready for the pre-season, and I realised I didn't want it anymore. I didn't want to live for a sport and only a sport, I wanted to just live."

Liam first tore his rotator cuff when we were seventeen and it led to months of me reminding him that he was more than just a hockey player and trying to stop him from thinking his life was over if he wasn't on the ice. He made it to his junior year of college before he injured it again. Then again at twenty-five. It played up quite a bit the following season as well but it wasn't bad enough for him to have to sit out.

Between Kai and my hockey coach (and his high school coach) Dad, I had heard a lot about this shoulder injury and its impact on Liam in college and professionally.

"I told you there was more to life than skating around on rink. Multiple times if I remember correctly," I said it with a level of familiarity that we didn't have anymore, but the longer we talked, the easier it was to fall into our old rhythm.

"You definitely did, but that doesn't change the fact that, at some point when I was a kid, hockey chose me and kept choosing me the bigger and more assured on the ice I got."

I didn't mean to, at least not consciously, but my thoughts wandered to an underwear advert that had been plastered around the city not long ago. Liam had been all chiselled abs and thick, muscular thighs that I wanted to sit on, curled up against his chest, which looked like both marble and the softest pillow you would ever sleep on. I could almost feel his arms and those solid biceps wrapped around me in the tightest hug, surrounded by the smell of his almond body lotion. I knew he wouldn't have switched that out even after all these years, just in case it screwed up his game.

"You alright there, Len?" I could hear the teasing tone in his voice.

I felt hot, which meant that my cheeks had probably gone a little pink. Blushing usually went unnoticed on my brown skin, but Liam would notice. He always noticed. I took a sip of my hot coffee in the hopes that I might be able to pass it off as the reason my cheeks were flushed. My fingers started toying with the ring on my thumb.

I cleared my throat. "I'm fine. Your parents must be excited to have you home for the holidays."

I hoped bringing up his parents would distract me from thoughts of black and white shirtless pictures, blown up to thirty feet and dotted around the city I lived in. I may have avoided the man himself, but I knew the exact location of every one of those billboards.

"They both are and they aren't." He shrugged.

"Meaning?" I knew his parents almost as well as I knew my own. They loved having him around. I couldn't imagine why they wouldn't be ecstatic about getting him for two weeks at Christmas.

"They are happy I'm coming home but aren't thrilled that I am retired and single at thirty. They liked my job. They liked my ex-girlfriend."

It made no sense for me to feel a sharp stab of jealousy at the fact that Liam recently had a girlfriend. He wasn't mine, and I'd been in a mostly happy relationship for most of my twenties, so it wasn't like I had a leg to stand on. But jealousy pulsed through me nonetheless.

I swallowed it.

"Why aren't you more upset about it?"

He shrugged. "She wasn't who I thought she was."

"You getting off on speaking cryptically today, Muller, or what?" I teased. He used to talk in near riddles when he saw me getting into my own head and wanted me to snap out of it. It always worked because I always found it annoying and had to call him out on it.

"Definitely not. Old habit." He smiled.

"You don't have to tell me if you don't want to," I said.

"Melanie wasn't all that happy about me retiring when she thought I still had a good four or five years left in my career. She made it abundantly clear that she was only in our relationship because I was Gunner the NHL player, not just Liam Mulligan."

Ouch.

"How long were you together?"

"She saved me from a hoard of overzealous fans on my twenty-fifth birthday and we kind of just fell together."

"Her loss. I—"

I was cut off by a phone ringing. I knew that ringtone. His mother was calling.

"Sorry, it's Mom."

I nodded my head in understanding as he answered the phone. I stared at the lid of my coffee cup and pretended that I wasn't listening to his conversation.

Four

LIAM

Michelle Salisbury seemed to have a sixth sense for calling me at less-than-ideal times. Like when I was having a conversation with the first woman I ever loved for the first time in over a decade. I had no idea if our brief conversation was all we were going to have before she disappeared into the ether again. Our parents still lived next door to each other, but I wouldn't put it past her to change her destination at the last minute to avoid me.

"Hey Mom," I answered, keeping my eyes on Lenny to prove to myself that she really was there.

"Liam, honey, are you at the airport?"

"Yeah, I've been here about half an hour. Excessively early as always."

I noticed the corners of Lenny's lips curl into a smile. Being early to everything was a trait I had acquired from her. She was born a month early and had been early to everything ever since, eventually dragging me along with her. There were worse traits to acquire.

"Good, you'll let me know just before you take off, won't you?"

"Course I will. Anything else?"

"I had a lovely chat with Stassie earlier... You know, it turns out little Alana is coming home for Christmas this year after all."

I couldn't help but snort at Mom calling her 'little Alana'. The woman, currently looking at the lid of her coffee cup like it was a piece of modern art, was only an inch shorter than me and I was 6"4'. Then I caught up with the rest of her sentence.

"What do you mean 'after all'?"

"She was supposed to go to Aspen with that boyfriend of hers, but they broke up a couple of months ago, so she's coming home. I think she might also be flying today. Oh, maybe you'll be on the same flight! That would be nice, wouldn't it?"

I didn't tell Mom that I was standing right next to her. Instead, I reassured her that I would text her before my flight took off and I would see her in a few hours before I hung up and turned to look at Lenny.

"Why did you and Kai break up?"

I saw surprise cross her face for a moment before she schooled it back to neutral.

"How do you know about Kai?"

Everything I knew about her from the last twelve years, I had learnt from a game of telephone that I never signed up to play. She left me and I respected that it meant she didn't want me in her life anymore. I didn't ask any questions about her, but people told me about her anyway.

"Mom mentioned speaking to Stassie today about you going back there for Christmas because you could no longer go to Aspen, what with the fact that you broke up with your boyfriend. As for how I know his name, I've picked it up over the last eight years, whenever Mom thought I just *had* to know about the wonderful things you were doing with him. So, why did you break up?"

"He asked me to marry him, and I didn't say yes," she said with a shrug, not looking up from her coffee cup.

I didn't want to look too much into the fact that the relief I felt that she wasn't engaged to another man was on par with the excitement I felt when I won the Stanley Cup. I decided to ignore it instead.

"Why didn't you say yes?" I asked. It wasn't the kind of question you could say no to, and I'd never heard anything to suggest that they weren't happy. In fact, I had been waiting for the day that Mom sheepishly informed me that they were getting married.

"You know, I've been asking myself that question every day for the past two months and I still don't have a concrete answer. I knew that I would need one, because going back home for Christmas was my only option unless I wanted to spend it alone, and people would ask. You know how everyone knows everything about everyone else. They were definitely going to ask. I've been thinking about it for weeks and I've still got nothing. The only thing I knew for sure was that I didn't want to marry him. I couldn't get my mouth to form the word 'yes'. He was a good guy. He was a safe guy. He was for sure the marrying kind, but the yes wouldn't come. It's hard to come back from a failed proposal."

Lenny looked annoyed that she didn't have a concrete answer for why she didn't get engaged and despite my better judgement, an idea formed in my head. It was probably a terrible idea, but it was an idea, nonetheless. One that might save us both, but mostly her.

"Do you want to pretend to be my girlfriend?"

She snapped her eyes from the coffee cup to me. "Come again?"

"Hear me out, we both don't want to have to deal with the fallout from other people, but mostly, our parents lamenting over the fact that we both recently broke up with our long-term partners, even if the reasons are valid. So, what if we gave them a distraction?"

I was figuring this out as I went along but given that she hadn't immediately shut me down, it felt like maybe there was a chance of this hare-brained idea of mine working.

"You can't be serious?"

Now would be the time to back out. To laugh it off, and we could go back to being civil to one another. We hadn't spent the last four years living in the same city and yet quietly, mutually agreeing to avoid each other for no reason. Her bakery was five minutes away from where the Panthers trained and I had never stepped foot in it despite my teammates always telling me that the hazelnut brownies there were to die for.

They weren't wrong. Lenny had always made a great brownie. So much so that I had insisted that I wanted a tower of brownies from Sweet Nothing as my birthday cake for my thirtieth. Best brownies of my life.

"I'm serious."

She took a long sip of her coffee.

"How would this work?" she eventually asked. I hesitated for too long because she continued. "Well, we are both freshly out of relationships, so, to some, it would seem like quite a quick turnaround for us to be in a new one without some crossover somewhere."

"We were friends once upon a time. That gives us a more solid foundation for a relationship than if we were just straight-up strangers. No cheating necessary."

"Except we are kind of strangers now. So, what happened? How did we go from near strangers to supposed lovers?"

It stung a little that she was right. We were near strangers now, even if falling back into conversation with her now had been as easy as stepping out onto the ice.

"You have a bakery right next to where I trained, why

would it be so ridiculous that we bumped into each other?" I pointed out.

"Because I have a bakery five minutes away from where you trained, and I didn't see you once. We've lived in the same city for four years and this is the first time I've seen you in person. Did you just spend all that time actively avoiding me?"

Yes.

"What, like you actively avoided telling me that you were moving to Michigan instead of Massachusetts?" I said instead, with a surprising amount of anger considering that I'd forgiven her for it a long time ago.

Lenny's mouth gaped before she closed it again.

I sighed. "Can you blame me? You left me and I was the one entering your space. I thought the least I could do was leave you alone when I got there."

She scoffed. "And yet here you are, standing in front of me as we board a flight home, saying we should tell people that we are dating and have been for...?"

"I dunno, a month or so. Like I said, it's not like we weren't friends before."

There was a time when no one knew me better than her. She still might be the only person I could say that about.

"They won't believe it," she said. It was funny how easily I could still read Lenny. She had the same look and tone about her as when I would dare her to do something slightly stupid. She'd say she'd take the forfeit but there was always a moment when she came around to the dare and it was just a case of coaxing her to commit.

I had her in that spot.

"That's where you're wrong. Our mothers married us off in their heads when we were kids. Just because they didn't spend our entire childhoods telling us they thought it, didn't mean that they weren't secretly rooting for it."

I could see her thinking it through. Making the pros and cons list in her head.

Against all odds, she was going to say yes. I knew it.

Five

ALANA

The reasons to say no were glaringly obvious.

Say no because it will open a whole can of worms, and besides, how much did I really care if people talked about me? Say no because you don't want to lie to his parents. Or your own. Say no because no matter what he says, someone will hear that we are together, trace the timelines of our previous relationships and assume there was some crossover. Say no because he's still Liam Mulligan, an NHL superstar, even if he no longer plays and news of him supposedly seeing someone would get out and you like your private life private.

Say no because you loved him and let him go once and it broke you, so putting yourself through that again is foolish. There is no way this could end happily. He's gone on to do great things and you have done great things too, but on a much smaller scale. He's black-tie galas and you are sweatpants covered in flour stains and you didn't think it would work when you were eighteen, so why would it work now?

But when I looked at Liam, really looked at him, I saw the scar that bisected one of his eyebrows. The green eyes that sometimes looked blue. The thick brown hair that still looked like it was begging for me to sink my fingers into it. His slightly crooked nose and the birthmark on the side of his neck. The sheer size of him and the fact that he was the only person who had ever made me feel small. The fact that he was once the person who knew me best. I couldn't bring myself to say no. I knew that the next two weeks would be easier if we gave them another story, but I was fine with writing this story with *him*.

So, I said something else and tried to ignore the fact that this was a much easier yes to give.

"You came to Sweet Nothing's fifth birthday party. Someone from that team of yours convinced you to come and you finally said fuck it and crossed enemy lines. The party was a couple of weeks after things ended with Kai."

A flicker of triumph flashed across Liam's face. He knew I'd say yes. How, I wasn't sure. Maybe because even after all this time, he still knew me better than he knew a hockey play. Then, he ran a hand over the back of his neck. He was about to say something he didn't want to.

"Might not work. My parents know I've never been there."

"When did this last come up?"

He shrugged. "I don't know. Maybe over the summer? Might have been earlier."

"Then we'll be fine. You had never been there when it last came up. It doesn't even have to be a fuck it moment. Maybe you decided to stop being rude and came to thank the person who made you a tower of brownies for your birthday."

His eyes widened. "How do you know that?"

"I know when your birthday is, and how many Liams could there be turning thirty on that day, with a specific request for the number seventeen to be added to a tower of hazelnut brownies?"

He blinked at me slowly, like I had just sprouted another head or something.

"Okay fine, we saw each other again when Teddy made me go to Sweet Nothing's birthday party so I could thank the person who made my birthday brownie tower. Five months after my birthday," he tacked on at the end.

I rolled my eyes and noticed that my fingers had stopped playing with my thumb ring. "Less sarcasm would be great, considering this was your idea and I am just trying to make sure that people buy it."

"Even though I am closer to thirty-one than I am thirty, thank you for the brownie tower. I think they are even better than when we were kids," he said sincerely.

"It's a blend of dark and milk cocoa powders. And you're welcome." I just about stopped myself from saying that I made sure that they were the best brownies I had ever made. I'd made them twice. There was nothing wrong with the first batch, not really. I just wanted them to be perfect and they weren't the first time, but I nailed the second batch.

"So, you're saying yes then?" He sounded hesitant.

"Against my better judgement, yeah. I'm saying yes."

The look of excitement and relief on Liam's face when I said it threatened to make butterflies take flight from somewhere I thought long dormant within me.

Six

LIAM

Even though I thought I had her, I was fully prepared for Alana to shut me down. I had prepared myself for the 'no' because the more I thought about it, the more I realised it was ridiculous of me to suggest to a woman I hadn't seen in twelve years, by her own choosing, that we tell people we were dating. Two months after her eight-year relationship had ended. Mine had also been long-term, but at least it had ended closer to the beginning of this year than the end of it.

Now that she had said yes, I was equal parts excited and terrified.

I wasn't super excited about lying to either of our parents and her brother, but I was so tired of people asking me how I was holding up after everything. I was fine. I had been bummed when the relationship ended but the more time I had away from her, the more I accepted that it was a good thing that it was over. The only thing I was good for was keeping her profile up. It hadn't taken me long to enjoy not having a camera shoved in my face when I was doing something boring like waiting for my coffee to brew all for the sake of 'content'. In fact, the relationship ending probably made the reality of my life without hockey a lot easier because I wasn't around someone who was always asking me about it.

If there was one thing I knew about Alana, it was that she gave exactly zero shits about hockey. That applied to most sports, which was always funny because she was a cheerleading co-captain and had to attend a lot of sports events back in high school, but she really didn't care about hockey. It was her apathy to hockey and her belief that there was life outside of the sport that got me through rehab in our junior year. Finding myself with someone like Lenny now made sense. And I could talk about her all day long.

"You got any other backstory bits you want to add or are we just going with that?" I asked, just to be sure we were on the same page.

"Don't think so, no. How hard can it be to figure the rest of this out on the fly? I mean, I've gathered that you and Teddy are still close as anything, not that he brought you up much, but you said he would be the reason you got dragged to a party, so I just assumed. Am I wrong?"

I shook my head. Behind her, Teddy was my closest friend. Had been since eighth grade.

"No, we're still close. He was part of the reason I made the move to Detroit. I couldn't pass up the chance to play with him one final time."

"Always the poet," she muttered to herself. "Anyway, it's not like that much time has passed since we started supposedly dating, so it should be pretty easy. Besides, you were right, we did know each other quite well, a lot of it might end up being muscle memory."

As if by magic, our gate was called, and I picked up my well-worn duffle and the backpack that Lenny had shucked off her shoulder sometime after I handed over her coffee. We both started towards our gate.

It was only as we joined the queue at the gate that she noticed I had her bag over my shoulder.

"I can take that, you know," she said. She held her hand out to me. I shifted the strap up higher on my shoulder.

She huffed and dropped her hand.

"This is lighter than you used to pack for a carry-on. You finally figured out how to pack light?"

"Yes and no. I stopped doomsday packing. At least when I'm going to certain places. Like home. I could say the opposite for you though." She gestured to my duffle, which was almost bursting, but still within the weight limit.

"The thing about spending so much time on the road is that it gets annoying having to pack all the time. You get really good at stripping everything down to the bare bones. It turns out that the skill also translates to longer trips."

"You mean to tell me that you have managed to pack everything you need for what...two weeks? Into that one bag?" Her mouth was slightly open.

I nodded.

"I'd say teach me your ways, but I know I wouldn't be able to swing it when travelling in the winter months."

"You still got that sweater obsession?"

"It's not an obsession, Liam. Sweaters are an essential layering piece. Need I remind you that we were raised in a state that gets snow?" She was pouting at me as she handed her ticket over to the clerk. It was checked quickly and then she moved on to mine.

"No, I remember that we were raised in a state that gets snow. I also remember that you wear sweaters year-round. Which I think is what makes it an obsession." I followed her down the tunnel, ignoring the flirty eyes that the clerk tried to give me as she handed my ticket back.

Lenny noticed, though, and a furrow between her brows

appeared for the length of a heartbeat before her face smoothed back out.

"I can take my stuff now," she held her hand out again.

"Where are you sitting?"

"17F."

So she was the reason I couldn't choose my preferred seat.

"Well, it's your lucky day, I'm 17E." It was a dreaded middle seat, but that didn't seem so bad now I knew who had the aisle seat. If I was lucky, she might switch with me mid-flight to give my legs some room. Like she used to.

"Of course you are," she grumbled as she walked down the tunnel. I let her put some distance between us for now. She could only get so far, anyway.

When I got to our seats, a man was standing very close to Lenny. His head came to her shoulder, and he looked like he was trying to say something in her ear. Lenny had a resigned look about her; it was one I was used to seeing on her.

She was trying to figure out how to get this man to back off without angering him to the point that he got abusive.

Melanie used to love finding herself in those situations because it gave her a chance to say that Liam Mulligan was her boyfriend. They usually backed off after that.

Lenny's eyes flicked away from the man to me, and I saw relief bloom in her eyes when she saw me. "My boyfriend is gonna need to get by you."

The way she said 'my boyfriend' made my blood feel hot, which could not be more inconvenient if it tried.

The man seemed to take a moment to hear what Lenny said and when he did, his head turned to look behind him. There was a split second just before he recognised me that he looked annoyed that I was impeding his opportunity to hit on

Lenny, and then when the recognition hit, I tried to figure out if he was a fan or if he had simply seen one of my many billboards in the city. Billboards that I would have happily burned down instead of constantly seeing them throughout Detroit. Mom told me New York was worse. Which I could believe because my *mother* was telling me about how she kept seeing me in my underwear around the city while she went about her day.

"*Gunner?*" Well, that answered that question.

"Hey man, what's up?" I said as I slipped Lenny's backpack off my shoulder and handed it to her. She dropped down into her seat and started rummaging around her bag.

"I'm all good. What about you? What are you doing here?"

"Yeah, fine thanks. We're going home for Christmas." I flicked my eyes to where Lenny was trying to disappear into her backpack. She looked up for just enough time to roll her eyes at me. I smiled.

"Oh, what happened to that blonde girl?"

The one thing no one ever warns you about when you get a modicum of fame is how much people start commenting on shit independent of what you're 'famous' for. They also never warn you about how it never gets any less jarring when people you have never met ask you about your personal life.

"We are no longer seeing each other," I responded.

"You didn't waste any time moving on, did you? Guess there isn't much else for you to focus on now that you've hung up your skates." He tried to playfully elbow me like we were old friends. I struggled to keep a neutral face.

"Hey babe, do you have my headphones? I can't find them in here and if you don't have them, then I've forgotten them." Lenny was standing again, looking at me and pointedly ignoring the man in between us.

"I think I might. Hey, sorry man, do you mind moving out of the way so I can give my girl a hand?"

The man nodded and moved out of my way, clapping a hand on my shoulder as he walked past. Just in case he was still looking at us, I made a point of looking through my bag for a moment, pulling out my headphones and giving them to her before putting both our bags in the overhead bin.

As I sat down next to Lenny, I waited for her to give me shit about calling her 'my girl'. It wasn't quite like her calling me 'babe' because she called everyone in her inner circle babe after a while. Although I was pretty sure it was the first time she had ever called me that.

"You get that a lot?" she asked instead, nodding in the direction the man had walked.

"What?"

"Comments on your personal life."

"Oh yeah, kind of, I guess. Depends on the person and how much they know about me." Fortunately, most of them only talked about my career and tried imparting knowledge about how I could make my game better.

"He knew enough about you to know that there used to be a blonde in your life. That's so weird. What have I signed up for?"

"We haven't entered a legally binding contract, Len. If you want out, just say the word."

"The word was 'no' about half an hour ago when you asked. We're in this now." She offered me a humbug.

I never travelled without humbugs. There was always one in my mouth when we took off and when we landed. The guys jokingly gave me shit for it but also respected the superstition. When one of the newer guys asked how it came about, I said I couldn't remember, it had always just been a thing for me.

Teddy had found my answer hilarious, but I never bothered to figure out why.

Looking at the bag of humbugs in Lenny's hand, I realised now, three years later, why Teddy had found it so funny.

It was Lenny's way of dealing with take-offs and landings and I'd pestered her enough once to give me one. Then she never stopped giving one to me until suddenly, I had my own supply, and it was a habit I couldn't break. I'd been so distracted looking for headphones that I had left my own humbugs in my bag.

I took one from Lenny.

"Thanks."

"You're welcome," she said before putting the earbuds she hadn't forgotten in and opening the book in her lap.

I sent a text to my mom to let her know I was about to take off and put on my headphones.

Another thing I had taken from Lenny? No talking, headphones in, for the duration of any and all flights.

Seven

ALANA

"Shit." I stopped just as I walked into the arrivals lounge giving Liam no choice but to walk straight into me.

"What?" he asked as he wrapped his arm around my waist to stop me from falling forward. My hand clutched his forearm. I let go just as quickly, as if I had been burned by the thick, corded muscle there. The rest of me, however, sank back into the heat of his chest like I belonged there. It took me a moment to remember why I had stopped.

"I forgot Dad was picking me up from the airport."

"Fail to see why that is a problem," Liam said, his arm still wrapped around me. There was no need for him to still be holding on to me. In fact, I kind of wished that he would let me go so I could sink into the ground and avoid this particular car journey home.

My thumb ring started spinning again.

"It's not. I just wasn't ready to start lying to a parent so quickly. And he's going to have all kinds of questions for you, so we really would have to hit the ground running."

I would swear until the end of time that I was not the kind of person who was capable of swooning because frankly, I am too pessimistic to believe such a thing was possible, but when Liam used his grip on my waist to spin me around so that I was facing him, his hand splayed across my lower back, I did nearly swoon. The smug look on his face told me he knew he'd affected me.

"All kinds of questions like what?"

"Oh, so you don't think your high school coach is going to have some thoughts on your retirement?"

"I don't think Rob is going to have any more to say than he already has to me."

My eyebrows scrunched together.

"I spoke to Rob when I was trying to decide what to do with my career. I wanted to know what made him decide to call it quits. I knew he would have a perspective on it that I needed to hear while everything was still so up in the air for me."

Robert Fitzpatrick was going to be the next best thing in ice hockey. That's what everyone told him. Heck, it was what he told himself. He had to believe it to make all the hard work worth it.

On the day of the last game of the regular season in his senior year of college, two things happened. One, my mom peed on a stick, and it came up positive, and two, he got body slammed into the boards in the second quarter. Except his knee didn't get the memo to go with the rest of his body and he ended up with major damage to the joint.

He could have played again. Every doctor, physio, therapist, and coach told him that if he didn't try to push himself too quickly, and put in the work, he could get back on the ice. He could still have been the next big thing everyone had said he would be. He could have had it all.

But during the really shitty parts of the rehab process, I was born, and Dad didn't know if he wanted it all. His career might have ended up costing him too much—always being out on the road, and having to return to the higher standards of excellence he was expected to maintain because he knew just how quickly things could turn nasty and abusive. It would keep him from what had become the most important to him —his wife excelling in her chosen career, his daughter, and then two years later, his son.

He found his way back to ice hockey on his own terms when Aaron started school and coached the team at my old high school. He is one of the best junior varsity coaches in the country. Not that you would know that to speak to him. He would rather wax lyrical about how great the rest of his family are than what he's managed to achieve on a coaching level.

Dad was the reason Liam pursued hockey in the first place, so Liam speaking to him about his retirement did make sense. What didn't make sense was the feeling that settled over me at the idea of Liam and Dad talking. It almost felt like jealousy.

"You spoke to my dad about your retirement decision?"

"Yeah...?"

"How often do you talk to my dad?"

"Not that much, really. Only when I needed an outside perspective from someone who also understood the sport. Don't worry, it was only ever about hockey. My mom was the person who gave me all my secondhand info about you."

"Oh, that makes sense," I said quietly, noticing the brief flash of sadness in his eyes. I shuffled out of his grip only to step backwards into someone else.

"Careful, sweetie."

I breathed a sigh of relief that it was just Dad I was stumbling into and turned around so I wasn't looking at Liam anymore. Even if it was only for a few moments.

"Sorry Dad, I didn't realise you were right behind me."

A knowing smile broke out on his face, and he cast his eyes between me and the man behind me.

"You did look like you were in your own little world. How long has this been going on?"

I could feel my heart pounding in my chest. The arrivals lounge suddenly felt too small, and I couldn't hear anything but the sound of my own blood rushing through my body. Now that the time to pretend was here, I couldn't do it. I couldn't lie. Not to my parents. Not to his parents.

But most of all, I couldn't lie to myself. I couldn't tell this dangerous lie that once upon a time, I wanted desperately to be the truth. I wouldn't be able to keep the line clear between fact and fiction. I'd break my own heart all over again, only this time I didn't know if I could mend the broken pieces.

Amid my panic, I felt a hand settle on the middle of my back, and that one point of contact brought me back into my body. I still couldn't bring myself to say the lie out loud, though.

In the end, I didn't need to. It takes two people to be in a fake relationship.

"Not too long, sir. We reconnected about six weeks ago," Liam said it with such confidence that even I believed him.

Dad looked at us both, me still leaning into Liam's touch. He simply nodded, slipped the backpack off my shoulder and onto his, and grabbed the handle of my suitcase. He turned with a mutter that sounded a bit like "finally" and started to leave the airport.

Liam removed his hand, grabbed his stuff, and followed.

As I watched the retreating back of my fake boyfriend, I realised that even though I had made Sweet Nothing's birthday party the start of this thing, I hadn't specified when it was. Yet Liam knew anyway.

When I was given my own phone at thirteen, I was told that I couldn't break big news via text. Even now, I had to either call or share big news in person.

Apparently, that rule did not apply to the adults who raised me because I knew the moment we pulled into the driveway that Mom knew that Liam and I had arrived back for the holidays as a couple. As far as I knew, Dad hadn't made a single phone call.

But there Mom was, alongside Liam's parents, looking like a kid waiting for Santa. Our moms' heads were dipping down to try and see the 'happy' couple through the window. They weren't going to see anything because we weren't sitting together. I was riding shotgun and Liam was cramped in the back. I almost felt bad that he was back there. But then I remembered it was a lose-lose situation. He would have the front seat even further back than I did, and I would have had to do the journey with my knees under my chin no matter whose seat I sat behind.

Also, he had walked straight to the back seat, and I was not going to turn down legroom when it was handed to me. I think it might have been his silent thank you for the fact that I let him have the aisle seat for half the flight. My legs had been mad at me for sitting in the middle seat ever since and being able to stretch out a little in the car had made them a little happier.

"You told her then?" I mumbled to Dad, who at least had the humility to look sheepish as he pulled into the driveway.

"Were you planning on keeping it from her while you were here?" he asked, his tone light.

"No, I wasn't, but I thought no big news over text?"

"Is that why you didn't tell us before you got back?"

No, I didn't tell you before I got back because Liam has been back in my life for hours, not weeks.

"Yes, that's why," I said with a surprising amount of conviction.

Dad nodded once and then stepped out of the car. As the driver's side door closed, Liam and I were plunged into a tense silence.

"You good, Lenny?" I hated how that name sounded from his mouth. I hadn't heard it in over a decade and I didn't think I missed it, but maybe I did. It sounded like home. It was dangerous.

We were using each other as a means to an end for the next two weeks. That was it. I had to remember that before I fell too far.

"As good as I can be walking into this particular lion's den," I admitted.

"This will be fine, Len. We let them fawn over us for a minute, then we go to our separate houses, and you won't have to see me again until tomorrow. Or maybe dinner time. Either way, it will be fine."

I laughed because even though I had no proof, I knew he was wrong. This was not going to be fine or over in a minute.

I was right.

Nine

Stassie had to be joking.

Something about us returning to our childhood homes had made a part of my brain assume that high school rules still applied. No sleepovers. No closed doors. No funny business. A.k.a, I would sleep in my room in my parents' house and Alana would sleep in hers. I had spent the drive from the airport thinking of ways to repeat the physical contact we had before her dad interrupted. I wanted to get her to soften against me again, like she needed me to keep her warm. The thought of her pressed up against me had me trying desperately to not get hard in the backseat of her father's car. It was safer if we slept in separate houses.

But I'd been an idiot who forgot who had raised us: Parents who hadn't had a 'no closed doors' policy because they trusted us to make smart decisions. We'd just pretended in high school they were stricter than they were so neither of our houses became the default party, or worse, hook-up, spot. If they had trusted us as teenagers, then why wouldn't they also trust two fully-fledged adults?

"That isn't necessary, Mom," Lenny said firmly.

"Don't be silly, honey. There is no need for you two to sleep in separate rooms in different houses if you're together now. Unless the idea of sneaking around is what—"

"Mom! We don't...that's not...we've not..."

If I wasn't feeling similar to Lenny right now, I would have found it cute how flustered she was getting.

"We are taking things slow. I really think it would be best if we were in separate rooms. In different houses," Lenny tried again.

"If that display at the airport is taking it slow then I want to know what full steam ahead looks like," Stassie teased.

My eyebrows drew together as I tried to figure out what that meant. A quick look at Lenny confirmed she was just as confused.

"What are you talking about?" Lenny asked. Stassie pulled her phone out of her jeans and slid it over to her daughter.

Lenny picked it up slowly and her nose scrunched. I leant forward to see what she was looking at and realised that Rob had sent photographic proof of our blossoming relationship. That was why our mothers had been so excited on the porch, waiting for us. That picture had captured something, a palpable heat that was evident through the screen.

I usually had a sixth sense for knowing when someone was taking a photo of me—people weren't as subtle as they liked to think they were, but I had not noticed this photo being taken. Given that it had been ninety minutes since I'd held Lenny against me and I could still feel where her body had slotted in against mine, it was unsurprising that I had been so unaware of my surroundings. But still, I'd had no clue.

Lenny's head tilted forward, and she pinched the bridge of her nose, letting out a deep sigh before she handed her mom's phone back to her.

"Fine, we'll sleep in my room."

It was only when she started to leave that I caught up with the fact that we had lost that battle. I offered a weak smile to Stassie and mumbled something about being right back to my mother before I hastily followed Lenny. Noticing, on my way past, that my dad seemed rather bored with the whole thing.

She was at the bottom of the stairs, trying to figure out the best way to get her suitcase up them.

"What the hell are you doing?" It came out harsher than I intended. I was doing a lot of that today.

"I can't believe we didn't see that coming, to be honest," she said to her suitcase.

"Why did you agree to it?" My voice was softer now.

"It was either agree to it or deal with them assuming one of us was sneaking the other into the house in the middle of the night like we're fucking teenagers. And let's be real, I am too lazy to do any kind of sneaking around, so our parents would be keeping an ear out to see if they can hear your hulking body creaking about from A to B. And it wouldn't go unnoticed if they heard nothing. I know you were quick on the ice, but I don't think that speed translates to stealth-like behaviour. At least this way we can control something in this shit show."

I hated that she was right. They would expect us to sneak around, especially with the illusion of passion Rob had captured. We had houses with squeaky floorboards and staircases that didn't have it in them to be quiet when you wanted them to be. It would be obvious that neither of us was trying to take part in a late-night rendezvous.

I hoisted my duffle onto my shoulder and nudged Lenny out of the way, grabbing the handle of her suitcase and carrying everything upstairs. I didn't need her to tell me where her room was. I'd been there often enough.

I paused when I opened the door to her room. It was almost exactly the same.

"The Jacob poster is gone," I commented as I settled our stuff in the corner of the room. I heard her laugh quietly and she opened the door of her closet, pulling out a rolled-up piece of paper.

"It was up until about three years ago when Kai came here to meet my family and insisted I took it down. I don't know why he cared so much. We didn't even sleep here. But he wouldn't stop questioning how I ever got laid in high school if I'd expected boys to deal with the extra eyes on them." She never brought people to her house. I was probably the only person outside of her family that dealt with the extra eyes. They hadn't bothered me.

I reached my hand out for the rolled-up poster. She quirked an eyebrow but handed it over. The blue tac was on her desk where it always was and then I was putting Jacob back where he belonged.

"Do you not find that weird? Kai couldn't get over how weird it was," she asked. I shrugged.

"I got used to it. It's weirder that his eyes weren't following me around the room. Besides, I always found its presence reassuring, it meant I could sleep well knowing that the vampire wasn't going to sneak in and watch you sleep."

"Why do you remember that in such detail?"

"Because it was all you read for what felt like an entire school year and then you made me watch the films so many times. I could probably still recite them *all*," I replied. I wasn't mad about it. I liked that she had shared that with me. Her running commentary was what I remembered most.

"You're welcome."

"I will say, I was always surprised that you went werewolf over vampire when you, too, like the cover of darkness."

"It seems like more effort than it's worth to be a vampire.

Besides, who wants to be around someone with the skin of a killer?"

"Bella."

A bloom of pleasure unfurled within me when Lenny laughed.

Ten

ALANA

It had been so long that it was easy to forget that once upon a time, Liam had been just at home in my room as he had been in his own.

Watching him stick up the Jacob poster he bought me when we were sixteen threatened to unlock a part of me that I had buried the key for. But I couldn't let it. If anything, now that I had signed us up to share a room for the next couple of weeks, I had to keep the part of me that was a little bit in love with Liam Mulligan firmly locked down.

"It looks better now though, right?"

I smiled and looked away from his proud face as I sat on the edge of the bed. Liam perched on the other side and suddenly, the king-size bed felt too small for the both of us. And we were just sitting on it.

"Do you think they think we're up here christening your bedroom?" I heard in his voice that he was teasing, but underneath was something deeper. Huskier. It was like he had subconsciously turned on his bedroom voice now that we were on a bed. I hated that part of me wanted more of that. I wanted it deeper, broken, *desperate* in my ear. I wanted the power that came with knowing that I was the one who had done that to him. The thought flashed through my mind that he was probably really pretty when he begged.

I cleared my throat. "It wouldn't be a christening. That happened a long time ago."

I don't know why I said it. Especially because it was a lie.

The truth was my childhood room had never seen a hint of two-player action. I didn't date in high school and Liam knew that. There had been exactly one chance for me to have sex in this bedroom and Kai told me that he was not going to have sex with me under my father's roof. He respected my dad too much to defile his daughter. No matter how many times I insisted that Coach Fitzpatrick (because that was what he called him even when Dad insisted he call him Rob) gave exactly zero shits who was defiling me, as long as it was consensual and I was being safe. Instead, I had to take down a Jacob poster.

Liam was kind enough to not call me out on what he probably knew was a lie.

"They probably wouldn't think that anyway, what with the fact that you told them we were taking it *sloooowwwww*."

Liam laughed as he flopped onto his back. I could see a strip of skin between his sweater and sweatpants. How had I only just noticed he was wearing sweatpants? Sweatpants that clung to his muscular thighs and teased the cut of muscle by his hip bone. I could feel the body heat coming off him and I was regretting not standing my ground with Mom and insisting we sleep in separate houses.

"I doubt they're thinking that because it's been barely five minutes, and I don't know about you, but I need a tiny bit longer before I am raring to go." I tried to go for a teasing tone, but I missed the mark and crossed straight into flirty.

I looked over my shoulder, taking my time to drink up the

sight of him lying on my bed just ready for the taking. His face though, was almost unreadable.

"I dunno, Len, your ass in those leggings is a good start. It wouldn't take me long after that." If possible, his voice sounded deeper now and despite myself, I looked down. In truth, the sweatpants did a pretty good job of concealing everything, but still, I looked. Stared. Studied. Tilted my head to see if there was even a suggestion of a bulge.

There wasn't. But I hadn't exactly been subtle, and his deep laugh filling the room made me want to fold in on myself and disappear.

"I was joking, Len. I mean, your ass probably does look good in your leggings, but I haven't really seen it, what with the fact that you had a long coat on and when you removed that, it revealed a sweater that would probably be too big on me."

I told myself it meant nothing that all I wanted to do was stand up and lift my sweater to reveal what it was hiding. It wasn't important that I wanted to feel his eyes on the actual curves of my body or prove that, yes, these leggings did make my ass look great. It was a great ass, leggings or not. It didn't mean anything because I stayed seated, swathed in my massive sweater, fiddling with the ring on my hand instead.

"It might be a tight fit, but I think you'd squeeze—" I cut myself off. Liam laughed again and stood up while I buried my head in between my knees and wondered if I had made myself small enough to become invisible.

"I'm sure it would fit just fine, Alana."

Liam rarely called me by my full name. Sometimes, I wondered if he even remembered what it was. It sounded like a whole new name in that deep, almost dirty voice. It made my thighs clench. It shouldn't have affected me like that, but it did, and now I needed him to leave so I could take a deep breath for the first time since he'd handed me my coffee at the airport.

Fuck, had it only been a few hours? I was already feeling strung out and choked by feelings I had done so well to keep locked up.

I heard the bedroom door open, but not close, and then the tread of Liam walking down the stairs. When I could no longer hear him, I uncurled from my ball and lay back on the bed. It was still warm from his body. I rolled into it.

Eleven

LIAM

There was an *atmosphere* in the kitchen when I walked back in. It was the kind of silence that told me that I had just been the topic of conversation.

I couldn't say that I was surprised, but I thought they would have at least put off the debrief until we weren't in the house. Or just taken the conversation next door, where there was even less chance of one of us walking in on them. We were always moving in between each other's houses, so I wouldn't have found it odd if I had come back down to a ghost town. I would probably have preferred it. It would have given me a chance to breathe for a minute.

"You all settled in?" Stassie asked, a small smile teasing the corner of her lips.

"I mean, our stuff is in Lenny's room," I replied. I was going to unpack but then I laid down, brought up christening her bed and her ass in those leggings. When she started talking about things being a tight fit, I couldn't be in that room with her anymore. Not when she was looking at me like that and we were on a bed.

"Are you hungry? I was about to make a start on dinner

but I'm sure I can rustle up a snack for you if you want," Stassie asked, although she was already in the process of pulling together a snack board full of my old favourites.

"So, how are you, son?" Dad clapped a hand on my shoulder.

"I'm good, Dad, just like I was when you asked me two days ago." Ever since I announced my retirement, my father had rocketed to the top of my most frequent callers. He firmly fell into the camp of people who thought they knew my body better than me and didn't understand why I retired when, generally speaking, I was still physically capable. He believed that, with every phone call, I was going to tell him that I made a mistake and was working on getting back on the ice professionally. He ignored the fact that I was nearly thirty-one and would have to compete with kids over a decade younger than me to even get on a team. No one was picking me after a year out of the game when a kid in his prime was raring to go. Nor should they. I was done. No matter how much it disappointed him. And oh, how it disappointed him.

"Ah, yeah, but now I can see the white of your eyes and figure out if you're lying to me when you answer."

I laughed. "And what is the verdict?" I asked.

"The jury is still out." He clapped me on the shoulder again, only this time he hit the shoulder that had sent me into retirement, and I pitched forward.

"Wrong shoulder, Dad." I winced.

"Sorry, I forgot which one was dodgy. Is it still bothering you?" he asked.

"Nah, usually it's fine. As long as I don't overuse it, it feels as expected." I rubbed over the shoulder, mostly out of habit, not because he had hit me hard enough to do any actual damage. I could see from the look on his face that he hadn't liked my answer, and I knew before he even started speaking what his next sentence was going to be.

"With a shoulder that's feeling fine, you could still be out there on the ice."

"But then who would I test all my new bakes on in the middle of the day, Robert?" Lenny asked as she walked back into the kitchen. I wondered if my dad remembered that Lenny only used his full name when he was pissing her off.

I smiled to myself as I looked at her walking into her domain. The sleeves of her sweater were rolled up past her elbows and I could see it. I could imagine walking in on her creating something new with her hands and flexing her forearm muscles, her right arm now sporting a winding pattern of flowers that I wanted to study at length. She would ask me to test what she was making and then brace herself for whatever comment she had managed to convince herself it deserved. She would hit me on the arm attached to my good shoulder and call me a liar when I inevitably told her it was good.

"Then he should definitely be back on that ice," Dad joked.

"There are other ways to exercise, Bobby. Surely you must know that," Lenny said as she pulled flour out of a cupboard and turned to Stassie, who was putting the finishing touches to her snack board. "I imagine you were about to start dinner but I'm really craving pastry. Can I make a pie? Obviously enough for everyone. I assume they are all staying for dinner?"

Stassie nodded. "That's fine. There's some chicken you can use and I'm sure you can figure out the rest with what we have in. I stocked up in anticipation of your arrival. This is all done, Liam. Enjoy." She gestured to the array of crackers, meats, and cheese on the board in front of her. I loved Stassie-sized snacks.

Wordlessly, everyone started leaving the kitchen and I remembered that Lenny liked to be alone when she cooked.

No part of me wanted to follow our parents into another room, but I also knew that I couldn't stay while she worked.

"You don't have to leave. You can make yourself useful and chop things if you like," Lenny said. She was looking in the fridge and slowly pulling various ingredients out.

"Put me in, Coach," I teased as I washed my hands.

"I think I'd rather you call me Alana than Coach. Unless you have some authority issues you want to talk about."

"Nah, Lenny, all good here. Just tell me what you want me to do."

"Chop."

She threw a carton of mushrooms at me before she washed her hands and started making pastry.

Twelve

ALANA

Why I agreed to let Liam stay in the kitchen was beyond me.

Especially because the last time I'd let him stick around while I made something, I'd realised that I was madly and hopelessly in love with him. I had just found out that I was being made valedictorian and would have to give a speech at our graduation ceremony.

I'd known that I'd had better than average grades throughout high school, but I never imagined they would be 'best in your year' level grades, so I never thought about the possibility of being valedictorian.

I hated public speaking. And being the only person being looked at by large crowds. Anything, really, that made me the centre of attention.

So, the day after I found out, I started baking at two a.m. Liam didn't sneak into the house so much as confidently let himself in through the back door with his key, like it was the middle of the day and not the early hours of the morning.

"Why are you awake?" he'd asked as he settled into one of the chairs in the kitchen.

"I could ask you the same question," I'd replied, beating

together a batter with a manual whisk so I didn't wake up the rest of the house with my late-night stress baking.

"Woke up to pee, saw the light on, and now here we are."

"You took quite the gamble on it being me in here."

"It was going to be either you or Coach. I figured I would get away with it either way."

We fell into a comfortable silence, and I focused on my whisking while he sat there and watched me with sleep-soft eyes.

I don't know what it was about him sitting in my kitchen in the early hours of that particular morning, watching me make brownies for the hundredth time, that made me realise that I was in love with him. But when I looked over at him, his head resting on his folded arms, half asleep, it hit me out of nowhere.

I was in love with my best friend and future NHL star. I didn't see how those two things were going to work together. I'd ruin our friendship with my new feelings, or his career would take off and be his focus, and I'd get left on the side-lines. Either way, I'd lose.

So, I left.

The last time I'd let him stay in the kitchen, teenage Liam had been half asleep, sitting down at the dining table. Present-day Liam was fully awake and still wearing those fucking sweatpants.

And present-day me wished that I hadn't told him that he could stay. But I knew if he left, he would be subjected to more passive aggressive comments from a father who didn't understand why he would give up everything he had worked for when he, in theory, still had at least three years left in him. Plus, both our mothers, who were nosy at the best of times, would have more slightly intrusive questions than ever before. I could guarantee one of them would ask if he was satisfying me sexually and, although flustered Liam was one of my favourite Liams, I didn't want him to be subjected to that when I wasn't around to protect and deflect.

"It's really cool that you know how to cook like this," Liam said, his voice bringing me back to the room. A room I hadn't realised I'd zoned out of. I'd been lost in staring at his hands, one wrist adorned with an Olympic rings tattoo, chopping mushrooms. An act that should not have been erotic in the slightest, but Liam had the kind of hands that just looked...capable.

"You telling me you don't know how to cook?" I asked as I added a little cold water to my flour and butter combo, starting to form a dough. At least I had that to take my energy out on now that I had removed my jewellery.

"I can cook, but you came into the room and said, 'I wanna make a pie' and you're making a pie."

"It's just a pie."

Liam laughed. "I bet it will be the best pie I've ever eaten."

"I made you a pie once. You spat it out and said it was almost inedible," I said, the corners of my mouth turning up as I remembered.

"We were thirteen. And it was! You'd used so much salt."

"A good friend would have sucked it up. You put me off making pies for years," I teased, tipping the dough onto the floured counter and kneading. I didn't miss the way his eyes narrowed in on my forearms. Good. It wasn't just me being enthralled by innocuous body parts.

"I was being a good friend. Who knows if you would have achieved such great things if you had stuck it out with that particular recipe, and then much later down the line found out that what you had was actually horrible."

"Owning one bakery would hardly be considered 'great things'." It was only because I was still looking at his hands while I kneaded my dough that I noticed when they stilled.

That made me look up at his face and he looked borderline angry.

"Is the bakery successful?" I nodded. "Then it's a great thing, whether you own one or an entire franchise," Liam continued.

"If you say so." I knew he was right but sometimes it felt like I should be doing more.

Liam dropped the knife and walked around to my side of the kitchen, settling so close to me that I could feel the warmth coming off his body and the scent of sea salt and almond flooded my senses. Somewhere inside me, that smell felt like coming home.

"You were fifteen when you said you wanted to open a bakery one day. That was your dream. You wanted to create something. You wanted to bring people happiness in the form of baked goods. You wanted to spend hours making something that could be gone in a matter of minutes, but that didn't matter because those minutes could be the only bright spark of someone's day, and you loved the idea of being responsible for that. You can take simple ingredients like sugar, butter, and flour, and turn them into the most incredible creations. That's not nothing. You had a dream when you were fifteen and you made that come true. There are a lot of people out there who can only imagine achieving their dream."

"You did," I said quietly. It felt like an easier thing to say than responding directly to the rest of what he said. I distracted myself by wrapping my pastry in plastic wrap to rest while I started on the pie filling.

"Yeah, I did. I worked hard for years and had a great group of people around me that helped it happen. Luck also had a huge part to play in it. Luck that I didn't ever do some serious damage to my body. Luck that I came up around a time when there were a lot of great defensemen but not a lot of great shooters. Luck that I got to work with some really great teams who made me better. Honestly, I was lucky I got out with all my own teeth. I never really thought about what I would do with my life once I retired. A lot of what I did on that ice are non-transferable skills. But if your business falls apart tomorrow, and it won't, you could still bake. You could still try again. You still have a lot of great transferable skills that will get you far in life."

"Do you not have a degree?" I was sure he was drafted during his senior year and had graduated.

"Yeah, in English and Ancient Greece."

I couldn't help but laugh. I'd forgotten that was what he was going to double major in.

"Oh yeah, you really backed yourself making it to the NHL, didn't you?"

"Damn straight. But see, not a single transferable skill in sight. You are way more impressive than me, Len."

"Your name is on the Stanley Cup, though."

A flash of surprise crossed his face. I watched that final, mostly because Kai had wanted to, but I also wanted to see Liam win it. He had been incredible in that game, scoring a hat trick and winning it for the Panthers in the dying moments of overtime.

"That is pretty cool."

He stepped away from me and walked back to his half-chopped mushrooms. I hated that I missed him being close to me.

I focused back on my pie filling. It was just a pie, but it would be the best pie I'd made in a while.

Thirteen

LIAM

The first bite of Lenny's pie almost elicited a deep, throaty moan out of me, but I managed to stop myself from vocalising it. Which was a good thing because the dinner table was suspiciously quiet. The only sound was the scrape of silver on china.

I felt the weight of Mom's glare on me while she watched every moment between me and Lenny. We weren't acting any differently from how we used to. We were just sitting side by side, eating. There weren't any bumped elbows or bashed knees. We both occupied our own space and didn't encroach on one another. It was a practised routine that we had brought out of retirement.

In the end, I couldn't take the silence anymore.

"Why don't you just ask?"

There was a pause, and then three of them asked a question at the same time. I only caught fragments of each, and they laughed at their eagerness.

"Do you want to try one at a time?" Lenny asked, her voice a combination of annoyance and amusement.

Stassie started. "How long has this been going?"

"Six weeks," Lenny replied.

Then it was Mom's turn. "How did you two reconnect?"

I took this one. "I went to Sweet Nothing's birthday party and the rest is history."

Rob was next. "How did you two not bump into each other before then?"

"The world may be small Dad, but it is big enough that you can manage to not bump into your old neighbour when you both live in the same city," Lenny answered easily. There was an unexpected sting from the way she referred to me as her 'old neighbour'. We were so much more to each other than just people who happened to live next door to each other.

"Was it like no time had passed?" Mom asked, a wistful look in her eyes.

I flicked my gaze to Lenny to find her already looking at me. The panic in her eyes was minimal, but I could still see it.

"Yes, it was simple," I answered. Today had been easy. We had fallen into a teasing routine like we had never stopped. I could still read her as easily as my favourite book. There were parts of her that had changed, but at her core, she was still the girl I grew up with.

I looked at her again and the panic in her eyes died.

"That's so sweet. You two look so happy," Mom said, the wistfulness now bleeding into her voice.

Lenny snorted. "Michelle, I have two weeks off from work for the first time since I opened the bakery. That might have something to do with why I look so happy right now." She looked at me again, amusement making her eyes shine. "But I will concede that he is very pretty to look at, so it hasn't been terrible spending time with him."

"I knew you were only using me for my looks," I teased, although I could feel my skin flushing at the compliment. I didn't think Lenny had ever called me pretty before.

"Spending time with you hasn't been awful, either. But

that might be because you stress bake brownies, and they are the greatest thing in the world.”

I had no idea if she still did that, but it seemed like a pretty good bet.

“Well, apparently my brownies were so good you had to come and thank me for them in person, so I am under no illusion as to why you have been sticking around,” she replied easily.

“So cute,” Mom’s voice cut through our conversation, and I was reminded that we were at family dinner. It was always so easy to get caught up in Lenny.

“Don’t tell anyone, Michelle, or it will ruin our reputation. No one has ever called Muller cute,” Lenny said. I snorted. She wasn’t wrong. I wasn’t a total beast on the ice, but I’d had my fair share of fights.

She then effectively ended the conversation by gathering up the empty plates and taking them back to the kitchen.

Fourteen

LIAM

I didn't think Lenny's bed was that small when we were up in her room earlier, dumping our stuff, but as she closed her bedroom door, the room lit only by the moonlight and two floor lamps, the bed looked tiny. The kind of small that had me wondering how we were both going to fit on it. I couldn't see how it was possible unless we pressed up against each other, which was not something I would be able to cope with. Mentally, emotionally, or physically.

"What side do you want?" Lenny's voice sounded strained.

"I'll just sleep on the floor," I replied, not chancing a look at her.

"For fuck's sake, don't be stupid. Just pick a side."

"What's wrong with the floor?" I knew it wouldn't be comfortable, but it was still a better option than lying shoulder to shoulder with her in a bed that would smell overwhelmingly like her vanilla body lotion with the scotch undertones of her perfume. That had been her signature scent since we were seventeen and I doubted she'd changed it. As long as both that perfume and her favourite body lotion were still being produced, she would stay loyal to them, and I knew they were still being produced.

The floor was the safe option.

"Is that a real question? You're a man in your thirties who has played a very physically demanding sport for over half of his life and has a mostly normal but definitely still dodgy shoulder. And that's the injury I know about. Fuck knows what you've done to that body in the last twelve years that I don't know about. The floor is not going to do you any favours, so pick a fucking side."

"I've broken a few ribs and received a lot of bruises. But I told you earlier, I've been lucky there have been no real big ones." I stopped myself from saying that the reason I felt so lucky to not have done anything worse than my shoulder was because I didn't think I could get through an extensive rehab process without Lenny there. She had been key when I was seventeen, and given the fallout of my retirement, I didn't necessarily have the best people in my court when she wasn't around.

"Only a professional sportsperson would consider broken ribs a non-serious injury. Your ribcage *only* protects your heart and lungs," she muttered, mostly to herself.

"They really weren't that bad. You got a spare blanket?"

"I dare you to suggest that you're going to sleep on the floor again. Please continue to pretend that I am going to let you get away with the dumbest idea you've ever had."

I could tell she was getting legitimately annoyed with me now, which was kind of sweet, but I couldn't resist messing with her just a little more.

"What's the forfeit?" I asked.

"What?"

"There was a dare in there somewhere, so what's the forfeit?"

"It wasn't an actual dare. It would be pretty tame as dares go."

I shrugged one shoulder. "So the forfeit can be just as tame."

Lenny opened her mouth and then shut it again before drawing her eyebrows together in thought.

"You owe me breakfast in bed," she said eventually.

I looked around me at the floor, like I was deep in thought and then looked at her again.

"You still sleep on the right?" I asked. I got a pillow to the face, probably because she assumed I would protest again, but she had given me a forfeit that involved looking after her. I'd take that any day of the week.

"Sorry, that wasn't the answer I expected, and I was mid-throw when you opened your mouth. Yeah, I still sleep on the right."

"Then I'll sleep on the left." I threw the pillow onto the bed. "I don't see how we're both fitting in this bed."

"This bed fits three grown men in it. Trust me, we checked, although I don't remember why. One minute, we were putting the mattress on, next thing, Dad was measuring the width of the bed with his own body. Fortunately, I am narrower than my father and even with that hockey physique of yours, you're not that wide. We'll be fine."

I laughed at that image of Rob measuring the bed and sat on the edge.

"Noted. And now I owe you breakfast. Aren't you lucky?"

Lenny rolled her eyes at me and as she walked to her suitcase, she mumbled something that sounded an awful lot like, "You're an idiot."

I'd never felt more at home.

Fifteen

ALANA

I couldn't sleep.

I had been trying for the last ninety minutes and was still trying to create pictures out of the shadows on the ceiling.

I was lying to myself. I told myself the problem was that I was trying to fall asleep much earlier than my body was used to. But I knew that the real problem was the body lying next to me.

Liam slept on his back, which was fine. Except with him lying in that position, the pictures I was making on the ceiling were anything but innocent and that was making sleep feel all the more elusive. Under the cover of night, I could finally admit to myself that he was still painfully attractive to me. In fact, he was more attractive now than when we were teenagers. It was rude of him.

"I can hear you thinking." Liam's voice was thick and gravelly. The tone vibrated through me and settled in between my legs. Great.

"I'm not thinking," I replied.

"It was so loud it woke me up." I felt the bed dip and I knew when I turned my head that I would be met with his face. I did not need to know what the moonlight slipping through the edges of the curtains was going to do to his bone structure.

"I highly doubt that," I laughed quietly.

"You don't sound like you've been sleeping. What's up?"

I rolled onto my side to face him, accepting that it would be weird for me to have a full conversation with him—as it seemed to be where this was heading—with me staring at the ceiling.

Fuck the moonlight and fuck Liam Mulligan's bone structure for managing to look better in the half-darkness. Men didn't need cheekbones like that or eyes that damn near twinkled in the moon's glow.

"I don't remember the last time I was in bed before midnight and apparently my body has zero desire to go to sleep, so I'm just kind of lying here."

"Why did you come to bed so early?"

Now that was the question.

"I dunno. I got swept up in everything, and everyone was talking about going to bed and then we had that discussion about the bed, and I thought I was tired. Today has been long, so I should be tired, but it seems like I'm not, so here I am. Wide awake."

"Okay, why didn't you get out of bed or read a book or something?"

Another perfectly reasonable question that I didn't have an answer to.

"You were sleeping. I didn't want to wake you up. Just figured it would be annoying if I left only to crawl back in at close to one or two a.m. or something."

"It wouldn't be annoying."

"You're that deep a sleeper?"

"What the hell would you be doing other than getting into bed?"

"Nothing. Just, don't worry about it, go to sleep. I'll be fine. My body will get the memo." I wasn't so sure that it would, which meant I was also probably going to wake up at five a.m. like clockwork, too.

"No, I'm awake now. We're having this conversation. Why won't you do what you usually do?" He shifted his arm to bring it under his head. I watched his muscles flex in the moonlight.

"Let's start here, what is your sleep schedule like?"

"It's determined to stick to professional hockey time."

"Meaning?"

"Bed by eleven, awake by seven."

"Every day of the week? Your sleep hygiene is that good?"

"I don't really have much say in the matter at this point. I sort of operate on autopilot with it all."

"Why did we not think of this earlier as a reason why we shouldn't share a room? There is no way your dad would have let his Golden Boy's sleep schedule get messed up for a girl. Not when you could still get back on that ice." I was going for joking, but the silence went on a beat too long.

"Don't call me that," he whispered.

"What, Golden Boy? You've been called that for years," I pointed out. The first time someone took note of his ability on the ice, he was dubbed the Golden Boy. He was fifteen. His career lived up to the title.

"Never by you." There was a vulnerability to his voice that I had never heard before. I nodded my head once. It wasn't my favourite nickname of his anyway.

"Okay, I won't. The rest of my point remains. You sleep well. How would it not be annoying to be disturbed by someone when you were mid-REM cycle or whatever?"

Another pause.

"What's your sleep schedule then?" he eventually asked.

"I dunno. I'm in bed by one and awake by five most days,"

I mumbled. I knew it was bad. I'd tried to fix it so many times over the years with no success.

Liam blinked very slowly. So slowly that I thought he might have been falling back asleep.

"Alana, that's barely four hours of sleep a night. How are you functioning?"

"Ooh, a full name moment, must be serious. To answer your question, I function just fine. I sneak a nap in the middle of the afternoon to top up. I run a bakery and am the head baker. A lot of things depend on me." It was a weak argument at best, but it was the only one I had.

"That's...I...okay, turn over."

"Why?"

"You don't even sleep on your back most of the time, so I don't know how you were planning on sleeping like that. Get comfy, which in your case, is on your side." He twirled a finger around to make his point. I wanted to resist but turned over onto my side. He was right anyway; I'd forgotten that he would know that about me.

I felt the bed dip and rock before a blanket of body heat encompassed me. I waited to feel annoyed that someone was encroaching on my personal space but, once again, I found myself wanting to sink into his warmth.

"I'm going to hug you now," he said, his voice a whisper in my ear. He waited a breath and then draped an arm over my waist when I didn't object. He pulled me closer to him until his chest was flush with my back.

"You've gone from telling me you were sleeping on the floor to spooning. Quite the one-eighty from you there."

"It's all just one big ploy to get access to your fancy pillowcase."

"It's not fancy, it's a necessity to keep these curls in check." I flicked my hair, bundled in a pineapple on top of my head, to prove my point. He laughed softly, his breath brushing the back of my neck and making me shiver.

I closed my eyes and made myself follow the steady rhythm of his chest moving against me.

Just as I was about to fall asleep, I remembered what side of his body he was sleeping on. I tried to shuffle out his grip, but he held me firmly in place.

"Where are you going?" he mumbled.

"Are you okay to lie on your shoulder like this?"

"Len, can you leave me to worry about my shoulder, which is fine? Relax."

I shifted around and got back into a comfortable position as Liam pulled me in tighter. I almost made a joke about the fact that I could feel the soft outline of his dick against me but fell asleep before I could get the words out.

I woke up to the smell of sea salt and, for a moment, felt disorientated. Then I noticed that my head was resting on something solid and cotton. My fingers tangled in something soft, the steady pulse of a heartbeat in my ear.

I opened my eyes slowly, briefly expecting Kai to be the body underneath me. When I tipped my head up, I saw Liam. His eyes were looking down at his phone and the other arm was resting on the headboard. There was a sprawl of lilac and black ink peeking out of the bottom of his T-shirt, covering the underside of his bicep that I hadn't noticed before. It looked a bit like the Stanley Cup. At some point in the last twelve years, he had started needing to wear glasses, and I hated the tug of desire that pulsed through at the sight of them.

My breath caught when his eyes flicked down and caught mine.

"Oh, you're awake," he said, sounding wide awake.

"What time is it?"

"Just after ten."

So much for my body clock being dialled into five a.m. wake-up calls.

"How long have you been lying here?"

"I woke up a couple of hours ago. Didn't want to wake you," he replied as he locked his phone and put it on the bedside table.

"You've just been lying here for hours waiting for me to wake up?"

"It's not like I had anything else to do, and it seemed like you might need the sleep. I was going to get out of bed when you moved off me, but you never did. How did you sleep?"

I did a quick body scan and found that I felt more rested than I had in months. Maybe years.

"I slept really well." I was rewarded with a big smile that made the edges of his eyes crinkle.

"Good. I'm gonna grab a shower now if that's alright with you."

I lifted off him and he climbed out of the bed. As I fell back onto his pillow, I took in the broad expanse of his back and the curve of his ass in his boxers. I felt my face flush at the fact that there had only been two flimsy layers of cotton between us when we were spooning.

It would have been so easy to slip things to the side and—

As Liam moved around the room, two questions came to mind. One, when was the last time I'd been even remotely this turned on? And two, where had I packed my 'just in case' vibrator?

The answer to the second question was probably the packing cube with all my underwear. The answer to the first was about three weeks before Kai and I broke up. Which meant it had been three months since I'd felt the *need* to have any kind of sexual release.

Yet, less than a day in Liam's presence had changed all that. One hug, pressing me against a firm body. Solid, competent hands cutting up some vegetables. Being engulfed in his warmth as he slotted in against me and held me while I fell into one of the best sleeps I'd had in a long time. A threadbare T-shirt against the planes of a broad back and boxers that teased along the lines of a truly God-tier ass. It was maybe even better than mine. Damn hockey players.

A collection of seemingly innocuous things that, when combined, had me scrambling for my suitcase the moment my bedroom door clicked shut behind Liam.

By the time I found my vibrator, I had already wasted three minutes. I guessed that, at most, I had ten. Liam was not the kind of person who liked to stand under the hot water and ponder the meaning of life.

Luckily for me, I was so on edge that by the time I got back onto the bed and turned the vibrator on, settling it on my clit over my pyjama shorts, I could already tell that I would finish quickly.

It took less than a minute for me to find the bliss of relief and thirty seconds after I turned the vibrator off, Liam walked back into the room. I was pretty sure it wasn't obvious what I had just done. My skin didn't visibly blush, so that wouldn't give me away, and the covers hid enough of me that he wouldn't notice the muscles of my lower stomach and thighs still twitching as I recovered.

"You still skip breakfast?" Liam asked, and I sighed internally in relief that he hadn't seemed to notice anything.

"Not in a substantial sense. I save that for lunch and dinner, but I eat in the morning," I replied. No signs of breathiness or tells of desire in my voice either. Good.

"So, when you said you wanted breakfast in bed, what you meant was brunch?"

I forgot about that. That whole conversation felt like it took place a lifetime ago.

"Yeah, sure." I wasn't serious about it anyway. There was no way he was going to actually do it; the dare wasn't real and so neither was the forfeit.

Liam shook his head at me with a smile on his face.

"I'm going downstairs."

"Good luck."

"Why would I need luck?" Liam hesitated, his hand hovering over the door handle.

"Yesterday was just a warmup. They can't wait to get one of us alone and try to get more details. The morning is prime time to get that info because your brain is still waking up and you're less likely to be guarded."

"Shit, good point. How long will you take to get ready?"

"Twenty minutes." If I didn't procrastinate.

"I'll wait," he said as he dropped onto the bed, reaching for his phone and revealing the waistband of his boxers and the cut of his lower stomach again. I felt another pulse between my legs, and the slight pressure of squeezing my thighs together sent another aftershock through my core.

I hoped he didn't notice as I shifted my vibrator somewhere on the bed where he couldn't feel it.

I thankfully managed to walk out of the room on steady legs.

Sixteen

"I think we should go on a date," I said when a freshly showered Lenny walked back into her room.

"And why is that?" she asked as she sat at her vanity table, pulling her hair out of its pineapple and shaking her curls out. It was the first time I had seen her hair down in years. I was surprised by how much longer it was as she teased it back into shape, the ends now nearly touching the bottom of her shoulder blades.

"Because we're dating. It's Christmas in New York and it would be weird if we stayed holed up indoors for the next two weeks," I reeled off.

"We are only dating in the eyes of four people," she said as she twisted around to face me, the beam of sunlight from behind the curtains of her window made her brown eyes look golden.

"Who will think it is weird if we stay indoors for the next two weeks," I pointed out. I also really wanted to get out of the house and go somewhere, anywhere. I needed a distraction, so I was less likely to get lost in thoughts of pressing Lenny against any and all hard surfaces. Now that I knew what she felt like pressed up against my body in the middle of the night, how she sighed herself into an even deeper sleep as she had turned over and rested her head on my chest this morning, it made me imagine all the other sounds I could maybe coax out of her if given half the chance.

Getting outside would be good for both of us. It was unlikely that she had an exhibitionism kink, and I had been followed by enough cameras in my life to wrestle mine into submission.

"Alright, fine. What did you have in mind?" she asked as she expertly parted her hair with her fingers.

Absolutely nothing. Then I remembered a very particular thing about Lenny. "You still do that thing where you have to get a doughnut every time you see one?"

"Yeah, I do."

"Alright, you wanna go get a doughnut?"

"I thought you wanted breakfast. You can't eat doughnuts for breakfast," she said as she twisted the front section of her hair back and secured it into a bun on top of her head.

"Alright, Mom. No one said that we were only going to get doughnuts. We can get other food. Like a croissant."

"Please don't jokingly call me Mom. Not when I know what your dick feels like against my ass." She carried about her business casually, like she hadn't just short-circuited a part of my brain. There was no reason for it to behave like that. All she had said was *dick* and it was almost clinical the way she had said it. Except I could still vividly recall the feeling of her up against me and it had felt *so good*.

"Fine, I won't call you that again. We should also see the lights at some point before Christmas Eve. Oh, and I want to go to the rink at some point."

"Why?"

"Because I've never gotten to slowly skate around in circles holding someone's hand before binning it off and drinking boozy hot chocolate instead, and this feels like the perfect time to rectify that situation." I'd never thought about doing it before, but I wanted to do that with her. Desperately.

"You're supposed to do those things with a girlfriend."

I raised my scarred eyebrow. "Is that not what you are?"

She paused for a moment before she sighed. "Technically, yes."

"So, technically, you should be the one that I do what with. I mean, I am sure I could find someone else—"

"That won't be necessary. I will get back on a pair of knives for you," she cut in, her eyes locking with mine in the reflection. I fought the smile that threatened to break out on my face.

"When were you last on skates?" I asked out of curiosity. She twisted her torso around to face me.

"I dunno, a while."

"Have you ever slowly skated around with a date?" I don't know why I was asking; I didn't really want to know. Something about the idea of her skating with someone else sat oddly with me.

"As far as every man I've ever dated is concerned, I don't have the balance that is required for biking, skating, or skiing."

My eyebrows creased; Lenny could do all those things. Well. I'd taught her how to ride a bike, we'd been skating since we were six, and we'd been skiing together multiple times. In the same place she was supposed to be spending this holiday.

"But weren't you going to Aspen?"

"Yeah, that's where Kai's family always spend the holidays. If I was spending them with him, that was where we went."

"What the hell did you do when you were there then if you didn't ski?"

"Ate. Enjoyed the scenery. Slept. Enjoyed the hot tub in my room with a book. Drank a lot of hot chocolate. I was never there for that long, and everyone understood that with my handful of days off, I wanted to completely switch off and not partake in any kind of physical activity.”

“Why didn’t you want them to know you could do those things?”

“Okay, I told a small lie. I went on a date with a guy that first December at college and he couldn’t skate properly. He felt very hurt by the fact that not only could I skate, but I was also very good at it. He ghosted me and I dunno, I guess eighteen-year-old me internalised that and now I say I can’t skate for the sake of the fragile male ego.”

“So, can I take you on a slow skate date? I promise not to be offended when you skate better than me.”

“No, I think you should be embarrassed if I can out-skate you, Muller. I haven’t been ice skating for twelve years, whereas you were doing it professionally until mere months ago.”

“Still haven’t heard a yes.”

“I don’t know what I’m saying yes to anymore.”

“Doughnuts today. Ice rink later in the week. Date afternoon with the lights. I guess we can go to the city as well if you want?”

“So I’m saying yes to four whole dates?”

“Someone once paid good money to go on a date with me,” I teased.

“I hope it went to a good cause. What did you offer for this date?”

“It was a dinner date. I am offering you experiences that don’t involve being chained to a table surrounded by other people staring at us trying to figure out if I am who they think I am.”

“Skating with a professional ice hockey player is quite the experience, but surely it invites the same ‘Hey, don’t I know you from somewhere?’ problem?”

“Wouldn’t know. I haven’t skated in a public skate rink

since turning pro, but I like to think I cut a slightly different figure when I'm decked out in all the pads, so being out of them is the disguise."

"No way in hell you aren't being recognised the moment you put a pair of skates on."

"What does the winner get?"

"Huh?"

"I think I won't be recognised on an ice rink, you think I will, so what does the winner get?"

"Well, what do you want?"

A montage of X-rated activities flashed through my mind.

"A year's supply of brownies," I said aloud.

"Fine. I'll get back to you on what I want."

"Are you ready to go?"

"Yeah, I just need to put a sweater on."

I watched her move from the vanity and squat down next to her still-unpacked suitcase. I'd unpacked while she had been in the bathroom, making use of all the pockets of space in her room that I knew she was unlikely to fill because they had always been empty when we were teenagers. I forgot that I wouldn't need to show that level of consideration because Lenny showed no signs of unpacking. Instead, she seemed perfectly content to simply lift things and move them somewhere else in the suitcase until she found what she wanted. She let out a noise of triumph as she pulled out a sweater.

A million years ago, I lost a sweater. It had been as close to perfect as you could get. It didn't feel too tight around my neck, the sleeves were the perfect length, it was soft all the time and was so perfectly snuggly that I wanted to live in it. And I did, until it went missing. I had worn it to a practice and assumed I had left it in a locker or on a bench in the locker room. But it never showed up, no matter how many times I checked lost and found. I mourned the loss of it for about a month and then let it go and searched for a new favourite sweater.

I never found one.

I was now looking at my favourite sweater, draped over the curves and edges of Alana's body. I thought I was imagining it, but no, it was definitely my sweater. It looked just as soft as it had been thirteen years ago, the sleeves just as perfectly long. The neckline looked a little looser, but it still looked like the perfect sweater.

It looked perfect on her.

Lenny caught me staring and quirked an eyebrow like she was daring me to say something while she flicked her hair out from under the neckline of the sweater.

"Nice sweater," I said as I stood up. "Let's get you a doughnut." I held my hand out to her. She stared at it, and I expected her to say something, but she simply put her hand in mine and I led her out of the room.

ALANA

Walking around town with Liam Mulligan was an exercise in pretending that you didn't know that people were staring at you. Whilst also being pinned down by the weight of all their stares.

Once upon a time, I was used to those looks. When Liam was around, I was shrouded by his presence and the way everyone loved him. It was a position I was happy with because while they were looking at him, they weren't looking at me, and Liam played the part of being the superstar well.

But back then, he had just been playing at being a superstar. I mean, he was always great, but it was still unclear if he was just *high school great*. But he made it to the big leagues, and he'd been great there too. He'd lived up to the hype, to the promise. He was the Golden Boy. People had been so devastated when he announced his retirement, they wanted to stop playing Fantasy League if he couldn't make up the team.

"Remind me again why I let you drag me out of the house?" I asked, trying to avoid looking at the family across the street who looked like they were about ready to accost Liam. I would end up taking photos if they got the idea that they could approach, and if I did it once, then everyone else who was pretending they weren't staring at us would come over. It would become a revolving door of phones being passed to me while they pawed all over Liam. He wasn't theirs to fawn over. That didn't mean he was mine, but he wasn't theirs.

"I believe I promised you doughnuts," he replied, looping his arm around my shoulders and pulling me closer to him. I fell into him easily.

"Are we walking to the city for them? Because we've walked past two places that do them and I am without a doughnut. The rule is whenever I see a doughnut I buy a doughnut."

"Fair enough. I see your point and I raise you. Why would I buy you any old doughnut from those places when I could buy you the best one that also happens to be your favourite?" I felt the gentle press of his lips on my temple and felt both warmed and chilled by the easy affection. I couldn't be out here getting attached to all this. We were *fake dating*.

But it was hard to not get attached when he remembered something as minor as the fact that, even now, I thought that the best doughnut in the world came out of Westchester Bakes. My dad had bought me one the day Aaron was born, and it was my first taste of how food could change your life. Years later, I realised that I wanted to make other people feel the way that doughnut made me feel and started baking.

"How are you so sure that I haven't found a new favourite?"

"Because they were your first food love," he said simply as he threaded his fingers through mine and kept us walking.

∼

There was a queue for Westchester Bakes, which wasn't unusual, especially at this time of year. It did, however, serve as a reminder to me that when we were younger, not only did Liam bring me my favourite doughnuts regularly, but he used to *queue* for them. For me.

As we joined the back of the queue, he turned around so his back was to the line and grabbed my other hand, holding them both.

"I forgot how cute you look in winter," he said, his green eyes looking blue in the crisp sunshine.

"Thanks?" It was all I could think to say in the immediate aftermath of a sincere compliment from a man whose eyes were literally sparkling at me.

"It's a compliment, Len. I dunno, I guess I forgot that you always preferred the colder months because the weather finally matches your stylistic choices. I still haven't met anyone who loves knitwear and a coat as much as you do. Winter suits you."

"Thanks. Winter doesn't—"

"Liam. Mulligan. Well, I never." I was cut off by the person in front of us, hidden behind Liam's back. I knew the voice, though. I'd know Chantelle Smith's voice until the end of my life. She had been my co-captain on the cheerleading squad our junior and senior years, which she wasn't jazzed by, but the squad couldn't pick one of us, so we shared the captaincy. She held that against me for those two years because cheering was her everything and it was just something I did because I happened to be a good tumbler. I also needed to kill time while my ride home was otherwise occupied. She also held Liam being my friend against me. She was convinced that I was the reason Liam didn't want to date her. I wasn't. I begged him once to go on one date, so she'd leave me alone.

However, I couldn't say that I wasn't happy about the fact that he never did. I had always been secretly happy that I never had to see Liam date anybody. Why that was, I didn't know until that night in my kitchen, when it all started to make sense. When he told me that he had a date for our high school prom, it ruined me. I changed my moving date to prom day, so I didn't have to deal with witnessing that in any way. It was the one and only time I had utilised the fact that my dad was revered at that school. It meant that the principal just accepted that the senior valedictorian wouldn't be finishing out the year or attending graduation.

Liam let go of one of my hands and turned around, managing to shift me so that I was pressed against his chest with his arm around my waist.

"Oh, and Alana? I thought you weren't coming back this year."

That was the problem with this place. Everyone knew everyone else's business even when I told no one except my parents of my original plans for the holidays.

"Plans changed and now I'm here." I shrugged.

"But what happened?"

"How are you doing, Chantelle?" Liam cut in, and I watched her face change as she dragged her attention away from me to something lighter. Something flirtier.

"Good. What about you? Must be nice to get a whole Christmas off now that you're out of the game."

It never ceased to amaze me how obsessed with Liam's career people were. It shouldn't, because he was kind of a big deal, but I had never been able to see him as the NHL's Golden Boy because even if we were no longer in each other's lives, he was still just...Muller. A guy who could tell you the most random facts about obscure Greek mythology and had an encyclopaedic knowledge of flowers. Someone who watched Mufasa die once, couldn't cope, and from then on, always walked out of the room when Scar started to take Simba to the gorge. He would come back just before

Hakuna Matata started with a Mars bar because I always used that part of the film as a chance to cry. I was always aware that he belonged on and to the ice, but whoever Liam was once those skates were laced was not the same person I got.

"I always got three days off, although it is nice to get a full two weeks with this one," he said as he squeezed me in tighter to him and suddenly, I remembered that we were supposed to be dating. I wasn't just standing here waiting for someone to ask Liam out before he politely turned them down and we carried on with our lives. For all intents and purposes, he was mine.

"When did this happen?" Chantelle asked, her eyes finally noticing Liam's arm holding me against him. His fingers had managed to find a space between my coat and sweater, and I could feel the heat of his palm on my stomach. The touch was making me feel tingly.

"A few weeks ago," Liam replied easily.

"How?" I heard the disbelief in her voice, but it was also borderline angry. Judging by the brush of lips against my temple, Liam heard it too.

"Sweet Nothing was having a little birthday party and that seemed like the perfect opportunity to thank Len in person for making my birthday brownies. I asked if she wanted to hang out and hanging out turned into dating, and now here we are."

"Stassie mentioned that you had a bakery in Detroit, Ally. Congrats."

She sounded sincere, but she'd used a nickname I had never given her permission to use, so I knew she wasn't.

"It's Alana," Liam said before I even had the chance to think about correcting her.

Chantelle carried on like he hadn't said anything.

"Listen, Eddie is having a party at his parents' house on

Christmas Eve. It's a lot of the old gang and I'm sure he would be happy to see you. Both of you," she tacked on at the end.

"We'd love to," Liam answered just as Chantelle reached the front of the queue. As she stepped into the bakery, she turned around to give us one last look.

"Starts at seven. I trust you still remember where the house is?"

Everyone knew where Eddie lived. It was called The Big House because, well, it was big.

"Yeah, I remember where Eddie's family lives," Liam answered and the door closed behind Chantelle, putting a blissful barrier between us for a short while.

"Is there a reason you just signed us up to a party? I only agreed to four dates and now you want to bump it up to five," I teased as I turned around to look at him. His arm didn't leave my waist.

"It might be nice to see everyone for a bit. I'll make it up to you. You can make me watch *Breaking Dawn* and I won't make a single disparaging comment."

"Wait, if you're going to give me one film where you don't make a single snide comment, then I am making you watch *Batman and Robin*." Liam rolled his eyes just as someone walked out of the bakery, and he freed me. I tried to ignore how cold I felt without him pressed against me.

"Wait here, I'll be back when I'm back," he said as he stepped inside the bakery before I could say anything. I could see through the window the way people's eyes snapped to him, Chantelle's included. I watched in real time as he morphed into Liam 'Gunner' Mulligan. The easy smile, and the open body language, exuding almost puppy-like energy, but a line of tension ran through his shoulders. I could see people talking to him, getting just a little too close. The woman behind the counter batted her eyelashes and would not stop smiling while he placed his order. I turned away from the window and pulled my phone out of my pocket, busying myself with checking my email. It was a pointless task. No one was emailing me. They were under strict instructions not to bother me unless there was a legitimate emergency. And they wouldn't tell me that over email.

I was reading a book that I had abandoned over the summer when I felt Liam return.

"One praline and coffee doughnut and a flat white, milady."

I locked my phone and looked at Liam. His shoulders were looser, the performance now dropped, with my favourite doughnut and my go-to coffee in his hand. Clearly, at the airport, Liam hadn't just heard my name, seen me standing there not hearing it and brought me my much-needed caffeine, he'd noticed my coffee order as well. He *remembered* my new coffee order.

"Thanks, I think you might owe me more than just the one snark-free film. I remembered while you were in there that my parents do that Christmas Eve lock-in at The Seamus Pub every year, which means I was getting the house to myself until one a.m. Instead, I have to go off and be social." I took a long sip of my coffee and let the warmth soothe me from the inside out.

"Oh yeah, mine are doing that as well. I forgot about that. Were you not going with them?"

"I wasn't supposed to be here, so it was too late for me to get added to the list, which meant I was going to be alone."

"I would have been there," he said.

"*Alone.* Locked doors, big lights off, *Jingle Jangle,* and the fancy whiskey from the back of the cupboard."

"They never changed the locks," he replied casually, which meant he still had his keys. The keys to a childhood home that wasn't technically his, but also very much was. "And anyway, wasn't Aaron gonna be at home?"

"No, he spends Christmas Eve with his friends somewhere not in the house."

We started walking down Main Street, our feet carrying us on autopilot to our favourite bench. It wasn't anything special, but it had the best dedication we had ever found.

For our Dad, who would have hated being surrounded by this many people.

Liam looked around before we sat down and I watched several pairs of eyes flick away, a terrible attempt to cover up the fact that they were staring.

"Are you stared at wherever you go?"

"No. I mean it happens, but not in the way it is happening here. Although I think it is less about me and more about *us*."

That made no sense. "What about us?"

"We haven't been seen together around here since our senior year."

"And that warrants them staring at us like we're giraffes at the zoo?"

"No, but I also can't say I blame them," he said with a shrug.

"I think you broke Chantelle's heart, though. She probably saw those shoulders and thought she was finally getting to shoot her shot with her high school crush, only to be denied once again." I changed the subject before I was forced to confront feelings that I was not in the headspace to deal with.

"Chantelle asked me out every month for two years and I never said yes. My answer to that question twelve years later is still no. She's not my type."

"Really? Because she looks an awful lot like Mel—" I cut myself off, but it was already too late.

"You been checking up on me, Lenny?" The smile on his face was downright sinful. Teasing always was a good look on him. At least to me.

"I might have cast an eye over your Instagram when I

couldn't sleep last night. You haven't culled her from your page yet," I admitted. I'd been surprised when I saw her in his photos. I'd deleted all traces of Kai from mine while I waited for my birthday cake to bake.

"I announced my retirement and stayed clear of social media. Given that she broke up with me not too long after that, I haven't had the chance."

"Whatever. What I was saying still stands. Physically, they are very similar. You can see why I would think Chantelle would be your type."

"That's fair, but that wasn't what I meant when I said she wasn't my type."

"Then what did you mean?"

"I don't tend to want to spend time with people who make it a habit of talking shit about my best friend," he said.

"Who, Teddy?" From what I remembered, Chantelle got on just fine with Teddy. In fact, I always got the impression that if Liam didn't exist in all his glory, then Chantelle would have been all over Teddy.

"No. You," Liam said simply.

"Oh," I replied, sending us into a comfortable silence for a moment while we ate.

"Still got it?" he asked as I scrunched up my empty bag and licked the sugar from my doughnut off my thumb.

"Never lost it," I answered. A Westchester Bakes doughnut would always be the one I associated with after-school sugar rushes and discovering new flavour combinations. It would always be the thing that sparked a fire within me that I would eventually turn into my job, which I still found new ways to fall in love with every day. Or at least most days. It was the doughnut I associated with good days and bad days and just because days.

"Come on, let's keep walking," Liam said as he stood up and held his hand out to me. I placed my hand in his and he immediately tucked our joined hands into his coat pocket to keep at least one of our hands out of the winter chill. Our hands being in there gave me no option but to press myself as close to Liam as possible.

"Anyone would think you haven't been home for ages," I teased, taking a sip of my coffee.

"Well, I haven't. Not properly anyway. Nor have you. And don't try to lie to me—just because you've been back to your parents' house does not mean that you've been home. When was the last time you queued in that line for the sole purpose of getting a doughnut?"

"I dunno, it's been years. But I will also say that I stopped queuing long before I left because *you* did it for me."

"Fine. When was the last time someone waited in line to get you a doughnut?"

"About fifteen minutes ago," I said.

"Don't be a smart ass."

"Being smart has almost always been a character trait of —" I stopped abruptly as we walked past a block of units that we used to walk by all the time. It was the block of units that held my dream bakery space. Liam once found me pressed against the glass, visualising what it would look like. Where the counter would go, where the display cases would be and how I would set up the kitchen.

"It's still empty," I said, extracting myself from his side.

"Oh, it wasn't the last time I was here," Liam said from right behind me. I pressed myself up against the glass again. The space had changed a little, but the bones were the same. I could still put the kitchen in the same place. In fact, it looked like I would be able to recreate the Detroit bakery almost identically. I could *expand.*

I had been thinking about expanding for a while, but the issue was always the same. I didn't have the capacity, time, or money to do it. I still didn't. I stepped away from the window and turned around to Liam.

"You okay?" he asked. I nodded as I laced my fingers with his again and nestled into his side. He accommodated me easily.

"Can we go home now?"

"Yeah, sure."

We walked home, pressed together in silence.

Eighteen

ALANA

Aaron was in my room, sitting on my bed and throwing a marbled black stress ball that he bought me when I was fourteen up in the air. He startled when I caught the stress ball straight out of the air, and I felt proud of my stealth mode.

"Jacob's back," he said composing himself and pointing at the newly reinstated poster.

"Yeah, courtesy of Liam." I threw the stress ball at him. He caught it.

"Ah, yes, Liam. I heard you two were together now. Not from you, though, which hurt my feelings. I thought we were closer than that." He threw it back.

"It's all very new. If it makes you feel better, we didn't tell anyone until yesterday." When we came up with the idea.

"Is that really a good idea?"

"Why wouldn't it be?" I threw the ball back.

"Oh, are we pretending that I didn't know you were hopelessly in love with your best friend and literally *left the state* with no warning to avoid confronting those feelings?" he chuckled as he threw the ball back.

"I didn't run to..." I trailed off, realising that it was pointless to lie to Aaron. He was the only person I ever told about my feelings for Liam, and I only did it because he was like a dog with a bone and he could tell something was up in the weeks before I left.

"Okay, fine, so I ran to avoid that. But that has nothing to do with what is happening now. We're not actually dating," I said instead. Except the words felt odd in my mouth. It was technically true, but in the aftermath of our morning, it felt less fake than it had yesterday.

I watched confusion fall over Aaron's face.

"What do you mean?" he eventually asked.

"Vault rules?" I asked, passing the ball back to him. When we were younger, Aaron and I created the 'vault' where we could tell each other anything and it would only stay between us. No matter what.

"Of course."

"Liam and I didn't bump into each other six weeks ago. He saw me at the airport yesterday and, well, he just retired and broke up with his girlfriend, who, by the way, was only with him because he was a hockey player and had zero interest in him without the ice time, which is frankly ridiculous." I took a deep breath. "And I just broke up with Kai and neither of us wanted to talk about those things, so he suggested that we divert our parents' attention while we were here and what better way to do that then by telling them that we were dating?"

"You've definitely diverted their attention, but was it the wisest of decisions?"

"Do I think it was smart to fake date the first man I ever loved? No, I think it was incredibly stupid. Up there as maybe one of the dumbest things I've ever done, just behind bleaching my hair and fucking my curls up a few years ago. But I can't tell you how much I needed to not talk about how things with Kai ended once I got here, knowing that everyone probably knew that we broke up. Liam's idea gave me a way out of doing that, and I can help him in the process as well. Things with him feel like they always did, and it's easy and nice. There are worse people to try and divert attention with. Besides, I've done the unrequited love thing with him before and got out of it fine. I can do it again."

I couldn't. Judging by the worried look on Aaron's face, he knew that too.

"He still lives in Detroit, Ally, and you've got deep roots there. You won't be able to run away and attempt to never see him again when the New Year comes around, and whatever arrangement you have ends but your feelings haven't."

He was right. "I'm not going to pretend that I've thought that far ahead, Aaron. I'm just going to live in the moment and take each day as it comes."

And try not to fall in love with Liam. Again.

"So, you're going to date Liam? Outside of the house?"

"Well, it would be weird if we stayed inside at what is arguably the most romantic time of year with all the lights and trees and all that shit. If we're supposed to be in the early stages of a relationship, then we would still be trying to spend as much time as possible together, getting to know each other better."

"I don't think you need to get to know someone better when you've known them since you were three. Yeah sure, there was an interlude in your friendship, but you did the awkward hormonal years together, so you're basically bonded for life. You know each other's origin story. You know you get on, that you like each other. And you know that you find him attractive." He waggled his eyebrows.

"Everyone finds Liam attractive, that doesn't make me unique."

"There is a difference between thinking someone is objectively attractive, which I think he is, and finding them sexually attractive, which you think he is."

I was reminded that there was probably, definitely, a vibrator under my duvet.

"So what if I do? That's not a crime. You don't have to worry about me, Aaron. I'm fine. I'll be fine."

That might have been a bigger lie than telling people that Liam was my boyfriend.

He got off the bed and handed the stress ball to me before wrapping his arms around my waist. Despite everyone telling me that one day he would be my big little brother, he never did quite manage to grow taller than me, and so his head rested on my shoulder as he hugged me tightly.

"This one has the power to ruin you for good, so yeah, I have to worry about you, Ally. But I won't bring it up again. If you need me for anything, I'm here. I'm always here," he said quietly in my ear.

There was a gentle knock on the door and Liam's head popped around it.

"Am I interrupting something?" he asked as Aaron dropped his arms from me and stepped away. "Aaron, didn't realise you were back."

"No, I was just leaving. Good to see you, Liam," Aaron said as he squeezed my bicep once and then walked out.

"You okay?" Liam asked as he stepped further into my room.

"Yeah, I'm fine," I replied automatically, although it was unclear whether that was true or not. Aaron wasn't wrong. This did have the power to break my heart, and I didn't know if thirty-one-year-old me had the strength to get through it this time.

Nineteen

LIAM

Lenny was cleanly on her side of the bed when I blinked my eyes open at half past seven. Part of me was sad that I wasn't pinned under her weight like I had been for the last couple of mornings, but another part of me was happy to be able to get some space from her.

I was still surprised by how much hanging out with her felt like coming home.

That was a dangerous thing to feel for a woman who had run away from me once and was capable of doing it again. Space, even for a moment in the morning light, would help me remember what we were to each other.

A fake couple.

She chose the moment I got out of bed to roll over onto my side. When she was met with an empty mattress, she grabbed my pillow and hugged it to her, sighing as she settled again.

I left the room before I could try to take the pillow's place. Once I got downstairs, I picked my keys off the hook by the front door, slipped on a pair of shoes and jogged to my parents' house. As I unlocked the front door, I waited for the alarm to start sounding but nothing came, which meant at least one of my parents was awake.

"Liam?" Mom called out as I closed the door behind me. I found her in the kitchen with the newspaper crossword spread out in front of her and a coffee in hand.

"Hey Mom," I said as I poured myself a coffee.

"What brings you over here?" she asked as she put her pen down.

"Do I need a reason to come and see my parents?"

"No, of course not," she said before taking a long sip of her coffee.

"Why do I feel like there is a but coming?"

"*But* there is a beautiful woman in your bed, and you've left her there," she said with a smile on her face.

"Technically, it's her bed and she's still asleep. Probably will be for a while."

"You leave her in bed alone a lot then?"

"We haven't exactly got to the sleepover stage," I answered. It wasn't a lie. "Anyway, I am partly here for a reason independent of seeing you. I need skates."

"What for?"

"Don't get your hopes up, I'm just taking Len to the public ice rink, and I know I have skates here, so I don't have to hire a pair."

"I wasn't getting my hopes up, I respect your decision to go out on a high," she said, and I knew she meant it.

"Can you get Dad on board with my decision while you're at it?"

"I've been trying, honey, but you know what he's like."

"Most parents would be happy that their kid made it to a professional league at all, not mad at them for retiring before it damaged them beyond repair," I retorted.

"He is proud of you," she insisted.

"I know, Mom, but it would be great if every conversation

we had now didn't revolve around him telling me that I should still be out there on the ice."

"He'll get there. He's just having a hard time adjusting. He got used to you being at the top and now you're not there anymore."

I just about managed to stop myself from rolling my eyes.

"I had to retire at some point. Would he rather I kept declining until I was forced off the ice? Did he want to see me get slammed into the boards and get an injury I couldn't come back from? Would that have made his adjustment easier? It's been eight months since I retired and he's still not there yet. I gave eighteen years to the sport, Mom, and I didn't want to do it anymore. It's as simple as that." It wasn't her I was frustrated with, so I tried not to sound annoyed. I didn't feel like I was succeeding.

"How does Alana feel about it?" she asked quietly.

That caught me off guard.

"Feel about what?"

"The retirement," she clarified.

"Oh. Don't think she cares," I said. The few times it had come up she seemed pretty indifferent to the whole thing.

"You don't talk about it?"

"Not really. You know her. She's never cared about hockey. I mean she cared if I liked it and wanted to do it, so me not playing doesn't really come up often." It had always been one of my favourite things about Lenny, the way she viewed my life off the ice as just as, if not more, important than my life on the ice.

"And that's okay with you?" she asked gently.

I shrugged. "Why wouldn't it be?"

"No reason. I just wondered if she was supporting you through this transitional time of your life."

"Yeah, she is." I'd felt more supported by her in the last few days than I had in the last eight months by my dad. "She doesn't bring every conversation back to hockey, which is great for reminding me that I am a person beyond putting the puck in the net. Do I have a pair of skates lying around?"

"Yeah, there's a couple of old pairs upstairs that you left here in your last off-season. Does Alana have skates?"

"Don't think so, but she'll be better in rentals than me. This body is used to a certain kind of skate, and I don't want it to be a public skate rink that takes me out. The irony would be too much, and Lenny would never let me live it down. I'll just go grab a pair and head back next door before Len wakes up," I said as I drained my coffee and rinsed the mug before putting it in the dishwasher.

"You seem happy, Liam," Mom said as she picked her pen back up. I thought about it for a moment.

"Yeah, I am."

"Is there a reason your cold arm is wrapped around me?" My question was mostly muffled into the pillow my head was still buried against. It was cotton and smelled an awful lot like almond, which meant it wasn't mine. Great, Liam was a witness to my burrowing for comfort.

"It's cold outside," Liam replied, sounding much more awake than me.

"And why were you outside?"

"Had to go next door."

"Are you being cryptic on purpose?" I asked, reluctantly lifting my head from the pillow.

"No, I just figured this would wake you up quicker." There was a smirk on his face that I wanted to slap off. Or kiss off. The second thought was worrying. But his lower lip looked pouty and like the most kissable thing in the world right now, so I couldn't be blamed for going in that direction.

"What, because it's very annoying?" I asked, shaking off thoughts of kissing and moving his pillow back to his side of the bed.

"Exactly. To answer your question, I went next door to get

some skates because if you remember correctly, you promised me a skating date."

"Hmmm, I've thought about this, and I agreed to four dates. So, when you signed me up for a Christmas Eve party, I decided that it was going to replace your skating date." I booped his nose with my finger and rested my head on his chest. That was better.

"Alana," he whined. My full name in his mouth was such a rarity that it always made butterflies take flight in my stomach, but this time they settled somewhere lower. It was too early to be this turned on, and it was too ridiculous to be turned on by someone calling me by my name.

"Liam," I retorted.

"You promised you'd come skating with me." He still sounded whiny. I imagined he still looked pouty as well. I didn't look at him because I didn't want to be plagued with fantasies of kissing his pouty lips while he helped me release the tension slowly building in my core.

"Did I, though?"

"Okay, fine, no you didn't promise. But you did say you'd come."

"No one is stopping you from going to the rink on your own, buddy," I teased. I was going. I was always going. I hadn't realised that I missed going skating at Christmas time until it was floated as an idea by someone who wouldn't care if I was a better skater than him. But teasing was something I knew how to do with him, and I was having way too much fun making him pout and whine. If I kept it up, I could probably get him to beg.

And the fantasies were back.

"The whole point of having a fake girlfriend is to deflect from awkward questions, and you think me going to an ice rink on my own when people have seen us walking around holding hands isn't going to invite awkward questions? About you and other things, *friend*."

"Then you should have picked someone who liked being outside." I laughed. Liam shifted his arm so that his hand was now resting on my waist. His fingers brushed the strip of bare skin between my shorts and T-shirt, and I burrowed further into him to avoid moaning out loud at the touch. I was now half lying on him. I'd feel embarrassed if he wasn't effectively keeping me pinned against him.

"Come on, Len. Don't tell me you haven't missed skating," he said.

"Are you sure you're not projecting?"

"No, I've skated in the last eight months. Now I wanna skate in circles with my very capable date." He squeezed his arm around me, and I melted.

"And show off all that hockey speed."

I felt his muscles tense for a moment before he relaxed again.

"Wanna tell me what made you all tense just then, Muller?" My fingers started drawing patterns on his chest. It was solid under my touch. I wasn't paying much attention to where my fingers moved, but I felt the stutter of his breath underneath me when I brushed over his nipple. I hoped he would answer my question soon so I could focus on his answer instead of the fact that he had sensitive nipples. A fact that could be a lot of fun to play with.

"It's nothing," he mumbled.

"Try again." I shouldn't have, but I gently pinched his nipple.

He let out a deep breath that almost sounded like a moan, but he covered it by clearing his throat. "Do you have an opinion on my retirement?"

I lifted my head again, not sure that I'd heard him correctly.

"Should I?" I asked.

"Just say whatever came to your mind when I asked." His eyes were closed like he was braced for impact. If it were anyone else, I would think my answer through so that I didn't risk hurting feelings. But this was Liam, who could sense when I was pulling my punches and hated it when I did. So, I said exactly what I thought.

"I don't really care…No that's not quite true. I care, but I care in the sense that I care whether you're happy or not. I don't think you should still be out there if your heart isn't in it. I don't think you should have kept playing because, in theory, you had the years left in your body. I don't think you owe anybody any more than what you have already given them. And I think it is a tad sad that some people you've allowed close to you have made you think that being a hockey person is all you are capable of."

I don't know what reaction I expected from him, but it wasn't for his body to start shaking with laughter.

"I asked because Mom brought it up and obviously, we haven't really talked about it. But I told her I didn't think you cared all that much beyond whether I wanted to do it or not. So it's nice to know that you haven't made me a liar in that sense."

It had been coming back to me slowly just how well Liam knew me and how well I knew him. With everything that clicked back into place between us, I felt more and more like myself than I had in years. It was hard to tell if it was because I was back home or if it was because I was around him again. Or if it was a magical combination of both.

"Alright, let's go skating. Do not judge me for the fact that I might be shit. I've not been on skates for a while."

"I think it might be like riding a bike."

"Except I haven't done that for ages either, and this involves blades and ice, which is a recipe for disaster."

"You'll be fine. I'll be there."

I wanted to give him shit for giving himself so much importance, but it did feel nice to know that he would be there to catch me when I inevitably fell on my ass.

"Is this a cover of Mariah Carey? Why use a cover when she is right there?" I was focusing on the music playing through the ice rink, and the weight of my ring as it spun around my knuckle. It was easier to focus on those things than the fact that Liam was on his knees in front of me. He was only tightening the laces on my skates, but he was doing it with a level of care that drove my mind to other places. And he was *on his knees.*

I had spent months feeling indifferent to sex, and I thought that I hated feeling that indifference, but it was actually easier to deal with than my current predicament of getting turned on at the drop of a hat. I could only attribute that to Liam. It was quite inconvenient. I was at an ice rink, surrounded by people I sort of knew and who definitely knew my parents.

And I was wet.

All Liam was doing was tying my laces and my body was acting like it had never been touched before. And maybe it hadn't. Not like this, anyway. Gently. Assuredly. Like I was something worth taking care of.

"Yeah, it's a cover," Liam answered quietly, bringing me back into the room and out of fantasy land. He tapped my skate twice.

"You still do that?" I asked.

"Do what?" He looked up at me and the intensity in his eyes while he was on his knees before me made me choke on air.

I cleared my throat and averted my gaze before I answered, "Tap the skates after you've finished lacing them up."

"With everything you know about sports people, and me, you think I stopped tapping skates after I laced them?" He laughed as he confidently rose to his feet, before sitting on the bench next to me and tightening his own skates.

"No, I guess you wouldn't stop. I just forgot you did that."

I watched as he quickly and methodically secured his laces, tapping them both when he finished, before standing up again and holding out his hand to me.

"You ready?" he asked. I slid my hand into his.

Liam led us to the rink like someone who was used to having to walk on concrete in blades. I crossed the short distance like Bambi. Liam found it hilarious, and I wanted the ground to swallow me whole. I used to be just like him, perfectly at home making that walk like it was nothing.

Fortunately, the second my blades touched the ice my legs didn't give out and leave me in a heap. When he was sure I wasn't going to fall flat on my ass, Liam let go of my hand and pushed off in the direction of flow on the rink, leaving me to try and remember how to propel myself around the ice and follow him.

As a reminder that Liam was not even a year into his retirement from professional hockey, he was back in less than a minute and came to a dead stop in front of me. A dead stop that should not have been sexy because all he was doing was *stopping* on some ice. But with the stopping came a wave of his cologne. I could feel his breath against my cheek and the sun hit his eyes just right, making them look like they were actually sparkling. So, it was all very sexy.

Then there was his smile. His smile almost took my breath away.

"You're showing off, Muller," I said, only sounding a little breathless.

"Just finding my sea legs," he replied, lacing his fingers through mine and gently tugging me along as he started skating again.

"Bend your knees and lean forward, almost like you're going to fall over," Liam said when he realised I wasn't going anywhere.

"Babe, if I lean forward like I'm going to fall over, I am going to fall over."

"Alana, if you think I am going to let you fall then you really do not know me at all. So, lean forward slightly and push off on your toes. Keep your knees bent so your centre of gravity stays low."

It was becoming increasingly obvious to me that the reason I let this man call me Lenny was because I would never be able to function if he called me by my full name all the time. It was a weapon. It had the power to take me out completely. It made my legs wobbly, my heart feel like it was trying to escape from my chest, broke me out in goosebumps, and made me want to get down on my knees and force that word out of him like a broken, gravelly prayer.

He'd used it twice today, which was maybe a record, and it was ruining my life. We were supposed to be having a Hallmark Christmas movie day, and I was wondering how quickly we could leave this ice rink, throw all pretence about this relationship out of the window and fuck it out. Repeatedly.

I almost forgot what he said and then remembered that he was giving me quite practical advice to get me off this spot that I was starting to grow roots into. I shifted my body forward and Liam skated back slowly, dragging me along with him. I started to use my legs to move forward, helping him with his task, which he was taking very seriously.

"I'm remembering another reason why I told people I

couldn't skate. It was because I grew to hate it when I had to do it slowly like this," I said just as one of my legs decided it didn't want to be underneath me and instead wanted to go out at some kind of angle. Quicker than I thought possible, Liam was at my side and caught my skate before it could slip too far out and leave me in a pile on the ice. One of his hands settled on my hip and somehow, I managed to stay upright.

"Told you I wouldn't let you fall. You wanna try again?" The heat of his fingers felt like it was searing through my leggings onto my skin. I needed to get away from him.

"No. Can we just call it a day? I've been on the ice. Can we be done now?"

"Do you really wanna be done?" Liam asked and I knew that I wouldn't be getting off this ice.

The ice was Liam's life. It was his one motivation for so long and now, suddenly, it wasn't. He could say it was the right decision all he liked, and I did think that it was the right one, but that didn't mean that he wasn't missing being on the ice in some capacity. Even if it was just for fun. If there was one thing I knew for sure, it was that Liam couldn't do that when he was a professional. Just fuck around on the ice for fun.

I could give him that, even if it felt like my legs were going to give up on me. That probably had more to do with the man currently holding me up than the thin blades on slippery ice anyway.

"No, I don't wanna be done. I want to fast forward through the training montage where I learn how to skate again and just be at the end where I'm skating circles around you."

"You could out-skate me once upon a time. I am sure it's still in there somewhere. No extensive training montage required."

"Yeah, but then you decided to make being an ice skater your entire personality and we couldn't just fuck around anymore. I could only be your stand-in goalkeeper or something. Although, I guess that wasn't for nothing. When are you going to thank me for making you the ice skater that you were?"

In actual fact, I'd done nothing. During the season, it was one of the only ways we could hang out with each other, so he had extra 'shooting' practice once a week. Although that was what we passed it off as when we booked the ice time, all I would do was stand there and he would shoot the puck at me in the gentlest fashion possible. The puck never made it off the ice because he was too worried about accidentally hitting me in the face.

"You're right, all my hard work had nothing to do with it. It was all you. Being around you was always murder for my ego."

I couldn't figure out his tone and I stopped. Then I realised that we had been moving forward, so maybe skating *was* like riding a bike.

"Wait, am I actually bothering you?" Falling into an old dynamic with Liam had been easy. He used to tease me for always studying; I used to tease him for having so many eggs in the hockey basket. That was our thing. But at the end of the day, we still hadn't seen each other for over a decade, so maybe now he thought that I was just being bitchy.

"No, Lenny, you're not. I know you're not being mean. I've always known you're not being mean. In fact, it's always been quite nice knowing that there was someone in my life who treated ice hockey like it was very unimportant and reminded me that I need to have a life outside of it. I've had a lot of people blowing smoke up my ass for a very long time and I think I missed you not giving a shit about hockey and calling me an ice skater."

We were moving again, slowly, but my legs were starting to find their rhythm as I pushed forward and followed Liam.

"I mean, technically, you are an ice skater. Yeah, there were other things you had to do but you were a person who skated on ice."

"And now you're an ice skater, once again," he said as he let go of my hand, spun around, and took off again.

The loss of his hand made my hand feel cold, but I didn't slip or fall. In fact, I felt fine. I knew I could take it from here. I used to be good at this. Dad had put me on the ice the moment it was safe to and taught me and Liam at the same time. Aaron had joined us at some point but hated it and immediately lost interest. At some point, Liam latched onto hockey, and Dad latched onto that, and I moved on to cheerleading because the fact that I could do the splits had to be put to use somehow. But I'd still been on the ice a lot. And as I moved forward, muscle memory kicked in and I felt stronger. I found my centre of gravity and stability on my blades and was able to put power behind my strides.

And so, I started to chase Liam.

Except this was Liam and he moved quicker than me, so before I had even made it three-quarters of the way around the rink, I could sense him behind me.

Just like muscle memory was propelling me around the rink again, muscle memory also made me brace for impact, but still stay loose, when I knew Liam was close.

Sure enough, as he reached me, his arm wrapped around my waist, scooped me up, and carried us forward.

"Going to have to try harder than that to catch me, Len," he said into my ear before carefully putting me down on the ice, making sure I was secure on my blades again before letting me go.

"What do I get if I catch you?" I asked.

"The satisfaction of knowing that you're a better ice skater than me," he suggested.

"That does not sound like a good enough win, but sure, I'll take it."

"Stick to the very inside so we don't piss other people off," he said as he pushed himself just ahead of me.

I nodded. "You get a two-second head start, so you better put those ice skater quads of yours to good use."

He smiled and drove off his left leg, putting so much distance between us with just the one move that I regretted giving him two seconds. One would have sufficed.

There was no way I was going to catch him.

Twenty One

LIAM

The thing about Lenny was that she had always been a better skater than me. She played down her ability like she did with most things, but I knew it wouldn't take her long to find her pace on the ice once she got used to being back on skates.

It took ten laps around the rink for her to catch up with me. Which was probably for the best because it took about that long for my body to let me know that it was not fit for long bouts of skating anymore. My knees started aching and my quads were beginning to protest from exertion.

Lenny wrapped her arms around my waist once she reached me.

"Tag, you're it," she said, sounding breathless. As she spun around in front of me, her eyes were a sparkling caramel and she had the brightest smile I'd ever seen on her face, causing the corners of her eyes to crinkle.

"I see you've found your grounding on the ice," I said, shifting so that she was now by my side, one arm still around my waist. I looped mine over her shoulders and we started skating at a more leisurely pace.

"And I see you've lost yours. There is no way I should have

been able to catch you." Her tone was teasing, and her other hand hit me playfully in the chest.

"You were always a better skater, if I remember correctly. For a long time, before you became my goalkeeper, Rob used you as a way to get me to move faster on the ice."

"Oh shit, yeah. I forgot about those sessions. Dude, you used to get ruined by me. I was so fast on that ice, I could skate circles around you."

"You really did make me a better skater. I learned how to be nimble on that ice because I used to have you skating circles around me before you switched to back-springs and school chants. I can't believe you told guys you weren't good on the ice just so you could protect their egos. If they couldn't hack it, that was their problem, not yours."

"Yeah, that may be true, but when you're young and trying to find love, you make all kinds of concessions. And then with Kai, I just kept it up because I wanted to use the rare time I had away from the bakery to be off my feet as much as possible. Skating, skiing, being made to go outside in general, really got in the way of me relaxing and resetting by a fire in a cosy knit with a bunch of books."

"Wow, I really ruined your holiday plans by demanding that we go out on dates, didn't I? How many books did you bring back with you?"

"Like ten. I've finished two so far."

It was then that I remembered that Lenny was a quick reader. A scarily fast one when she wanted to be. Her dad was her ride to and from school and when we turned sixteen, and I got my licence, it became me. Both her dad and I had hockey practice after school, and although there was a period in the school year where our practices aligned, a lot of the time they didn't, so Lenny spent a lot of time at the rink waiting for one of us to be done so she could go home. She finished a lot of books during those practices. Thick ones, too. Ones that would have taken me weeks to even find the motivation to want to read. She read them like it was nothing, and she loved it.

Rob would always ask her about what she was reading on the rides home. Sometimes, it was the classics. Then there were a lot of werewolves, which then became a lot of vampires, which then became regular re-reads of *Twilight*. Even though Rob had no idea what her obsession with that book was about, he always asked if she learnt anything new from the re-read. And was always interested in the answer.

When I started doing most of the driving, I also took over asking about her reading. Even when the books started to take a steamier turn, she still gave me a breakdown and left me feeling every bit the horny teenage boy I was. Who then took out all that sexual tension in the shower.

It always felt like I'd read more books than I actually did because of those car journeys.

"How have you already finished two books when we've only been back four days?" Other than outside the bakery when she was waiting for me, I hadn't seen her reading once.

"Other than the first night, you have gone to sleep much earlier than me. I wasn't joking when I said that I was more of a one a.m. bedtime kind of girl, so while you've been having fun communing with Morpheus from eleven p.m., I have been downstairs sipping a hot drink and getting lost in the pages of a book. Or two."

I smiled at the Greek mythology reference. Where Lenny had books, I had Greek mythology. I'd downloaded so much information into her brain about the whole genre, she probably had just as much knowledge as I did. If not more because she retained information better than me, and once she knew something, she never forgot it.

"What have you been reading?" I asked. Her face lit up

and she took a deep breath before launching into her spiel, her fingers lacing through mine still over her shoulder.

"Well, the first was a thriller that kept me up way later than I anticipated because I couldn't stop reading, which I guess is what you want. It involved stolen identities and a mystery boss, and it ended up being the ultimate long con. I thought it was super obvious what all the plot points were going to be and the twists it was going to take, but it managed to keep me guessing. I was surprisingly happy with how it ended, and you know how much I resent endings sometimes."

"You wonder why some people even bother with the rest of the book if they haven't figured out how they are going to finish it properly," I reeled off. It had been a recurring theme in our car discussions.

"Exactly. Anyway, the other one was a romance novel. Friends pretending to date to save a Christmas tree farm. It seemed suitably festive. I had no idea it was going to end up mirroring my life so closely when I decided to bring it home with me."

I noticed that she was still calling Westchester home. She'd lived in Michigan for over a decade and yet, she was still calling this place home. I still called it home as well, but that was because I *felt* at home here more than I ever did in the places hockey took me. Yes, my parents were still here, but my bones just felt at peace in Westchester. Although now that I was thinking about it, I had felt a sense of calm wash over me the moment I heard Alana's name called out for a coffee and found her at the airport. A calm I hadn't felt since she left. A calm I didn't even know I was missing until it came back to me.

"The verdict on that one?" I asked, rather than dwell on thoughts of home.

"It was great. I loved it. I think I might make it one of those books that I always re-read when this time of year comes around. It feels like a delicious hot chocolate, a blanket, and a fire on a cold winter's day." She sounded so at peace, surrounded by all these people skating.

"Sounds perfect."

"It was. Speaking of sounding perfect, I'm hungry and if I remember correctly, this rink is stacked with food and drink trucks so we must be able to find something decent to eat. Let's get off the ice now while you're still on two feet, number seventeen."

She extracted herself from my side, leaving a coldness in her wake before she slipped out of the masses and skated to the exit. I waited for a gap in the crowd and followed her.

"I know you don't know what the hell you want to do with your life now that you've retired, but I think you'd be a good coach. I mean, I wasn't a total newbie, and I didn't need to be coached in the ways of ice hockey, but you did make the whole skating thing a lot easier. I felt safe. I think that's a good trait to have, being a calming presence or something," she said as I joined her off the ice.

I hadn't considered coaching yet. It didn't feel like that was where my skill set lay. That and I wasn't the best loser. I had no idea if I'd be capable of picking a team back up after a loss. I typically needed to fester in the disappointment for forty-eight hours and ever since college, I needed to do that in solitude.

But Lenny was being completely sincere right now and I thought maybe she was on to something. I had no idea how to even start getting into coaching, but I felt like I could do anything with her believing in me.

Twenty Two

ALANA

Maybe it was because going around in circles and trying not to disrupt the flow of skaters wasn't very conducive to fangirling, but once we were on solid ground again, people would not leave Liam alone.

It was slow at first, like they were scared to approach, but then one brave teenager came up to him, told him he loved him, and the floodgates opened.

Men that were around our dads' age came over and clapped him on the shoulder like they were proud parents and said variations of how he was the best thing to come out of Westchester. Teenagers who were at our old high school kept calling him a legend and letting him know that Coach Fitzpatrick was always saying how proud he was that he managed to produce both Liam Mulligan and Teddy Carter. I didn't doubt that my dad was proud of them, but he was not the sort of person to keep bringing up his success stories. He'd had a lot over the course of his career, so I wondered who the bragging was really coming from.

As the dads and teenage boys gave way to a bunch of women, I stopped hanging around in the background like I was Liam's shadow, took his skates bag, and wandered over to a food truck that served nothing but fries. Several concoctions caught my eye but, in the end, I went with fries covered in rosemary salt and doubled the portion just in case Liam managed to extract himself from the crowd before I'd eaten them all.

I was almost halfway through eating when I felt someone hanging out behind me. I think he was trying to sneak up on me, but it felt like the atoms in the air around me had changed, and the little ball of anxiety that had settled in my chest when the crowds started gathering eased, which could only mean that Liam was behind me.

"You done being the best thing since sliced bread?" I asked. The woman sitting next to me looked over at me with a look of fear in her eyes, like I'd started talking to myself after being silent for the last fifteen minutes. I ignored her.

"What do you think was the best thing before sliced bread?" Liam responded. The woman visibly sank in relief before perking up a little. I tried to keep ignoring her.

"Getting through the First World War."

"Wait, do you know when sliced bread became a thing?" There was no free space at the table I was sitting on, so Liam squatted down next to me.

"1928," I replied, swiping to the next page of the book I was reading on my phone, only to discover that it was the beginning of the next chapter. I locked my phone and looked at him. Only instead of looking at his face like I intended, I found my eyes were drawn to the way his thighs bulged in his jeans while he was in that position. I blinked slowly to try and erase the X-rated images that had taken residence in my brain and managed to look at his face. His cheeks were pink from the cold and the dusting of stubble on his face made him annoyingly more attractive. His eyes looked more grey than green, a colour I had never seen before.

"Huh, then yeah, you're probably right. Any of these fries for me?" I slid the box over to him and looked back down at the table, my brain still trying to figure out why his eyes looked grey.

"Help yourself."

"Thanks," he shoved a handful of fries into his mouth. "Yes, by the way. I've finished being the best thing since sliced bread. Although I very much don't think I am that, before you try to give me hell for saying such a thing."

"Me? Give you hell for saying you're awesome. That could never be me."

"I don't know, Gunner, I think you're pretty great," said the woman sitting next to me. I turned my head to look at her and saw that she had a very flirty face on, one finger twisting a strand of hair.

Liam swallowed.

"Yeah, thanks. I was only ever as good as the team around me, and I played with some great teams."

Well, that answer sounded scripted.

"You and Teddy proved to be a lethal combination on the ice," she said.

"We grew up together. I knew how to read that man on the ice, and he could do the same. It came in handy. We were a good team."

"Were you only a great team on the ice?" Her words were dripping with innuendo, and I struggled to not burst into laughter. I had no real frame of reference, but something told me neither Liam nor Teddy was the kind to share off the ice.

"Teddy was a great wingman. Wouldn't be with my girl-friend without him."

"Oh, I didn't realise. I'm sorry," she said to me.

I shook my head. "No worries. You're not the first to flirt with my boyfriend in front of me, I doubt you'll be the last." I had a lot of conflicting feelings about that truth. I was starting to think that maybe, just maybe, I was a jealous person.

At least I was when it came to a certain retired hockey player. Kai used to say it was cool how chill I was when other women flirted with him, but the truth was, I hadn't really cared. He'd never given me any reason to think he would take anything beyond just flirting.

Liam didn't give me a reason to think that either, but something inside me still wanted to mark him as *mine, mine, mine* whenever someone so much as batted an eyelash in his direction. It was confusing and new. I didn't know what to do with it.

"I can imagine," she said, nudging me in the side like we now shared an inside joke.

"Len, you can't sustain yourself on fries alone, so what do you say we go get more food? I'm all yours for the rest of the day," Liam said, bringing my attention back to him.

I ignored the muttered *"I wish he could be mine for the rest of the day"* from the woman next to me and looked around at the other food trucks stationed around the rink.

"What are your thoughts on burgers?" I asked.

"They are probably what sliced bread was invented for," he replied as he held out his hand, fingertips lightly dusted in rosemary salt.

As Liam started looking for a place to sit, a family cleared their table so quickly it was almost farcical. He thanked the dad of the family, who looked the most starstruck of them all, as we sat in their vacated seats and put our burgers on the table.

"How exactly is one supposed to approach eating such a thing?" I asked as I sat next to him, and he pushed one of the burgers over to me. It was stacked. There were too many layers to count, and sauce and cheese were dripping down the sides. The stick holding it together in the middle was there symbolically, as I didn't think it was making anything more structurally sound at all.

"I think you just get involved," Liam replied before he crammed as much of the burger into his mouth as possible. Barbecue sauce dripped out the sides and smeared along his chin as he bit down. I never thought I would feel envious of a condiment because it got to be in such proximity to his mouth, but I also didn't think chopping was sexy and he'd managed to achieve that. Who knew what else he was going to make attractive to me?

I picked up my own burger and followed suit, embracing the mess that ensued the moment I applied even a tiny amount of pressure to the top bun.

"Shit, this is so good," I said, throwing out any kind of etiquette and talking with my mouth full.

"Right? It's maybe the best burger I have ever eaten." Liam was studying his burger, looking for the best place to sink his teeth in next. He hadn't cleaned the sauce off his chin yet, so I reached over and swiped it off with one of my fingers. His stubble made it just a little harder to wipe off cleanly, but I managed it. As my finger left his face, his tongue darted out like it was trying to finish the job. It left his bottom lip looking wet and I had the urge to lean over and learn what it would feel like between my lips.

I'd never thought about kissing so much in my life.

In a bid to stop thinking about that, I licked the sauce off my finger. Liam watched the movement, and I realised why I had never seen his eyes look grey before. I'd never seen him turned on before. Or I'd never paid enough attention to him before to notice if he had ever been turned on in my presence. But as my finger left my mouth, I watched his green eyes darken to grey and it made my skin feel hot under his gaze.

I cleared my throat in a bid to try to clear some of the sexual tension that had blanketed us in the last minute. It seemed to knock the lust out of Liam's eyes a little.

"Thanks. Is it all gone?" he asked. His voice sounded different. Huskier.

"Until you take your next bite, yeah."

Liam laughed.

"How about after we eat these, we go for a walk? It will be dark soon and you can see the lights in all their glory. If you're a good girl, I might even buy you a hot chocolate." He winked and took another bite, getting more sauce on his chin.

Ordinarily, I would give him shit for saying the words 'good girl' in relation to me, but today, the words made me very aware of the steady pulse of desire thrumming against the seam of my leggings.

I took another bite of my burger to try and distract myself from it.

Twenty Three

ALANA

I woke up and rolled onto cold sheets. It was a harsh wake-up call from my lovely dream, which had been full of highlights from the day before.

Liam's assuredness on the ice and the way it seemed to yield to him like he was its master. The easy way he dealt with people coming up to him and singing his praises, while also keeping me out of it. The way his fingers tangled with mine while I found my feet in skates again. The press of his hand against my lower back, a brand against my skin even through my winter layers. The feeling of satisfaction that washed over me every time I managed to get a full belly laugh out of him. The warmth of spiked hot chocolate while we marvelled at the lights, and burgers so stacked that they left smears of sauce on full lips that I wanted to clean up with my tongue.

Yesterday, it felt like I was actually dating Liam. And more than it feeling real, it felt *right*. Especially the part where he was on his knees in front of me, which had taken an X-rated turn in dream world and had left me feeling needy.

I rolled over in frustration and stuck my hand underneath my pillow, making contact with my vibrator.

The cold bed was a good indication that Liam had been gone for a while, and I pushed up onto my elbows to see if I could figure out where he might be. His towel was hanging on the long radiator, so he wasn't in the bathroom, which suggested that maybe he had gone for a run. He mentioned yesterday that he might try and get one in. If that was the case, then I probably had more than enough time to satisfy this need.

I pulled the vibrator out and slipped it between my legs. The press of the point against my clit sent a shiver through my body. I couldn't remember the last time I had been turned on this quickly. Definitely not for the majority of my twenties. But this week, I'd been like a live wire and the barest of touches were setting my nerve endings alight. Sometimes Liam just had to look at me for my clit to perk up.

I clicked the vibe on and closed my eyes, letting images of what I wished had happened last night play in my mind. How I wanted to lick the cream from the hot chocolate that had ended up on his upper lip after the first sip and tease the plush lower lip between my teeth before coaxing him into a kiss. I could feel his hands sweeping up my back and holding me close to him, his thigh slotting in between my legs, a solid pressure where I would need him most. I could hear the sounds he would make the longer we kissed, and as my hands started to stroke across his body, they'd become desperate, low, *needy.*

The pressure coiling in my lower stomach was starting to build, and I tilted my hips to press the vibe harder against my clit. The promise of relief inching ever closer. I started imagining his hands, so big and slightly calloused, pressed against my naked skin, and his fingertips teasing the pucker of my nipples. The weight of him pressing me down into the mattress, and the kisses he would pepper over the line of my neck.

I felt my muscles tighten and I prepared to fly off the edge into sheer orgasmic bliss.

And then my vibrator died.

"Fuck!" I muttered angrily and punched the mattress with my free hand.

"I can help with that." My eyes flew open. I refused to believe that the voice I just heard was actually in the room, but there he was.

Liam was leaning against my closed bedroom door. How had I not heard it open? He was holding a tray with two plates of toast stacked with bacon and eggs, as well as coffee so hot there was still steam coming off it.

"What the hell are you doing here?" It was all I could think to say, even though it was pretty fucking obvious what he was doing.

"This is my room for the holidays as well and I'm bringing you breakfast in bed," he replied. His voice sounded tight. It made my body coil even further in anticipation. I was the reason he sounded like that, and it made me feel powerful.

"What's for breakfast?" It was such a ridiculous question to ask while my body still thrummed with desire and Liam looked a bit like he wanted to devour me. I was hoping that if I distracted him enough, we could just ignore the last few minutes.

"I went and bought that bread you like, the one with the cranberries in it, and toasted it. And fried some bacon and eggs. I wouldn't exactly say I made it. But I did bring all the very simple components together."

"Oh," I said stupidly. I loved that bread. I had tried to make it myself, but whatever Westchester Bakes did to it could not be replicated. And he'd gone out to buy it for me specifically.

"I'm just saying that I made this coffee too hot to drink right now and I don't think either of us minds eating lukewarm food," Liam said as he pushed off the door and started walking towards his side of the bed, settling the tray on the bedside table. So, distracting him hadn't worked.

"And why are you saying that?"

"Playing dumb doesn't suit you, Len."

I groaned. "Can we just pretend that you didn't see anything and then we can eat the breakfast you made in peace?"

"No," he said. I was surprised by his bluntness but also, it felt good to be so obviously and openly desired by this man. But still, thinking about crossing the line was very different to actually crossing the line.

"The moment's passed, anyway. Let's just eat." I tried to sit up, but he put a hand on my shoulder and kept me lying down while he crawled on the bed.

"I've changed my mind. I don't want a year's supply of brownies for winning, I want something else."

"Huh?"

Liam pressed both of his knees up against my thigh and looked down at me. "I wasn't recognised on the ice rink. I said I wanted brownies, but I want to change my prize."

Oh yeah, that bet. Except...

"Muller, you spent at least half an hour with fans. What is your definition of getting recognised? Because mine is the swarming of people who knew your name and wanted your picture. There is no way you won that bet."

"We said *on* the ice rink, and they all came up to me when we were off the ice. I won." He smirked.

I sighed. On a word technicality, he was right. No one came near him whilst he was on the ice. I was the sole focus of his attention, and he was mine.

"What's your amendment?"

His eyes flicked down my body. It was still mostly covered, but I felt naked under his gaze.

"What do you think I want?" His voice was dangerously deep now, his eyes that shade of almost-grey again.

"I don't know, that's why I'm asking." A small lie. What he wanted was written all over his face.

"Alright Alana, let me be explicit about this. I want to drape your legs over my shoulders and hold you open while I lick and suck—and gently bite if you're into it—your clit until you get the orgasm that your vibrator just left you on the brink of."

Like when he had asked me to be his fake girlfriend at the airport, there were a million reasons to say no. The biggest one was that this would complicate *everything*. But I had already made things complicated when I said yes to being his fake girlfriend.

And I'd had a better time this week as a result because even though we had said it wasn't real, Liam was taking the role of being my boyfriend very seriously. He didn't have to take me on a Christmas lights walk, but he did because he knew I loved Christmas lights. He didn't have to make sure that I was properly fed at every moment. He didn't have to go out this morning and stand in a queue to buy a very specific bread that he knew I liked when we were teenagers. But he did so he could surprise me with breakfast in bed, which I didn't even think he would remember he was 'supposed' to do. An oversight on my part because Liam always made good on his forfeits.

My fake relationship with Liam was the easiest one I had ever been in, and it hadn't even been a week. So why not add another layer to it?

I pulled the duvet off me and Liam inhaled sharply. "Amendment accepted. Oh, and Liam, I'm into it."

Within seconds, Liam was straddling my waist, keeping his weight on his knees. It was only now that he was sitting in front of me that I noticed the thick bulge in his shorts, visible even though they weren't exactly tight. I swallowed thickly.

"Fuck Len, you are so beautiful." He sounded almost breathless as his hands came to rest above my shoulders and he tipped forward bringing his face close to mine.

"You're not totally hideous." I tried to go for a teasing tone, but it ended up sounding desperate. Which, in some ways, I was. I saw a sly smirk break out on his face just before he ducked down and nuzzled against my neck, his lips brushing against me in featherlight presses that made me feel even needier.

"Are you all wet for me?" he whispered against my ear. He nipped at my lobe, and I tilted my hips up against him, bringing my clit into direct contact with his hard cock. It pulled an unexpected moan out of me that made Liam chuckle.

"So that's a yes, then?" he asked as one of his hands started trailing down my side until his fingers hooked into the top of my shorts.

"Shit," I said suddenly. Liam's hand immediately moved, and he sat up, still keeping the majority of his weight off me.

"What's wrong?"

"Nothing exactly. I just remembered that it's been a while since I bothered to extensively groom down there. So, like, there's hair there." I felt dumb saying it out loud, but I'd also been in this position before and well, it had a disappointing end every time.

"Is that it?" He sounded a touch amused.

"Well, yeah, I guess."

"Okay, fine. Can I get back to what I was doing then?" His fingers tickled along my waistband. His total indifference to something considered a deal breaker with others made me feel bold. It had been a long time since I felt bold in the bedroom. Figures Liam would be the person to bring it back out of me.

"Are you lying when you say that your shoulder is the only serious injury you've ever had?"

"No, shoulder is my one and only, and once again, I assure you that it's fine," he answered, not phased by this line of questioning.

"Great. Get on your knees at the end of the bed." I had never seen pupils dilate in real time quite like I did in that moment. I felt so powerful.

"Do I get a pillow?" he asked as he climbed off me and shuffled to the end of the bed. I took the second pillow on his side and threw it at him. He put it on the floor and sank to his knees. I took a deep breath before I lifted my hips and pulled my shorts down my legs.

"You're bare under your pyjama shorts?" Liam asked breathlessly as I scooted down the bed, bringing the apex of my thighs closer to his mouth.

"If I'm not on my period, yeah, usually," I replied as Liam's hands wrapped around my thighs and pulled me in the rest of the way. I expected him to say something else, but instead, he sealed his mouth over my clit and started circling his tongue around it.

"Oh my god," I moaned, my back arching and pushing my pussy down on his face. Liam seemed to relish in that and sucked lightly before getting back to teasing my orgasm out of me with the tip of his tongue. It had been so long since I had felt the warm press of someone's mouth on my sensitive flesh, while their stubble teased my inner thighs, that I had forgotten how much I loved it.

Liam was laser-focused, and I could only lie there and quietly moan into my hand to muffle the sound, as he brought me closer to the orgasm that had been buzzing under my skin since I woke up.

"I'm gonna—" I couldn't finish my sentence because my entire body fell over into complete bliss, and all I could do was ground myself by tugging on Liam's hair with my free hand.

Just as I started to feel more over-sensitive than felt good for me, Liam pressed one final kiss against my pussy and lifted his head. The bottom of his face was slick with my orgasm, and, combined with the dark look in his eyes and the smile on his face, he looked downright filthy. He let go of my thighs, a loss I felt more keenly than I wanted to admit, and stood up, not an ounce of self-consciousness about the evident, unattended bulge in his shorts. He walked back to the tray loaded with our breakfast.

"Now, we eat breakfast."

Twenty Four

LIAM

Lenny hadn't put her shorts back on, but she had covered her lower body while she ate her almost-cold breakfast.

The only sound in the room was that of cutlery scraping on plates and the occasional moans of contentment from her when she ate a particularly delicious mouthful. It was a surprisingly comfortable environment considering that we had just crossed a line in our friendship that we could never uncross.

Not that I wanted to go back. I wanted more. More of watching her fall apart against my tongue. More of the moans that she had to muffle with her hand to make sure she wasn't being too loud. I wanted *everything*.

"Why did you feel the need to tell me that you had pubes?" I asked when I saw that she had mostly finished her breakfast. I had a feeling I knew why, but I hadn't wanted to dive into it earlier lest it piss me off and ruin the mood.

"I dunno, not everyone likes to deal with that." She shrugged then took a sip of her coffee, now the perfect temperature.

I waited.

"My last two boyfriends said it got in the way of good oral sex," she said when the silence between us got a bit too heavy.

"But not penetrative?" I scoffed.

"They never had any issue with that," she muttered. Almost bitterly.

"What standards, exactly, did they expect?"

"Are we really having this conversation?" I nodded and she rolled her eyes. "I guess the ideal was nothing, a landing strip was acceptable, at a push."

"And they had no leeway with that?" This conversation was pissing me off exactly as I thought it would, but it was bringing with it an unexpected annoyance. Lenny had more important things to think about than having to remember to have hair removed on a regular basis just so her boyfriend would service all her sexual needs.

"Not a lot, no."

"You know that's crazy, right?"

"Yeah, and I also know that you are the first person to go down on me in over two years because of it."

Dual feelings of pride and anger passed through me at that.

"Do I dare ask if he held himself to that same standard?"

"No, and as such, I also have not given a blowjob in two years. You know I'm petty, and frankly, they call it a job for a reason."

"You didn't say yes because you didn't want a life without getting eaten out, isn't it?" I teased. Lenny took another long sip from her coffee, and I worried that I'd crossed a line, but she let out a soft laugh when she swallowed her coffee.

"It didn't even cross my mind that I would be signing myself for a lifetime without it. I was used to it not happening. The lack of oral seemed like a really small thing in what was otherwise a good relationship. Or maybe I just wanted it to be good because the thought of being single in my thirties terrified me. I had a good enough man right there, even if sexually, we weren't the most compatible. The bigger issue was that he was obsessed with you." The corners of her mouth tipped up into a hint of a smile.

"Now why did you have to tell me he was obsessed with me? I was so determined to trash-talk him for all eternity," I groaned. Lenny laughed, bright and free.

"I obviously can't say for certain because I wasn't there for the aftermath of the second huge event of his year, but something tells me that he was more heartbroken over your retirement than his failed proposal. At least that's what I'm telling myself so that I feel like less of an asshole for leaving him hanging in a lunge with a ring in a box, held proudly in front of him."

I shifted so I was close enough to wrap my arm around her shoulders.

"I'm sure I'm not the first person to say this, but if it's not a resounding yes, then it's not for you." I kissed her temple.

"Are you still hard?" The change of subject almost caught me off guard, but this was Lenny, and she didn't do feelings all that well. At least she didn't talk about them well; her love language was probably acts of service.

"Not completely, but not far off," I answered, and she nodded slowly before groaning in frustration.

"Fuck, I don't have any condoms, do you?"

"I didn't come home to my parents' house with the intention of having sex with anyone, so didn't think to bring any with me. Also, it felt presumptuous to think we would end up here, so I haven't bought any either..." I trailed off. "But my last screening came back all negative and I haven't been with anyone since I had it done," I added.

She sighed. "Yeah, I'm good too, but I'm not on birth control." She must have caught a look on my face because she continued, "It's not because we were trying or anything. I am still very much not having children. It's just that birth control made me feel like shit and I got bored of trying them all. Funnily enough, the thing that catches the sperm before it can do any damage *does* work. So, condoms are my form of birth control, as well as a very good understanding of my cycle, but mostly condoms."

I paused.

"So, let me get this straight. Kai didn't try to find some bullshit reason why he couldn't use condoms, but he found pubes offensive?"

"Like I said, Muller, he was kind, safe, and good."

"I know this is kind of my fault, but all this talk of your ex-boyfriend is making me less hard."

"Well, that's not what I want. Wait, I can bring this back. So, my initial plan was to sink down on said dick, but that's out of the question now. I was then going to suggest a mutual masturbation situation, but can I be honest and say that I don't remember the last time I came more than once—"

I cut in, "Surely at some point with your ex?" Her silence spoke volumes. "Did you have a satisfying sex life?"

"Orgasms are not the be-all and end-all of sex. I usually got one, but it felt greedy to ask for more, especially when the second one usually takes a lot of work."

"Yes, there is more to sex than orgasms, but you should at least have someone who wants to help you have as many as possible whenever you want and takes the time, when necessary. I mean did he forget vibrators exist?"

"No, he knew they existed. He found them a little emasculating during partnered sex, so..."

It was my turn to groan in frustration. "You've faked a lot of orgasms in your time, huh?" She nodded. "Just promise me that you'll never try and fake one with me. I can take it if you need an assist, and I understand that it might not happen every time or more than once in any given encounter, but please don't fake it."

She nodded again. "Alright, pick a place on the body."

"I've got a better idea. Let's have separate showers and go into the city because something tells me that, despite bringing the vibrator, you did not bring the charger, which means we need a new one. Plus, condoms."

"Are you sure?" She ran a finger along my covered length. I shuddered underneath the touch.

"Did we not just establish that not all sexual encounters need to end in orgasms?" I said, despite everything in me screaming to beg her to continue touching me with more pressure.

"Fair point." She removed her hand and then handed me her now empty plate before shimmying her shorts back on underneath the duvet. "I will go have a shower. You take all this back down to the kitchen. Are we gonna get the train or drive to the city? I should warn you, I haven't driven a car since that road trip we went on between junior and senior year, so you will be the one driving."

Suddenly, I remembered that Lenny hated driving more than anyone I had ever met. She only learned so she could say she knew how, and sometimes she drove me to and from the arena on days when she knew I was too tired to function. On the road trip she was talking about, I did most of the driving because despite her telling me that she was fine to drive, I knew she would spend the whole time with her knuckles clenched around the wheel, forgetting to breathe.

"I'll drive. I'll just get the car keys from Mom."

"Sounds like a plan," she said and then she leant forward and pressed a kiss to my cheek. It wasn't the first time she had ever done that, by any means, but something felt different about it this time. My cheek felt warm from it, and it felt that way long after she disappeared from the bedroom and I went to the kitchen to wash our dishes in the sink.

Twenty Five

ALANA

Liam was wearing my sweater.

Technically, it was his and I had just been borrowing it for the last thirteen years. He gave it to me because I was cold on the drive back from one of his games and it was in the backseat of the car. I had planned on giving it back, like I usually did when he lent me clothes, but something about this one was different. It was the perfect sweater, so I kept it a little longer than I usually did. Then I kept on keeping it because he never asked for it back. I'm not sure he even remembered I had it.

I was going to leave it behind when I left for Michigan, but my subconscious had other plans. I found it at the bottom of my suitcase when I was unpacking in my dorm room. I told myself that I would send it to him but every time I picked it up, I convinced myself that it still smelled like him, and I couldn't part with it. After a while, it became a physical reminder that Liam Mulligan, the NHL Golden Boy, had once been in my orbit. It was both a good and a bad reminder. Given that I still had it, clearly it was a mostly good one.

And he'd finally gotten it back.

It was tighter across the shoulders than it had been when he'd bought it, but other than that, it still fit perfectly.

"Nice sweater," I commented as I pulled on my jacket and wrapped my scarf around my neck, partially covering the bottom of my face. Liam stepped into my personal space and kissed my forehead.

"Yeah, it's the funniest thing. I thought I lost it and then it just...turned up," he said into the skin at my temple and a full-body shiver went through me.

"The borrower must have given it back," I whispered as he stepped away and pulled his coat on, an easy smile on his face as he then settled a baseball cap on his head and turned it backwards. As you do in December.

"Come on, Homily, let's go get mad at Christmas tourists."

"Babe, I think we might count as Christmas tourists. We don't live here anymore."

"Do you tell people you're from Michigan?"

"No, I say I'm a New Yorker."

"Exactly. It's in your blood. Let's go get mad at Christmas tourists." He looped an arm around my shoulder and pulled me to his side as he opened the door and led us to the car.

I did a lot of my best thinking when on transport, and so this car ride was also providing the perfect opportunity for me to overthink whatever the hell this morning was. I now knew what Liam's hands felt like when they grabbed my legs to pull me in closer to him. I had vivid details of what the stubble dusting his jaw felt like rubbing on the sensitive skin of my inner thighs. I knew that he could use his tongue like a weapon, and he applied the same amount of focus he had on the ice to making sure I finished. It was too much.

It was everything.

I wanted more.

"What are you thinking about over there?" Liam asked as one of those hands wrapped themselves around my thigh and squeezed gently. I felt a low tug between my legs.

"I'm thinking that driving into the city this close to Christmas for a condom run feels excessive. I'm also thinking that it's wild that we just had sex and even wilder that it doesn't feel weird at all. Even though it is very weird."

"You regret anything?" he asked warily.

"About this morning? No." I could tell Liam wanted to press me further, but he simply squeezed my leg again.

"What about you?" I held my breath.

"Do I regret basically starting my day with my face buried between your legs? No. Can't say I do. I feel like I should write a love letter to your vibrator for dying and granting me the opportunity to take its place."

"How long were you standing there for?"

"No idea. Time lost all meaning the moment I opened the door and saw you writhing on the bed, trying to get yourself off. Then I just tried to think of a plan of action that would end with me getting you off. It wasn't part of my original plan, but then again, none of this was part of my original plan."

"I thought your original plan was 'get my parents off my back'," I joked.

"Which has actually gone swimmingly because your mother insisted that I sleep in your room."

"The more I think about it, the more I am sure that Dad suggested that when he was bringing us back from the airport and Mom went along with it."

"The same man who faux-threatened a whole hockey team to stay away from his daughter? That man suggested his daughter and the kid from next door share a room?"

I laughed, remembering how scared the team had been

around me once Dad had given them a different kind of team talk.

"I asked him to tell his team that I was off limits because one of the keepers wasn't quite taking a hint, and he was happy to oblige. Nothing like the fear of Coach to keep people away. Although, I still don't know how it became a rumour that Coach Fitzpatrick was castrating hockey players and jocks alike who tried to date me. He's never actually given a single shit about my dating life and is mature enough to acknowledge that I am a grown-ass woman who most likely has sex."

"So why do you think he is the mastermind behind it all?"

"How much have you talked to your dad since you got home?" I replied. The fragile way he had asked me how I felt about his retirement, combined with the conversation I had overheard on the day we got home, told me that his dad still wasn't quite on board with Liam's decision to quit while he was ahead.

"On his own, hardly at all."

"Exactly." I tapped the hand on my leg twice.

"Always two steps ahead, that Coach," he muttered.

"Almost like he's one of the best high school coaches in the country."

"Funny that. Where are we going?" he asked.

"The city?"

"No, I meant what shop?"

"Why do you assume that I have a preferred sex shop?"

"I think you prefer buying online. But I also know that you always have backups, which in this case, is a preferred physical shop. The city is a big place. You gotta give me some direction."

"Go to the West Village," I said.

Twenty Six

ALANA

"This is *the* sex shop, isn't it?" Liam asked as he held the door open for me. I didn't need any further clarification on what he was referring to.

"The *Sex and the City* one, yeah," I answered. It also happened to be the first one I ever stepped foot in and therefore, it held a special place in my heart.

"I've never actually been in a sex shop before," he said as he laced his fingers with mine.

"There is probably somebody, somewhere, writing poetry about the symmetry of us both having first experiences in the same sex shop."

I felt flustered now that we were here. We'd established that sex toys were good. Liam had been the one to decide that we needed to make the journey to a decent one because he knew I wouldn't have remembered a charger, and wanted to make sure that I was sexually satisfied.

I was overwhelmed by the fact that I was having sex with someone who was actively interested in my pleasure.

"You alright, Len?" Liam's voice cut through my thoughts.

"Yeah, this is just all very weird. It's a good weird, but still...yeah, weird," I answered.

Liam just nodded and started wandering, gently pulling me along with him. He came to a stop in front of ropes of silk.

"Hypothetically, would you tie me up?" he asked casually.

"And just leave you there? Sure." An idea formed. Quickly.

"No, seriously." He squeezed my fingers.

"I am being serious. I wouldn't leave you there forever. But you, naked, limbs tied up, completely at my disposal. Yeah, I would do that. I could leave a vibrator on and then go bake a batch of brownies or something. Come back with gooey baked goods to you being an over stimulated mess. I'm up for that."

Liam was silent and when I turned to look at him, I saw his mouth was opening and closing. His eyes looked darker, and his neck was flushed.

"Have you thought about that before?" His voice was gruff. Broken. His question was accompanied by one of his hands dipping to his crotch and readjusting.

"Not until you asked, but the visual came to me as quickly as they do when I get a new idea for a cake."

Liam grabbed several silk ropes and pulled me further into the shop.

"For when we are not sleeping in your parents' house," he said. There was no doubt in his voice.

"Alright, what's one of yours then?"

"One of my what?"

"Fantasies. I just gave you mine practically wrapped up in a little bow."

"And it was a great gift. One that I can't seem to move past." He swallowed thickly and then shook his body out.

"Well, you can't have it, it's mine," I retorted.

"I always thought about taking you in a locker room," he threw out easily.

"What do you mean *always*?"

"Are you a suction toy girl?" he asked instead.

"On very rare occasions," I answered.

"So no to this section then. Are we talking dildos or bullets only then?"

Part of me couldn't get used to the fact that we were so casually having this conversation. I'd never been with someone where this kind of conversation was even possible.

"If I have you, then why do I need a dildo?"

"Because I won't always be around if you want something to fuck?"

"Firstly, wasn't this trip out of the house supposed to be just for a new vibrator because the one I have with me is now dead? I have other toys in a drawer in my bedside table. In Detroit. Secondly, if I'm that desperate, it's external stimulation only. I don't tend to have the patience to deal with anything else, and if I really do need it, my fingers do just fine."

"Toys? As in plural? And he never wanted in?" I could tell he was trying to be neutral, but there was always a hint of annoyance in his tone whenever he mentioned Kai.

"Yes, as in plural. And no, he never wanted in. What about you?" I'd never really leant much into the idea of being the one doing the fucking because I knew Kai would say no, but Liam hadn't batted an eyelid at the idea that I might want to tie him up and edge him indefinitely, so maybe he wouldn't run from this idea.

His eyebrows drew together. "Huh?"

"Do you need a dildo?"

"You wanna fuck me?" He didn't sound anything other than interested.

"Is it an option?"

"It could be. But again, not when we're sleeping in your parents' house."

Liam kept talking about a future between us like it was a foregone conclusion.

No hesitation. No questioning.

Just a certain belief that what we had created in these six days would stand up on its own two feet when we left the Westchester bubble.

And I couldn't forget that 'always' he'd mentioned, like it was nothing. This wasn't fake anymore. It arguably never was.

"I could apply that logic to you. Penetrative sex is still penetrative sex." I was mostly joking. There was no way that I was going much longer without knowing what he felt like inside me and getting him to come at least once while he was there.

"A fair point and I don't have a good enough reason as to why you can't peg me in the next week other than the fact that I am down for it, but not in my immediate future."

"I'll allow it then," I teased. Now that he had given me permission, I didn't really want to do it in my parents' house either. I needed a whole day for all the things I wanted to do to him with no risk of someone knocking for us to help with something mundane, like dinner.

We finally reached the display of clitoral vibrators.

"So many options," Liam whispered in my ear. I could feel silk brushing against the back of my hand.

"Less options when you eliminate all the brightly coloured ones that I don't vibe with. Pun only a little bit intended."

"Of course you only want your sex toys to come in black," he teased, picking up the sole black one available and studying the packaging. "Ten settings, silent, waterproof, rechargeable. I assume that ticks all your boxes?"

"Yeah, that should just about do it. And they don't have to be black. Any neutral colour will do," I clarified.

He walked away from me and headed towards the checkout desk, but not before picking up three boxes of condoms and two bottles of lube.

"Are three boxes really necessary?"

"I find in these situations, it's best to be over-prepared, and I do not want a repeat of this morning where I have to put off letting you sink down on my cock because we ran out."

"That's still sixty condoms. How much sex are we having in the next week?" More sex than I had in the last couple of years, that's for sure.

"As much as we want. You want anything else?"

"I want you to hand me that vibrator and I'll go pay for it." I reached out for it, and he held it up over his head. I stretched for it, and he flicked his wrist to keep it just out of my grasp. I could get it, he wasn't that much taller than me and we had a similar reach, but I knew it would be a point-less task. He was paying for this no matter how much I protested.

"No. You want anything else?" he asked.

"No, just the vibrator. And the condoms. Good call on the lube," I replied.

"Great, you might as well wait for me outside."

"So the woman behind the counter can flirt with you without my presence?" I was joking. I'd noticed her notice Liam the moment that we walked in. He was hard to miss, especially when he walked around looking like a living wet dream in his backwards cap. She had not stopped staring at him as he moved around the store. Even when she had been serving other people, she'd had one eye on Liam.

"She'd probably do it even if you were there." He shrugged.

"So you noticed her too?"

"The same way you can sense when a guy isn't going to leave you alone is the same way I always know when someone is going to toe the line of appropriate behaviour when I inevitably have to interact with them. So yeah, I noticed her.”

“I’m so glad I don’t have to deal with passionate sports fans.”

“You do still have to deal with men, though.”

“A good point. Alright, I’ll go wait outside.” I went to move, but his hand wrapped loosely around my wrist and pulled me into him.

“Wait, is preventing the flirting why you wanted to go pay? Are you trying to be all Momma Bear with me, or is it a jealousy thing?” He cocked his scarred eyebrow.

It was both.

“It’s neither. I’m chill. You can look after yourself, and if I worried about every person who was ever going to flirt with you, I would be permanently jealous and who has that kind of time?”

“I probably have that kind of time.”

“Then you should really get a job, Muller,” I teased and headed out of the store.

Fifteen minutes after I left him, Liam finally joined me outside. I sensed him standing next to me and heard an intake of breath when he looked down at my phone screen and saw what I was reading. Instead of talking, he took one of my hands and stuffed it in his coat pocket, pulling me closer to him in the process.

Five minutes later, I reached the end of the chapter and locked my phone.

“Was she just about to get railed by three werewolves?” Liam asked.

“Yeah, she was.” I sounded almost wistful. Liam picked up on it.

"Sorry to have stolen you from what I imagine would have been a fun time."

"What took you so long? Did you get lost after I left you in there?"

"No, I did get distracted though. Look what I bought." He released one of the straps of the bag in his hand and I looked at the contents. Most of it was as I expected, but there was an extra box in there that I didn't know about. I pulled it up slightly, keeping it in the bag but high up enough that I could see what it was.

"It's a cock ring," I said.

"It's a *vibrating* cock ring, which means we don't always have to worry about added external stimulation if I'm inside you because it will just be right there. Plus, it feels great for me so that's a bonus." Liam sounded so proud of his purchase.

It was ridiculous to almost feel like crying over a cock ring. I felt more emotional about this ring of silicone than I had when Kai had presented me with a ring of silver and diamonds.

I could feel tears prickling at the backs of my eyes, threatening to spill out with every blink I took. I buried my head in the fabric of the travelling sweater, revelling in the feel of his chest against me.

"You want a bagel? I'm craving cream cheese and lox." Liam asked, his hand squeezing mine three times in his coat pocket.

I sniffed and extracted myself from Liam's arms.

"A bagel sounds good," I replied. Liam did not comment on the fact that my voice sounded thick with unshed tears. I wasn't sure I would be able to explain to him why a cock ring had made me so emotional and thankfully, he didn't make me.

I'd forgotten how easy loving Liam Mulligan was. It was so easy, I never realised I was doing it until the thought struck me out of nowhere.

Just like a rainstorm.

Twenty Seven

ALANA

Sheltering from the rain in Macy's almost made me wish that we had just accepted that we were going to get drenched and headed back to our car anyway. Macy's was busy at the best of times. But two days before Christmas, while rain battered the sidewalk and threatened to cause shallow flooding in the roads, added a new layer of hell to an already hellish landscape.

Liam seemed unbothered by it as he led me around the packed store with one hand, and the other carried the bag from the sex toy store. I wasn't too sure whether he had a destination in mind or if he was just trying to find a place in this whole store that wasn't crammed. It seemed unlikely that he would find one.

In the end, he stopped in the men's section, specifically the sweater section. As concentration of people went, it was on the quieter side, but there were still too many to be comfortable.

"Why have we stopped here?" I asked.

"Well, you seem to be in the market for a new sweater," he teased. I laughed. If he thought he was keeping that sweater, he was sorely mistaken. I didn't have time to reply to him as a man, whose panicked expression morphed into awe when he noticed Liam, cleared his throat.

"Sorry to interrupt, are you Liam Mulligan?" he asked.

I slipped my hand out of Liam's and squeezed his arm. I could still feel the solid muscle of his bicep underneath his several layers. "You go be Gunner. Come find me when you're done," I said as I took the bag from his hand and walked off.

~

I wasn't sure how long it was until Liam found me again, but I had migrated away from the men's section and was now looking at party dresses that I didn't need. But like a magpie, I was drawn to shiny pieces of fabric.

I sensed his arrival in my atmosphere before I saw him.

"Look what I found," he said by way of introduction. I followed the line of his arm and was met with his hand waving some mistletoe around.

It seemed impossible, given that I knew the feeling of his tongue in my most sensitive places, but as I looked up at the mistletoe currently hovering between our heads, I realised we hadn't actually kissed.

I pressed a chaste kiss on his cheek and went to walk away. His hand caught my wrist and pulled me back.

"What the hell was that?"

"It was a kiss on the cheek."

"Which is not what you're supposed to do under mistletoe." He shook it over my head again.

"Muller, I am not kissing you for the first time in the middle of a fucking Macy's."

"It wouldn't..." he trailed off. I could see the moment it dawned on him that I was right. "How is that even possible?"

"A good question. I mean this morning kind of took an unexpected turn, and I guess we haven't got around to it." I shrugged. Liam's eyebrows knitted together and then he reached for something to my left.

"I think you need to try this dress on," he said, not giving me a chance to respond before he hooked an arm over my shoulder and led me to the dressing rooms.

Surprisingly, they were mostly empty. The woman who handed me a tag indicating how many items I had was not paying attention to us, which was probably for the best because Liam was practically vibrating next to me as he led us to the stall in the furthest corner.

Liam hung the dress over the hook in the room and then stood opposite me.

"Why are you staring at me?" I asked. I could feel the heat of his gaze, but he had drawn an invisible line between us.

"I'm thinking," was all he said in response.

"Well don't think too hard, Muller." I tried to lighten the mood.

"I do think you should try this dress on." He nodded to where it was hanging up. I couldn't think of anything worse than peeling off all the layers that I had on, but I had been looking at the dress for ages before Liam found me. It wouldn't surprise me if Liam had been watching me stare at it before he had walked over. I took my coat off and threw it at him.

He caught it with ease.

"Fine, but close your eyes."

I expected him to protest but instead, he turned his cap around and closed his eyes. I went about changing as quickly as possible.

As I zipped it up and let it settle on the contours of my body, I knew why I had been so drawn to it. I looked really fucking good, and suddenly, I was excited for Liam to open his eyes.

"Okay you're good," I said, and he spun the cap back

around and opened his eyes. First, they adjusted to the bright light of the dressing room, then the green darkened, and I felt my skin heat up underneath his stare.

"Fuck, Alana," he said my name as both a whine and a prayer as he closed the distance between us. He wrapped one hand around the back of my neck, his fingers tangling in my curls, and his eyes flicked down to my lips before he stepped in closer.

I'd never really thought about the fact that my favourite colour was a shade of green before it turned into blue. I kind of assumed it was because I loved the ocean. But no, it was the exact shade of Liam's eyes.

I don't know who moved first, all I knew was that I held his stare for a fraction of a second and then his lips were against mine. The first press was gentle. The thought that this felt more intimate than the fact that those same lips had been in between my thighs just this morning made me laugh, breaking the kiss.

Liam pulled back a little and raised his scarred eyebrow.

"That was not me judging your kissing skills. I'm just thinking about how funny it is that you ate me out before we even kissed."

"Some might say that was a better first kiss to have," he whispered against my lips.

I didn't bother responding with anything other than pressing my lips against his again. There was nothing gentle about our second kiss. It felt almost desperate. Decades worth of want and longing were finally finding a way to be let out. He nipped at my bottom lip, a gentle scrape of teeth before he soothed it with a swipe of his tongue.

I removed his cap with one hand and threaded my fingers through his hair as he pushed me backwards until I was pressed against a wall. When he slid one of his legs in between mine, I tilted my head back as the pressure of his thigh against me made pure want rush through my veins. As Liam started kissing my exposed neck, his cap fell from my grip.

The hand threaded through my hair ran down my body until he grabbed my upper thigh, and I moaned. Low and guttural. For his ears only, but still very aware that I was in a dressing room in Macy's. I felt Liam's smile against the crook of my neck and his fingers moved closer to the apex of my thighs. Slowly. The kind of slow that almost made me want to beg him to get a move on and touch me.

Just as I was about to cave, two fingers pressed against my clit, and I sighed with relief.

"I can feel how wet you are," he near growled into my ear.

"I've been wet all day. You're not good for me." My voice sounded so breathless.

"Nah, I think I'm great for you, babe. Do you think you can be quiet?"

"I don't own this dress," I responded.

"But you will, so back to my original question." His voice dripped like honey against my neck.

I nodded. "Yeah, I can be quiet."

Liam didn't say anything else. He simply slid his fingers into my underwear and started rubbing circles around my clit.

I laughed softly.

"You know I'm gonna get a complex if you keep laughing when I touch you."

"I promise, it's not you. It's just that I don't remember the last time I had an orgasm without outside, vibrating, assistance and you get your slightly calloused, very capable fingers on my clit, and I'm just about ready to burst."

He started rubbing faster and I grabbed at his shoulders to keep myself upright.

"I don't remember you ever being this good for my ego."

"Don't get used—" I didn't get to finish my sentence, because out of nowhere, the slow build of my orgasm crashed over me, and I had to bury my mouth into the fabric of Liam's sweater. He kept rubbing my clit until I tried to shift my hips away from him, and only then did he remove his hand. Then, because he was very good at finding new ways to destroy me, he stuck the fingers that had just made me come into his mouth.

"Sorry, didn't catch the end of that," he said when he finished sucking his fingers clean, smugness practically oozing out of his every pore.

"You're the fucking worst, you know that?"

He smiled as his fingers trailed down my side until they found the zip of the dress and slowly dragged it down. I could feel his erection on my hip, but he made no move to do anything about it, and I was frozen under his gentle touch.

"I'm going to go pay for this dress while you get changed," he said quietly as he peeled it off me. His eyes took in my body as he revealed it, bit by bit. I felt my nipples harden at the heat of his stare.

"You are not buying this dress for me," I managed to get out.

"Except I am. You want the dress. I saw you looking at it for ages, but you decided it wasn't worth paying over a grand for. Which is fair, but I was always going to buy it for you because you deserve the things you want, even if they might be a bit excessive. And now, having seen you in it, and getting to watch you come all over my hand while wearing it, I am definitely buying it for you. Consider it your Christmas present."

He let the dress fall to the floor and then ran his hands back up my body in featherlight touches that made me shiver.

"What were the sex toys for then?" Not that I wanted to unwrap one in front of our families.

"Our sex life," he murmured, a thrill went through me at the word 'our', "which is something completely different from this. They were basically a necessity. Make sure you act surprised when you unwrap this on Christmas Day."

"I'll be sure to give the best fake surprised face I can muster up."

He kissed me once more on the lips, lingering for only a moment before he scooped the dress and his hat.

"Just as long as that's the only faking you do around me," he said as he took the dress and sex toys out of the dressing room and left me to get dressed.

Twenty Eight

LIAM

Alana had whipped cream on the corner of her mouth, which would have been fine except for the fact that she kept sticking her tongue out to try and lick it away. Every flick of her tongue made her lips look a little bit slicker and highlighted that they were still kiss-bitten. It felt like one big tease, which only got worse when she accepted defeat and swiped the cream away with the tip of her finger before slowly sliding it into her mouth and licking it clean.

I knew she was actively fucking with me when she hollowed her cheeks out before releasing her finger with a pop. I groaned, my hands clenching around the steering wheel.

"You alright there, Muller?" she teased as she took another sip from her hot chocolate, this time avoiding getting cream anywhere.

"In a general sense, yes, I am fine. At this moment, no I'm not. You keep licking your mouth and teasing me with your tongue and I am *driving*."

"Are you usually this easily distracted?" she asked, her voice slightly muffled by the lip of her cup.

"Babe, you know how you said you've been wet all day,

which is something that has also been playing on my mind since you said it?" I saw her nod in my peripheral vision. "Well, I've been some kind of hard since I got my first taste of you and unlike you, I haven't even come once today. Add to that you sitting there, intentionally teasing me, and I'm a bit on edge."

I was usually quite good at being on edge, but this was sending me into overdrive.

"In my defence, you said you were fine this morning, and you left the dressing room so quickly there was no chance for me to reciprocate."

"There wasn't time. We had already been in there a suspicious amount of time considering you only took in one item."

"There didn't need to be a dressing room situation at all. You are the master of your own torture."

"Sorry for being unsatisfied with a kiss on the cheek and not wanting to wait until we got home to rectify the situation."

"I wasn't complaining about it. I personally am very satisfied right now." She licked the corner of her mouth once more just to ramp up the torture.

"We'll be home in like twenty minutes. Could you try to be unappealing and unsexy for that long?"

"Not possible, but I will stop messing with you," she said, taking another sip of her hot chocolate. I groaned because apparently, even that was sexy to me now. Lenny laughed.

"How was the city?" Mom asked before we had even taken off our coats. I almost thought we had walked into the wrong house before I remembered the Fitzpatricks were hosting dinner again. They were always the ones to host.

"It was busy. You know how it is, Mel," Lenny answered, hanging her coat up and picking up both our bags.

"Did you get what you needed?" Mom asked. A sheepish look fell over Lenny's face. I pressed my lips together to stop the smile from breaking out on my face.

"Yeah, I did. Just going to drop my bags off upstairs then I'll come down and help with dinner," Lenny answered.

I watched her walk up the stairs, not taking my eyes off her until she disappeared at the top. I was only half checking her out.

"You were always gone over that girl," Mom said quietly, drawing my attention back to her.

"She was always the best part of my day," I replied.

"Well, don't stand here talking to me," she said as she nudged my shoulder, and with that, I followed Lenny upstairs.

As I closed the bedroom door, something hit me in the face. I managed to catch whatever it was in the crook of my elbow and realised that it was a condom.

"I thought you had to help with dinner?"

"I do but..." she trailed off and I walked closer to her. She took a step back and ended up flush against her bookshelf.

"But you just couldn't wait to feel me inside you?" I growled into her ear and felt her shudder against me.

"No, I can wait. As I said in the car, I am perfectly satisfied." She tried to slip away, but I bracketed her against the shelves and her arms automatically draped over my shoulders. I looked down the long line of her body and realised that she had changed out of her leggings into a pair of shorts. I moved one of my hands and ran it up her thigh, raising goose bumps as my fingers trailed along before I reached the apex of her thighs and slid my fingers under the fabric of her shorts and underwear.

"Always so wet," I whispered against her neck, my teeth

teasing the sensitive skin in a way that made her clutch harder at my shoulders.

"Only for you," her words caught on a gasp as I slipped a finger into her.

"You're gonna feel so good wrapped around my cock."

I felt her hands undo the button of my jeans and pull the zip down before she pressed her palm against the hard line of my cock over my boxers. My hips stuttered against her, and I grunted into her skin.

"Of course this is what you're packing. You know, I used to get asked a lot if you had a monster penis because everyone just assumed I must be an oracle on your junk. I never said anything because obviously, I didn't know. All the girls assumed you must be skating with a ten incher because, well, you're a big guy and I just tried not to think about it too much. I'll be honest, I couldn't say that I thought they would be wrong. But it's so much worse than that. Not only does Liam Mulligan get to be an NHL superstar, 6'4", with muscles carved by the gods themselves—by way of a personal trainer and the best nutritionist going—and a face that is aggressively attractive. But he just *has* to have the Goldilocks of penises."

"You sound angry about it," I said, pulling back a little to look at her face. Her dark brown eyes were clouded with lust, but the line between her eyebrows suggested annoyance.

"You have no idea." She squeezed my cock once before she pulled it out and tucked the waistband under my balls, taking the condom and rolling it slowly down my length.

"If you don't hurry up and secure that thing, I am gonna blow before I even get the chance to put it to use." I gritted out. Her deft fingers moved faster to secure it, then she let me go.

"I don't remember you ever being this good for my ego," she quipped.

I ran my hands up her legs again and then cupped them under her ass. "Jump," I said as I palmed the flesh underneath my palms.

I could see the hesitation on her face. "Babe, can you just trust that I know what my shoulder is and isn't capable of? I promise you, it can handle this."

"If I even get a hint that you're in pain," she warned, pointing her finger in my face before jumping up. Her legs wrapped around my waist, and I adjusted my grip on her so I could hold her comfortably in my arms. Without a word, she reached down and pushed her shorts and underwear to the side before reaching for my cock and slowly sliding it inside her.

"Fuck," I sighed when she bottomed out.

"By all means, go ahead," she said as she settled her back against the shelves, one of her hands moving to grip a shelf. I looked down at where our bodies joined and groaned.

"I'm not gonna last long," I admitted.

"You don't need to. I'm not gonna come again, it will take too long, and I *do* need to go make dinner. I am loathe to admit that you were right, but I really wanna know what you feel like so I can think about something else while I cook. So, Muller, go ahead and fuck me." She clenched around me as she finished speaking and I moved my right hand to brace on the bookshelf and started moving my hips.

"Shit," I muttered into the damp skin of her neck as I rocked back in. Her fingers curled in the hair at the nape of my neck and pulled. My hips stuttered at the stab of pain before I found a rhythm inside her.

Lenny had her bottom lip pulled in between her teeth but I could still hear the little moans of pleasure she made as I thrust up into her.

"You feel so good," I panted. She released her lip and smiled at me in a way that signalled trouble.

"Oh yeah? How about now?" Her lips brushed against mine as she spoke. I thought she was going to kiss me. I wanted her to kiss me while I drowned in the pleasure that was being inside her.

What she did was both better and worse.

She caught my lip in between her teeth and pulled at the same time she squeezed around my cock. My hips stuttered again, and I came. She sealed her mouth over mine and caught any noises as my whole body gave itself over to my orgasm.

When I felt like every atom of my body was spent, she leant back and both of us tried to catch our breath.

"You don't play fair," I said. Barely.

"Maybe not, but are you not satisfied?"

"For now, yes." I pulled out carefully and set her back on the floor.

"Then I played fair enough, baby." She pressed a kiss on my cheek before she readjusted her shorts. "Your shoulder okay?"

"It's fine. I told you it could take it." Although I liked that she still asked.

"I know, but it's still good to check these things. I'm gonna head downstairs and start dinner. Take your time, maybe splash some water on your face, you look so flushed. And remember to take that fucking hat off unless you want me to jump you at the dinner table."

"You're really proud of yourself, aren't you?"

"I got you so turned on you lasted less than two minutes once you got inside me. Of course I'm proud of myself. Truly a wonder for my ego."

"I'm going to ruin you next time," I warned. Although I wasn't sure I could. Not more than she ruined me.

She smiled. "I don't doubt you'll try, Muller."

Twenty Nine

LIAM

Lenny was slowly driving me wild.

She wasn't even doing anything that exciting, just sitting cross-legged on her bed, holding a mirror in her hand and doing her makeup.

"Not to give you a complex, but staring at me like that is making me feel like I am running late. Am I running late?"

"No, we've got like an hour and besides, it's a party. Who arrives on time for a party?"

"Me, because I am early to everything even when I don't mean to be."

"Well, you're with me now and I am very good at making an entrance. So you've got time." I had also given her a time that was ninety minutes after the 'start' time of the party, knowing that she would be ready early. I was just as bad. I was already ready to go. Being early was usually great, except for when parties were involved.

"What else does being with you get me?" she teased.

"Fancy places. Almost any hockey game you want. Some swanky parties. The more I talk, the more I realise that you probably got the bum end of the deal because all my perks involve being outside and you are not an outside person.”

“I like being outside. Once a month and only on Saturdays.”

“I can agree to those terms.”

“Good. Can you also agree to hold this mirror? I gotta do my eyeliner.”

I moved across the room and sat opposite her, our knees brushing as I took the mirror from her.

“This okay?” I asked. She took my wrist and moved it around until she was happy. The gentle touch of her fingers on my skin made butterflies swoop in the pit of my stomach.

“You need to stop looking at me like that if you expect me to make it out of the house. I might just need to have my way with you instead.”

“How am I looking at you?”

“Like you haven’t eaten for hours.”

I laughed softly.

“It has been a while.”

“It’s barely been twenty-four hours.” She rolled her eyes and then blinked one shut, holding it taut before she started drawing a black line across her lash line.

“Yeah, a while.”

“You’re fucking ridiculous. Can you tilt it down a bit?”

I did as she asked until she hummed an affirmative.

“I am very much of the belief that you deserve to be eaten out at every available moment. Finish your wings and I’ll give you a quick one before you get dressed and then we can go.”

“Bold of you to assume that I still do the same makeup that I did as a teenager,” she said as she finished one eye.

“Bold of you to assume that I haven’t looked at everything you’ve posted online over the last few days and have seen proof that you do. Only you don’t bother with eye shadow anymore.”

"Yeah, I left that in high school. You're telling me that you never looked me up once over the years?"

"Didn't see the point. You ever look me up?"

She looked at me with both eyes.

"Never intentionally, but it's hard to ignore Gunner the NHL wonder when he insists on being the best to ever do it or some shit. And that underwear advert. Did you request it be on every billboard around the city?" She closed the other eye.

"Yes, I happened to love going to my place of work every day and being met by my own blown-up crotch."

Lenny snorted and then cursed under her breath.

"You can put the mirror down. I gotta go remove this eyeliner and start again."

She pressed her hand on my thigh as she untangled her legs from underneath her. She was wearing a sweater that was big enough to fall below her bum and nothing else except—

"Are you wearing a garter belt?" I asked as she stood up. I could feel lust coursing through my veins and settling in my groin at the thought.

"Yeah, I hate tights but I'm not in the mood to brave it with bare legs, so therefore, garter belt and stockings."

"There's a Claus joke in there somewhere."

"I'll leave you to think about it while I go sort out this eye."

Just as it felt like Lenny was gone for a tad too long, she came back in, eye now fully lined.

"Could you have just done your makeup in the bathroom?"

"I could have, but there was something nostalgic about sitting on the bed in my childhood bedroom, doing my makeup for a party with all our high school friends. That, and

I really could not be bothered to get up. You got your Claus joke yet?"

"No, I keep getting stuck somewhere between stockings, stuffing, and naughty."

She laughed as she started rolling a stocking up her leg.

"You're doing it again, Muller," she said. Her voice sounded like it was coming from far away. I was too focused on her fingers unfurling the fabric up her calf and onto her thigh before securing it to the garter belt.

"We don't have to go to this party," I said, still looking at her legs. I didn't see the sock coming until it hit me in the face.

"I have put on a full face of makeup and steamed the creases out of my dress, Liam. You are not going to be the only person who sees it."

"Fine, I'm going to wait for you downstairs because if I watch you pull that other stocking up, we are not leaving this bedroom," I said.

"That's the smartest thing you've said today," she replied.

She came downstairs wearing a tight red dress that settled just under the top of her stockings and highlighted the curve of her ass. Her heels made her already long legs look miles longer. I let out a groan and Lenny giggled.

"I need you to know that, although yes, I did pack this outfit just in case I had to go to a party, I had no intention of wearing it. I had cosy Christmas Eve plans that you ruined by accepting this party invite. And I'm a nice girlfriend, but I'm not that nice. Realistically, I could have worn nice jeans and a sweater, and it would've been fine. But now you are going to have to attend with the knowledge that if you inch this hem just a couple of centimetres, you're going to reach the sensitive skin of my upper thighs. And just above that, all you would have to do is slip my underwear to the side to get your hands on my pussy which, surprise, is wet."

There was so much about what Lenny had just said to dissect, but my mind kept getting stuck on the fact that she had called herself my girlfriend. Just girlfriend. Not a mention of the word fake anywhere.

Just a woman who wanted to cruelly tease her boyfriend because he made her go out to a party.

"You look beautiful."

Lenny clearly still hadn't learned how to take a compliment, so she rolled her eyes and went to get her coat. As she pulled it on, she studied me slowly, taking in what I was wearing. Black jeans and a dark grey knit sweater that she would borrow indefinitely if I gave her a fraction of a chance. It was an outfit simply unworthy of being in the same stratosphere as hers, but it didn't matter because Alana was looking at me like she wanted to drag me back upstairs.

"You look shit-hot too, Muller," she said, shaking her shoulders, and I guess clearing whatever fantasy she had going through her head, before opening the front door and waiting for me to catch up.

Thirty

ALANA

I didn't hate being at this party as much as I thought I would, but when we hit the two-hour mark, my social battery bottomed out, and suddenly, I needed to be back in my house in my sweatpants and one of Liam's t-shirts.

So, of course, I couldn't find him and ended up cornered by Eddie. I had liked Eddie just fine when we were in high school. He was the star quarterback, but he never cared about football the way people wanted him to. He was just good at it. He'd had a calming energy about him whenever we hung out, which had typically only happened in situations very similar to this one.

What I had forgotten about Eddie was that he used to have a crush on me. One that he clearly hadn't gotten over in the last thirteen years. Or maybe he had, but then the proximity made it come back with a vengeance.

"I'd heard you were around for the holidays," he said as a greeting, his eyes tracking up and down my body.

"Here I am," I said weakly.

"How have you been?" he asked. I was bored of this question at this point. The answer was complicated. Did they mean over the last thirteen years since I missed our high school graduation, in which case the answer was fine? Or did they mean recently, where I felt like I was on an emotional roller-coaster that I very much wanted to get off? Not even six months ago, I'd been with the person that on some level, I believed I was going to marry, and yet now I felt more at home than I ever had with someone else.

I couldn't even call it falling in love because it wasn't that. It was a phoenix finally rising from the ashes of a love that had long burned up but was getting ready to fly again.

"Yeah, I've been fine," is what I said instead. It's what I had been saying every time I was asked.

"You around for long?"

"Through to New Year," I said. I had a feeling I knew where this was going, and I felt anxious goose bumps prickle on my skin.

"That's plenty of time for us to hang out then," he said, his eyes still looking at my body, never my face. I think he was going for flirty, but it wasn't working. Maybe if there wasn't someone else, I would say sure, we could hang out. Eddie was as good a rebound as anybody. But there was someone else. And Eddie either hadn't been told or he didn't care and thought he could compete with Liam.

I knew the second Liam arrived. Sea salt and vanilla entered my radar because he now carried a piece of me around with him always. His hand snaked around my waist, and I sank into his warmth.

"Do you know what you're standing under, Len?" he asked. It was almost a whisper, but I was still looking at Eddie. I could tell that he had heard because he looked up. I tipped my head, which Liam took as an invitation to press kisses along my neck. Given that I was now slightly taller than him, he had much easier access. I laughed softly as my gaze reached the mistletoe hanging from the ceiling.

"Well, would you look at that," I said, shifting a little to get him away from my neck, then pressed a kiss to his cheek. I felt his cheek move as he smiled and when I removed my lips, he moved to stand in front of me, blocking my view of Eddie.

"Not getting with that this time, babe," he said. He gently grabbed my chin and angled my head down before he sealed his lips on mine. Part of me wanted to be embarrassed about this public display of affection but I couldn't think about anything but Liam.

The width of his palm on the middle of my back, holding me close, while his other hand curled around my neck to hold me at the right angle. The sweep of his tongue in my mouth and the pressure of his lips against mine. The slow build of heat that was gathering south of centre. The feel of his sweater in my hands, and the press of his thigh between my legs. I could feel him harden against my hip, and I broke the kiss before I really did forget where we were, and escalated things.

"That's better," he said against my ear. I shivered.

"Jealousy sure is an interesting colour on you, Muller," I whispered back.

"Chantelle mentioned something about seeing you two together the other day. You finally locked that one down, Liam?" Eddie asked somewhere over Liam's shoulder. Liam turned around in such a way that put him in between me and Eddie. In theory, the overprotective act should have annoyed me, but I found myself liking it.

"Wasn't screwing it up for a second time, Eddie," he said before looking back at me. "You ready to get out of here?"

"I'm fine if you still have people you want to catch up with," I replied on autopilot because it had only been a couple of hours and Liam was a social person. There was no way he was already done with this party. Even if I was.

"You wanna come with me while I catch up with people or am I just leaving you to disappear into a corner and think about the book that you could be reading at home?" There was a teasing smile on his face, and I wanted to hate him. For knowing me so well. For having the nerve to be so smug about the fact that he knew me so well. I hated myself a little bit for ever running away from someone who just made things *easier* for me. Always had and apparently always would.

"There are only so many times I can hear variations of, 'That's so cool' when I tell them what I'm doing with my life, and have the conversation not so subtly steered back to talk of you. So, I am fine in my corner."

Liam turned his head. "Thanks for the party, Eddie. It's been great to see everyone. We're gonna head out," he said as he laced his fingers with mine and started leading us to the door.

"Yeah, good to see you both too," Eddie called after us, only sounding a little disappointed.

"I really was fine to stay there for longer," I said as we walked home, cold fingers linked together, providing a faux kind of warmth.

"You're always fine to stay at places you don't want to be in anymore. I really wish that the part of you that is scared of asking for what you want in social situations, like leaving because you're tired or bored or just over it, was one of the things that had changed about you over the years."

There was no malice in his words, but his accurate representation of me still slipped through a rib and cut me almost fatally. I tried to change the subject.

"Are you sure you didn't just want me out of there to stop Eddie from trying to make a move once you had gone on to mingle?"

"I think that kiss would have turned him off from making

a move, so no. And if it hadn't, you would have shut him down anyway."

"What makes you so sure about that?" I don't know why I asked. I would have shut him down. Even if I wasn't in this situation with Liam, I would have shut him down. For the same reason I never gave him the time of day in high school. I just wasn't into him.

"You've never been into Eddie," he said. I waited for him to say something else, but that was all he said. We lapsed into silence.

"Want to tell me why you're annoyed?" Liam asked quietly when we were five minutes from home.

"I'm not annoyed," I answered truthfully.

"Then what's wrong?"

"I'm just thinking," I replied.

"You gonna enlighten me on what you're thinking about?"

"It's nice having you back in my corner, is all," I said. It was all I could say without everything spilling over. I felt Liam's gaze settle on the side of my face and I kept my eyes forward. I knew that if he saw my whole face he'd be able to read it, and I wasn't ready for that.

"I never stopped being in your corner," he eventually said, turning his eyes forward again.

I blinked back tears.

"How was everyone, anyway? You talked to more people than I did."

"Do you find it funny how people seem to revert to an old version of themselves when you put them back in certain situations?"

"Is that an answer to my question?"

"Yeah, kind of. Everyone behaved the exact way they did when we were eighteen. Some of them flirted with me because that was what they always did. Some of the guys only knew how to talk to me about sports. A couple were still a little bit scared of me because they remembered how I used to be on the ice. You tried to disappear into a wall," he teased at the end.

"I wasn't trying to disappear. I was talking to people. You saw me talking to people."

"I saw you talking to Eddie," he grumbled.

"Which you then promptly shut down in a bout of jealousy."

"I wasn't jealous," he shot back quickly.

"I was in that spot for ages before you came over and you only made your appearance when I was talking to Eddie. What is that if not jealousy?"

"It was me seeing you and knowing that you were ready to leave. It just so happened to be that you were under some mistletoe while you were talking to Eddie, and it's bad luck to ignore it. Or whatever that superstition is."

"You have so many superstitions and you don't know what's up with mistletoe?" I didn't either, if I was being honest.

"I have a lot of sports-related superstitions. They don't tend to carry outside of that."

"I see what you're doing here. It's interesting that you've shifted the conversation to superstitions so we can stop talking about you being jealous."

"I wasn't jealous. I'm...what was it that you said? Chill?"

"Oh my gosh, you're ridiculous. Fine, after whatever incident I said I was chill, I was not chill. I was maybe a little bit jealous." Or a lot jealous.

He smiled. "I really did go over because I could tell you were ready to go, but I also wasn't a huge fan of how Eddie was looking at you. Like he wanted to take you up to his room."

"Because only you can do that?"

"I'd fucking hope so, as your boyfriend."

I stopped. We were outside his parents' house.

"This isn't fake anymore, is it? We're actually dating, aren't we? You are getting a proper thrill out of saying that you're my boyfriend." I had said I was his girlfriend before we left, and I'd meant it. I was his girlfriend; there was nothing fake about it.

"This hasn't felt fake since I wrapped my arm around you in that bakery queue and Chantelle started talking to me. Actually, that might be a small lie. This hasn't felt fake since I left you in bed that first morning and came back just in time to hear you say my name when you came," he said.

"What...no...that's...you didn't...why didn't—" I'd been so sure I was quiet that morning.

"Why didn't I say anything? What was I supposed to say?"

"Is that why you started talking about how we should go on dates? So you could test drive a real relationship?"

"Yes and no. I did think we probably shouldn't stay holed up in the house because that would be odd. But yes, I wanted to date you and figured if you were thinking about me like that, it might not be beyond the realm of possibility that you could think about me as an actual boyfriend. I wouldn't call it a test drive. I very much want to keep you, but the dates were kind of a test drive."

"Oh."

"Yeah, oh. Now come on, let's get you a whiskey from the back of the cupboard and under a blanket. If you're lucky, I'll go down on you." He gently pulled on my arm and walked us the seventeen steps home.

"What do I have to do to get lucky?" I asked as I unlocked the front door.

"Exist on a day that ends in y."

There was a hand playing with my waistband. When I blinked my eyes open, Lenny was laughing to herself and when I looked down, I saw that she had placed a bow on my morning wood.

"Merry Christmas to you, I guess," I said, my voice groggy. Lenny turned her head, her mouth still turned up in a smile. The sunlight made her eyes look like the colour of burnt honey. I could stare into them for hours.

"Are you calling your dick a gift?" She sounded wide awake, and I remembered that for some reason, Lenny's body was incapable of sleeping in on Christmas Day.

"I think you called it the Goldilocks of dicks."

"Technically I called it the Goldilocks of penises," she said, lifting the bow up and throwing it onto her bedside table. "I also think gifts are supposed to be a surprise, so it would be a pretty shit gift."

"Why are you putting bows on my dick anyway?"

"You kicked the duvet off, and I got distracted by the bulge and couldn't carry on reading my book. I was going to do something else but then remembered we haven't had a conversation about that. Then I found the bow on the floor and here I am. Putting bows on your dick and finding it hilarious."

"How long have you been awake?"

"A couple of hours. I tried to get back to sleep, but you know me. An over-excited kid in a giant's body on Christmas morning." She shrugged.

"You can, by the way. The whole 'while I'm asleep' thing. You don't just have to place a bow on it."

"Same. Well, three weeks out of four in a month. Merry Christmas, by the way," she said, her eyes flicking above my head. I followed her eye line to find that while I had been sleeping, some mistletoe had appeared on the headboard.

"Where did you get this?"

"It was in the bag with the dress you had to buy. I hung it up before I started playing with bows. We seem incapable of kissing without mistletoe being present."

"I didn't have to buy that dress. I bought it because you wanted it. I would have bought it even if the dressing room thing hadn't happened."

She didn't say anything. Instead, she swung a leg over me and placed her hands on either side of my head before dipping down and sealing her lips against mine.

I wanted all Christmas Days to start like this. Heck, I wanted *every* day to start like this. Lenny pulled away just before I could press her flush against me and move things further.

"Come on, Seventeen, I'm gonna make cookies," she said as she got off the bed.

I reached for my phone and tapped the screen to bring up the time. "It's seven-thirty in the morning."

"It's seven-thirty on *Christmas* morning. There are no rules. Besides, what is better than oven-fresh cookies on Christmas morning?" I opened my mouth to say something, but she stopped me before I could. "If you make a vagina joke right now, you aren't getting shit. I'm shutting it down and cutting you off," she warned.

I closed my mouth. Then pressed my lips together tightly because I wanted to say something I shouldn't. This thing between us was too new. Too fragile. We'd fallen apart once before and had only just come back together. I didn't want to be the one to tip the balance. I had no way of knowing if it would tip in my favour.

In *our* favour.

But the thought came to me loud and clear as she walked out our bedroom with a bounce in her step.

I love you.

∼

"Where do you want me?" I asked as I walked into the kitchen.

"Not in this kitchen," Lenny replied, not looking up from her mixing bowl. She had flour on her cheek.

"You told me to come here," I pointed out as I stopped beside her and swiped the flour off her. She leant into the touch.

"Yeah, but that was before you got here, and I remembered that you are quite distracting."

"You can make cookies in your sleep. Anyway, if you really didn't want me here, you wouldn't have waited until I woke up before you came down to make cookies."

The idea that she wanted me around in her domain made me feel warmer than any fresh baked good could.

"A great mistake on my part. You are welcome to leave now," she said as she cracked an egg into the bowl.

"What kind of cookies are you making?" I asked instead.

"A burnt butter pecan thing," she replied. "Actually, I have a task for you, make those pecans smaller pieces for me, please." She gestured to a half-filled Ziploc bag. It would never cease to amaze me how quickly she could pull together ingredients for a bake. I'd been less than two minutes behind her, and she already seemed halfway done.

I picked up the Ziploc and whacked it on the counter.

"Wake up the whole neighbourhood, why don't you?" she muttered as she added butter to her mix.

"How else am I supposed to break them up?"

"You could've used a knife," she suggested.

"And give you both a chopping board and a knife to wash up? Because I know how much you love that shit." I whacked the bag down again. "I'm done now, anyway. Very brittle pecans, quick to break up." I handed her the bag of smashed pecans.

"Get out right now," she said. Lenny sounded almost angry, and I couldn't help but find it amusing.

"What have I done now?"

"You smashed some pecans to perfection with two firm slaps against a kitchen counter and you can literally hold me up against a bookshelf like we're not basically the same height. I'm finding the strength of it all, of *you*, quite overwhelming and this is a kitchen. And not only is it a kitchen, but it is also the kitchen in my parents' house. Who are here. Upstairs. And I know my parents don't think I'm some virginal woman nor do I care that they know I'm getting railed by the boy next door, but I do not need them to catch me having sex. In a kitchen. Which I am very close to giving in to unless you leave right now." She tipped the crushed pecans into the bowl and started beating everything together.

"I mean, I wouldn't say no to slipping..." I was cut off by a tea towel getting thrown at my face.

"I cannot stress enough how much I hate you."

It sounded an awful lot like *I love you*.

"You were the one who said they were close to wanting to

get railed on a kitchen counter," I pointed out, putting the tea towel back on the counter.

"Would you be less annoying now if I could have woken you with a blowjob?"

"I'd be high on endorphins, so I'd probably be more annoying."

"That's what you can do. Go for a run. That would also get you high on endorphins and, more importantly, would get you out of my kitchen."

I knew that she was aware that I was moving towards her, but she kept her eyes focused on the bowl in her hands as I stepped behind her and rested my hands on the counter on either side of her hips. There was a couple of inches of space between our bodies and I could see the way she was resisting sinking back into me.

"Oh yeah, you want me to go out and get all sweaty. Come back in need of a shower. You want to see my T-shirt plastered to the contours of my body, my thigh muscles stretching against my running leggings. My chest heaving as I try to get my breath back. My skin flushed pink. Would you help me out of my clothes? Would you join me in the shower and make sure that my tired muscles are soothed?" As I'd been talking, Lenny had stopped mixing her cookie batter and her back was now pressed against my chest, her neck tilted to the side letting me speak against the sensitive skin by her ear. I could see goose bumps erupting on her skin. I moved one of my hands to rest on her lower stomach and she sank further into me.

"No, don't do that," she said, her voice barely above a whisper. I kissed the juncture of her jaw, and she twisted her head to meet my lips with hers. Before it could get too heated, we heard the click of the lock in the kitchen door behind us. I knew before they made themselves known who was walking in on us. It could only be my parents.

"Well don't you two look cosy?" my mom said. Lenny

seemed to shake off the cloak of lust that had settled on us and returned her focus to her mixing bowl. I stayed behind her, my arm still holding her close, because as much as I also knew that my parents were aware that I had sex, I did not need them to see me sporting an erection.

"Merry Christmas Mel, Bobby," Lenny said, sounding just the wrong side of normal for her. Not that my parents would notice.

"Morning," I said.

"What are you making?" Mom asked.

"She tells me they are burnt butter pecan things," I answered for her because I could sense that Lenny had entered that zone she only reached when she was at the portioning stage of baking. Nothing else existed when she entered that zone.

"Very nice. Are your parents up, Alana?"

There was a moment of silence as Lenny finished rolling her last two cookies in a ball and placing them on the baking tray.

"They might be, but I haven't seen them. I guess you're over here early for a reason, so you can just do whatever you came here to do. These are about to go in the oven and Liam is about to clean up. So we'll be out of your way shortly."

"I am?"

She turned around in my arms and pressed against my erection with her hip.

"It's another counter and the task might be numbing enough that it gets Goldilocks to calm down," she said, her voice low enough that only I could hear her.

"You just don't want to wash up," I teased, rolling my hips into her just to watch her try to suppress a moan.

"That too," she thrust the empty mixing bowl into my hands and walked out of the kitchen. I strategically placed it near my crotch as I walked to the sink and started washing up.

"Dad is going to prep the turkey. We thought that would be nice, as you missed coming home for Thanksgiving. I'm going to get started on the veg before Stassie and Rob come down," Mom said, now standing next to me. It wasn't all that different to the way that Christmas had been when we were younger.

"Yeah, sure, I'll get out of your way. Although I imagine Len will be back to take the cookies out of the oven soon."

"Things going well with her?" Dad asked. I got the feeling this week, within my minimal interactions with him, that part of him believed that it was her fault I no longer played. How he had reached that conclusion, I didn't know, but he was treating everything around me as a reason instead of just accepting the fact that I was done, and nothing anyone could say was changing my mind on that one.

"Yeah, we're fine."

Better than fine. Official and everything. It was the best Christmas present I could have hoped for.

Aaron was standing outside the bathroom he shared with Lenny when I went back upstairs.

"She in there?" I asked. He nodded.

"She's probably been awake for hours, but she chose the moment I needed to pee to go have a shower."

"She has cookies in the oven so she will probably be quick, if that's any consolation."

"Was that a two-person job?" There was a teasing tone to his question.

"I just smashed some pecans, so no, it definitely wasn't, but she seemed to want me there," I replied.

"Ally always wants you there. The problem was always that she was scared you would stop being there, so she got ahead of it." His eyes widened in surprise. Almost as if he hadn't quite meant to reveal that much.

It had, stupidly, never occurred to me that Aaron would know the whole story, but clearly, he did. The only person closer to Lenny than me back then was her brother, but even if I had thought to ask, he would have kept the vault locked no matter how much I pleaded for answers.

"You know the whole story?"

Aaron looked down at his parents' bedroom door. It was still closed.

"Yeah, I know why she left. And I know how mildly annoying she found it when she started dating Kai, who was basically your number one fan. I also know that she was kind of irritated that you moved to Detroit and the only thing that softened that blow was the fact that she was happy that you and Teddy got to play together again. You have probably guessed that I also know that while she did make your birthday cake, you didn't go thank her for it in person six weeks ago, and decided it was a smart choice to fake date each other the day you both flew back for the holidays. And I think this whole thing was fake for all of two days and is now an actual relationship, and if that is the case, then I am happy for you both."

None of what he knew was surprising.

"It's not. Fake that is. Don't suppose you're going to tell me any more?" It was worth a shot asking. He had managed to tell me things without telling me the thing he knew I wanted to know most.

Aaron laughed as the bathroom door unlocked and opened to a billow of vanilla-scented steam.

"You know I'm not," he said as Lenny walked out in a towel.

"All yours, A-A-Ron."

Aaron slipped into the bathroom and closed the door with one final nod in my direction. Lenny looked at me.

"Put the sex eyes away. I have to take those cookies out of the oven, so we quite literally do not have time." She walked to her room.

"Really? Not even for one tiny, quick little orgasm?" I asked as I closed the bedroom door behind me and backed her up against the nearest wall.

She gasped as her back met the wall and then rolled her darkening eyes. "Yours or mine?"

I smiled.

"Always yours," I said as I pulled the towel from her body.

Thirty Two

ALANA

I wasn't arrogant enough to think I could get away with looking Liam dead in the eye and telling him that I was his gift for Christmas. Not only was I not arrogant enough, but I was also self-aware enough to know that if I pulled a stunt like that, he would never let me live it down. I didn't need him having that kind of power over me. Although, given that this morning he had kind of said exactly the same thing, maybe he would have let me get away with it.

Once I had come down from my orgasm high in that Macy's dressing room, I realised that I didn't have a gift for Liam, and promptly went into panic mode. I was a good gift-giver. Some might even say great.

And giving gifts to Liam used to be where I truly shined. I would spend weeks thinking about what I was going to get him, and it paid off every time. The soft look on his face when he opened a present from me would make my entire day. But I hadn't been in Liam's life for over a decade, and even though a lot about him was the same, he was still a thirty-year-old man who had nearly thirteen years' worth of new interests and desires. He'd probably lost some things I knew about him as well.

So, I had no idea what to get him for Christmas and I'd had almost no time to think about it. In the end, I saw a keychain of a grey wolf hanging on a display next to some scarves. I decided that if I couldn't give him a thoughtful gift, I could at least give him something funny to unwrap. I'd paid for it hastily on the floor above where he had left me. When I'd found him, he was hanging by the scarves I vetoed, studying one, which immediately made me wish I had bought him one of those instead. At least it would have been practical. Or re-giftable.

So, seeing him holding it in the shiny purple wrapping paper I'd wrapped all my presents in while he had been sleeping at six a.m. made my stomach turn. I wanted to walk over and snatch it out of his hand and tell him to pretend he'd never seen it.

It was making it hard to focus on everyone around me opening their presents because I could see him feeling out the weight and shape of the gift in his hands. He knew it was from me and I knew he was going to be disappointed with it, so I was trying out all the different excuses I could give as to why I'd chosen it in my head. None of them so far didn't expose the fact that we had only been back in each other's lives for seven days and not six weeks. Even though we were no longer lying, we *had* lied. And this shitty, *Twilight*-based, gift was proof of that.

"Liam, what have you got in your hands?" Mel asked. My hands went clammy and, not for the first time, I found myself grateful for the fact that my skin didn't turn red in any circumstances. I just felt overly hot instead.

He started to carefully peel the tape off. He was treating it like it was fragile, like it held the secrets to the universe. My tongue didn't seem to want to work in my mouth. I needed to justify it. To explain myself. To assure him that it was okay if he hated it. It was just supposed to be a joke because once, a thousand years ago, he had given me a wolf.

When the last piece of tape was peeled off, Liam pushed the paper down to reveal his gift. It looked even stupider in the cold light of day when I was not riding the high of coming all over Liam's hand. Liam smiled softly at the keychain, just like he always did whenever I gifted him something, and then he started laughing. Great. He was taking it as a joke. I didn't need any of my half-baked excuses.

He looked over at me. "Open yours from me," he said, his eyes sparkling with humour.

I picked up the brown paper package that he had handed me earlier and started tearing into it. As expected, the dress he had told me I needed to act surprised about was nestled in there, but then I noticed something sticking out of the neckline.

A russet wolf keychain.

I could feel everyone in the room looking at us. I guess they were trying to figure out why two people in their thirties were exchanging wolf keychains.

Eventually, Mom broke the silence. "Aww, isn't that sweet?"

I didn't know which one of us she was talking to or if she was even talking to either of us at all. I couldn't stop looking at the keychain. It was dumb, the way seeing something that I knew cost five dollars partially hidden in the folds of an expensive dress was making me feel.

Seen. Cared for. Understood.

Loved.

Even though I knew that the feeling had been resurrected over the last week, it hadn't fully taken flight. At least not until now. While I struggled to keep tears at bay over a damn keychain. That matched the one I had bought him.

Or maybe this was the first time I was accepting that it had taken flight. Maybe it unfurled its wings and took off this morning when I woke up and saw him sleeping next to me.

Maybe it happened when he walked into my kitchen as I was starting to bake and, just like I knew when we were teenagers, I knew it again now.

I was in love with him.

"Where have you gone?" It was Liam. I hadn't noticed him settle in next to me. Everyone else had left the room.

"Nowhere. You got me a keychain."

"You also got me a keychain." He put his next to mine.

"Yeah, I forgot I didn't have anything for you, and I panicked."

"You didn't have to get me anything. When did you even buy it?"

"I guess at the same time that you did."

"You know what this means right?"

We might just be in love with each other.

"Do not make an imprinting or a knotting joke right now," I said.

"You're no fun." He pulled me into his side and pressed a kiss to my temple as I rested my head on his shoulder.

"I'm very fun. Did you not see my bow earlier?" I gestured in the direction of his dick.

"Yeah, I did. Do you want to go unwrap that gift?"

I pulled away from him slightly. "You know I bought that keychain because I didn't think you'd let me get away with saying that I was your gift, but here you are, doing just that and expecting me to not give you shit for it."

"You can give me shit for it if you want. In fact, I fully expect you to. And I definitely would not have said no to unwrapping you." His palm tapped my hip.

Then I remembered that he had left me to get dressed earlier while he went to take my cookies out of the oven, just before they burned to a crisp, which meant he didn't know what was hidden under my clothes.

"Maybe later. I think you're gonna like the underwear I have on." I patted his knee as I stood up.

"That's...not fair."

"Nor was the fact that I had to portion up a whole batch of cookies with your dick pressed against my ass and pretend that it wasn't there," I said, heading for the kitchen. Just as I left the room, I heard him groan.

LIAM

It was too cold for me to be outside, but I'd woken up restless and I didn't want to wake up Lenny, so here I was, running.

Or at least, I *was* running. I had managed two kilometres before I gave up and turned around. I was now walking back home via the bakery.

As I joined the queue of Westchester Bakes, my phone rang. A picture of the second greatest person I knew, spread-eagled on the ice after a particularly brutal practice, lit up my screen.

"Hey Teddy," I answered.

"If it isn't my favourite right-hand man," Teddy replied.

"Ah, you miss me?" I teased.

"On the ice, not anymore. In general, shockingly yes. I feel like it's been ages since we talked to each other."

"It's barely been a week. But how are you? You're in Boston, right?"

"Yes, we are in Boston. And I'm feeling pretty good about it. The whole family came to Boston for Christmas, and it's been nice to have them around. How's home?"

"Home is...nice," I replied. Home was starting to feel less

like a place and more like a person. A person whom I had left in bed.

"Nice?"

"Just say what you want to say, Teds," I sighed. I knew this hadn't just been a friendly call. We did talk more often since I retired, but we mostly sustained our friendship on random memes and miscellaneous text updates in between physically seeing each other.

"My mom has both of us on Google alert and she got one a couple of days ago, for you. It was a bunch of pictures and a whole article about how you had found yourself a mysterious woman. You have a new girlfriend?" he said bluntly, also sounding a little hurt.

"Yeah, I do."

"Why am I finding this out via Google and not from you? I wasn't even aware you were dating, and I know you're not on the apps, so how the hell have you found yourself a girlfriend?"

I took a breath. "It's Alana."

Teddy was quiet but I knew he knew who I meant.

"As in Fitzpatrick? Coach's daughter?" he finally said.

"He's not been our Coach for years; I think you can call him Rob now. But yes, as in Fitzpatrick."

"How did that happen? When would you even have crossed paths with her? You've been very skilled at avoiding anywhere she may be the entire time you've been in Detroit."

I thought about lying to him, but there didn't seem to be any point now that it was official. Also, he knew I didn't go to that birthday party because he had and told me it was a great time. So, I told the truth.

"I bumped into her at the airport and, with the fact that our parents are still neighbours, we couldn't avoid each other anymore, and now here we are."

"But again, I ask, why is this how I am finding out that

two of my closest friends have finally figured their shit out and started dating?"

"Because part of me is still worried. You know her, she operates like a fox and is prone to running if startled. She could still wake up one day and disappear again. I didn't want to jinx it by telling people outside of the ones we were spending the holidays with."

"She hasn't run yet. You definitely should have told me," Teddy said.

"There is still a 'yet' in your sentence though, Teddy."

"Liam, you don't hang out with someone in the vicinity of *Macy's* that close to Christmas unless you're down for life. In fact, I think the fact that you got Alana out into the city that close to the twenty-fifth is the biggest indicator that she isn't going to run. Not this time."

"You sound very sure about that, man," I laughed softly as I reached the front of the queue.

"I know I don't need to remind you, but she never stopped being my friend. I know who she was as a person in her late twenties, and now into her thirties, and she's not like she was back then. And I know it's not the best example, but she didn't get engaged to a man she had been with for years. Do you know how hard it must be to stick to that conviction? You don't say no to a proposal, but she did, and she stuck to that answer even though everyone kept getting on her case about it. So, if she's hanging around Macy's and getting on ice rinks with you, I feel pretty confident when I say she won't run now. She knows what she wants, and it looks like it might be you she wants now. She won't run again."

"You're probably right. Hang on," I said to Teddy just before I ordered a pistachio croissant and a hazelnut pain au chocolat.

"You get over your aversion to pistachio since I last saw

you, dude? Wow, Alana has really changed you as a person," Teddy asked as my pastries were boxed up.

"No, they're for Lenny. Or at least, one of them is. I'm hoping she will leave me with the pain au chocolat, but no stress if she wakes up and decides she wants Nutella in pastry form," I replied, paying for my order and taking the box before slipping out the door.

"You'll just eat the pistachio one? Liam, you hate pistachios."

"I wouldn't eat it, there is other food in the house and one of her parents or Aaron will eat it. Does part of me hope that she will go pistachio over hazelnut? Yes, but I'm not fussed if she doesn't. I have other options, and I want her to have options."

"Jeez, I forgot how bad you used to have it for her. Did you wake up especially for this pastry run? For options?" I could hear the smile in his voice.

"No, I woke up and thought maybe I should go for a run because I was feeling restless. I got 2k in and gave up. Now I'm talking to you and turning the walk back into a pastry run."

"I need a boyfriend like you. Or a girlfriend. Or just *someone* who treats me as well as you are treating her. If she does run, can you please come back to me? I swear I would treat you so right."

"Thought you said she wasn't gonna do that?"

"Yeah, and she's not. But in an alternate universe, she does, and then we become the new power couple, and everything is great."

"Alright, I'm going to leave you to your daydream," I laughed.

"You gonna watch the game?"

"I can't promise that I will, but I can be there if you need me afterwards," I answered.

"No, I'll just work extra hard to make sure we win so I

won't have to pull you away from your warm bed to help me wallow in my sorrows."

"Great, well shoot sharp and I'll talk to you later."

"Later, Liam."

Rob was in the kitchen when I walked in, a pen poised over a crossword clue.

"Morning, Rob," I said as I set the pastry box on the counter.

"Morning, Liam, you been for a run?" he asked.

"I went on half a run, aborted it, and bought pastries instead."

"A wise choice," he said.

"Just you up?"

"In the house yes, but Stassie and Aaron went for a pre-breakfast walk."

"They couldn't persuade you to join them?"

He tapped his puzzle with the end of his pen. "It seemed like the only time I might get to myself to get through my crossword."

"Oh, I'll leave you to it," I said as I picked the box up.

"No rush. Actually, there is something I wanted to talk to you about. I want you to know that this comes from a place of love and there is no pressure or expectation attached."

He set his pen down and I started to feel nauseous, like I was about to get told off for something.

"Sure, what's up?"

"My assistant coach told me he was leaving at the end of the season, which means I am in the market for a new one. Now, I don't know if coaching is something you would consider, but I would like to offer you the position."

"Oh." It was the only thought in my head. There was a lot

about retirement that I'd been enjoying. The free time. Not having to worry about being at the rink on time. Life was less stressful when I didn't have to go through my entire game day routine. And the day-before-a-game prep. And the post-game wind down. I loved sleeping in my own bed every night and I didn't miss the travel. But on some level, I did miss hockey. Skating with Lenny the other day had reminded me of how much I liked being around the ice.

High school hockey would require less of me than pro hockey did. It would keep me close to the ice and would open me up to a whole other aspect of the sport that sounded interesting to me. I was wary about orienting my life around the sport again, but I was looking at a man who managed to be a successful coach for years and raise a family, so I knew that balance was possible. I was more wary of the fact that if I said yes to this, then it would mean me putting roots back down in Westchester. A place that Alana very much did not live, even if she did still call it home.

"You don't have to give me an answer right now. I appreciate that it's a lot to consider. Let me start with this, I know you've never coached before in the capacity that I am asking you to, but you did help me with the summer programs for a few years before you went pro, and you were great at that. You have a very analytical way of viewing the sport that I think would be invaluable. But more important than that, you respect when enough might just be enough. I know the past few months can't have been easy for you, with people constantly telling you that you shouldn't have retired, but you've stuck to your guns and that is an admirable trait. You know that life outside the rink is sometimes more important, and I think that kind of understanding might be crucial to some of these kids when faced with the reality that going pro might not be in their timeline. Plus, you work as a nice counterpoint to me. You made it to the NHL. I peaked in college." He gave a self-deprecating laugh.

"You didn't peak in college, Coach. I wouldn't have been half the player that I was if I hadn't had you in my corner every step of the way. If you say the way I view the game is analytical, it's because of the way you taught me to play it. I got good at shooting because you made me run drills until I could find any pocket of the net in my sleep. You were the one who taught me that balance is important. You set realistic expectations for every single one of those players on that ice, and we were all better for it. Plus, you have those kids of yours who turned out pretty well, and I don't know if they would be the same people if you were always travelling for hockey."

"One of my kids could not be more apathetic to hockey if they tried," he pointed out. I smiled.

"Apathy is better than hatred if you ask me. And she'd hate it. If you picked professional hockey over her and Aaron, she would have learned to hate the sport and maybe even you, and then who knows where we'd be?"

She wouldn't be in my life, that was for sure. And my life without Alana in it was like the sun without the moon. It just didn't work. Even when she left me, she was still somewhere in my orbit, and I was better for it.

"I'm not asking you to do that either. Pick this sport over her. I know that she has a life in Detroit, and I know that you must have some roots there too. Asking you to move back here would be a lot and if you decide that staying there is what is best for you, for her, then so be it. But I want you to know that the offer is on the table."

"When do you need to know by?"

"End of January."

"Okay, I'll think about it."

"I'll let you go take those up to Alana now," he said as he picked up his pen and immediately filled in a clue.

Thirty Four

ALANA

There was a shift on the bed that jogged me awake and as I blinked my eyes open, I saw Liam settling on the edge, two plates in hand.

"Morning," he said.

"You sound like you've been awake a while," I replied, my voice cracking as it tried to find its way back to consciousness.

"Awake enough to have run 2k and bought you a pastry. Pistachio or hazelnut?"

"If I say hazelnut, are you just going to smile your way through eating the other one?"

"No, Rob's downstairs. Aaron and Stassie might want to fight for it when they are back from their walk. Just figured you would want options."

"Stand down, you can eat your hazelnut croissant," I said as I sat up and reached for the pistachio pastry. "Why did you only run 2k?"

"I could not be bothered, and it took me that long to accept it. I talked to Teddy on the way back, so that was nice."

"And how is the Teddy bear?" I asked just before I let out a moan at my first bite of pastry. I saw Liam's eyes darken.

He cleared his throat. "They're in Boston. He spent Christmas there with his family, so he is well and truly settled before their game later today. Is while you're having a moment with your breakfast a good time to tell you that there are photos of us out there?"

I couldn't say I was surprised; it had occurred to me that this would happen. I thought I would care more, but I actually felt indifferent to it. I wasn't hiding being with Liam and in some ways, I accepted that it came with the territory.

"Photos of us doing what?" I did still need to know for sure that someone hadn't managed to catch our dressing room tryst on camera.

"Teddy mentioned something about us frolicking in front of Macy's and the ice rink."

I sighed in relief. "Oh, well that's fine. For a second, I worried that we got caught in the dressing room."

"I think Teddy would have been a lot more scandalised if that was the case, but he seemed pretty chill. Plus, he couldn't tell that it was you in the pictures."

"So he thought you had a mystery girl?"

"Yeah, he did. Was kind of surprised when I said it was you. Then a little bit annoyed that I hadn't told him directly. You know Teddy." Liam was peeling flakes off the top of his pastry and very intentionally not looking at me anymore.

He was right, I did know Teddy. Well. We had never stopped being friends. All week, Liam and I had been skirting around the reason we hadn't seen each other for years. Liam knew me well enough to know that I wasn't going to start talking about my feelings unprompted, and so while we found our bearings around each other, he had let it go.

But I knew he could only let it go unspoken for so long and we couldn't exactly move forward as a couple with it still hanging between us.

"Why did you go to Michigan?" His voice was quiet. Tentative.

And there it was. I took a deep breath, knowing I couldn't deny him the truth anymore, and jumped straight in.

"I had exactly zero intention of falling in love with my best friend. The same best friend that everyone told me I would end up marrying one day. One, because I thought you were a stupid boy, even if you were *my* stupid boy, and two, because it's just too fucking basic. How many films have been made about that? So, imagine my surprise when I'm listening to Lacey talk about how she loves her boyfriend so much she's going to have sex with him and when I ask her how she knows she loves him she says all these things that sound familiar to me. Then a couple of days later, you walk into my kitchen at three in the morning and sleepily hang out with me while I bake, and I realise *you* are the reason the things sounded familiar.

"And then I just felt very stupid, because at no point did you give any indication that you saw me as anything more than a pseudo-sister. But I couldn't turn it off once that switch had flipped. Then I remembered that we were going to college together. And I knew you would know that something was wrong because I couldn't keep it in anymore. These feelings that were blooming for you. So, I knew there would come a point where I would start to feel irrationally jealous or sad or angry at you if you started having casual encounters with people, like I wasn't dying inside to have you. I convinced myself that if you knew how I felt, you'd give me this speech about how you did love me, but it was like a sister. Or you'd give some spiel about how you couldn't commit to a relationship because of hockey or college or because you liked having casual sex and didn't want to be stuck with one person. With me. And because I made it weird by confessing all these feelings, you would slowly pull away. In my head, I was losing you anyway and I figured there was no need to drag it out any longer. And I got into Michigan. So, I broke my own heart and ran away."

Liam was silent for what felt like forever, and I tried to distract myself with the pistachio topping of my pastry. I felt him move up the bed until he was sitting next to me. I waited for him to get me to look at him, but he just started talking.

"It is really basic to fall in love with your best friend, but if you'd told me, I wouldn't have told you that I loved you like a sister. I would have told you that I loved you too. Because here's the thing Alana, I juggled hockey and school and *you* throughout high school with great ease. I didn't go to every party or always hang out with the guys because I wanted to hang out with you. Coming out of the rink on a day when we lost was fine because I would walk into that parking lot and see you leaning against the side of my car with the bottom of your face buried underneath your scarf and your hands in your coat pockets. And that became the best part of my day."

I wiped under my eyes, and I realised I was crying. Liam took my chin in his hand and tilted my head to look at him. He swiped his thumbs over my cheekbones and something else clicked into place.

"The day I met Kai was the same day I got this tattoo." I gestured to my right arm. "I got it as my final hurrah to you—"

"What flower is it, by the way?" Liam cut me off.

"Don't ask questions you already know the answer to."

Queen of the Night. A flower that only blooms at night-time and then dies at sunrise. Liam discovered its existence when we were thirteen and told me about it because it reminded him of me.

"Fine, how many Queen of the Night flowers are tattooed on you?"

"I think you know the answer to that too," I said quietly.

"Seventeen?"

The number on the back of every hockey jersey he's ever worn.

I nodded. He blew out a slow breath.

"What were you going to say?"

"The day I met Kai was also the day I decided I was going to put my unrequited love for you in a locker as soon as my tattoo was finished. Then, with my arm still wrapped, I literally bumped into Kai and away we went. It's funny because I never actually got to fully put you in that locker in my mind. I ended up with this man who had been very invested in your collegiate career and where you were going professionally. But that's not the point. What I'm trying to say is that I've just realised why I didn't say yes when Kai proposed. The moment Kai started to get down on one knee, I closed my eyes because if I couldn't see him do it then maybe it wasn't happening. But when I closed my eyes, the only thought I had was that if he really loved me, hell if he really *knew* me, then he wouldn't be asking me to marry him in front of all those people, the fact that we knew them was kind of redundant. And as soon as I had that thought, it was immediately chased by the thought that there was someone who knew me well enough to not do something like that so publicly, and I couldn't ignore that."

Liam wiped under my eyes again and pressed a kiss to the space between my eyebrows.

"I asked you once if you would still be my friend if I didn't play hockey and you said, 'The fact you play hockey is the least interesting thing about you'. I don't think you ever told me what you thought was more interesting about me, but I do know that you said it with the utmost sincerity. When I floated the idea about retiring while I was rehabbing my shoulder, I jokingly asked Mel if she would still love me if I didn't play hockey and she hesitated to say yes. Suddenly, all I could think about was how you didn't hesitate. You never hesitated."

"We are having this conversation in our thirties because I hesitated," I pointed out.

"Hey, everything happens for a reason, right?" He kissed my forehead.

"You're very pretty. That is more interesting than the hockey. Tall. Everyone loves tall. You were one of those people who liked ice time and conditioning in equal amounts, so you would have always been cut. That's interesting. It shows complete dedication. Dedication is interesting, right? You know obscure flowers, which while niche, is interesting." One of his hands moved to cup the back of my neck and his thumb swiped along my jaw, making my skin erupt in goosebumps. "You like books, and you understand the importance of *the* hand flex. On that, you have very interesting hands that are capable of very interesting things, like stick handling, although I guess that is hockey-related."

He smiled before pressing a kiss just below my ear, making me shudder.

"Len, I am about to show you something and the answer to your inevitable question is going to be eighteen."

He brushed his lips against my cheek and then stood up, his fingers finding the waistband of his shorts.

"Muller, I've seen your dick before, you didn't need to announce that," I said, not that I was complaining. I was always down to see it now that I had.

"It occurred to me about five minutes ago that you haven't seen me completely naked because if you had, we would have already had this particular conversation."

"That's ridiculous, I've definitely seen you—" Except I hadn't. Shirtless, yes. He'd had his dick out enough that he could fuck me with it, but fully nude? Yeah, that hadn't happened yet.

"Yeah, wild right? Almost as wild as the fact that I learned just how good you taste before I kissed your mouth," he said as he pulled his shorts down and let them puddle on the floor. He was half hard as he pulled his top off as well.

"What am I looking at? Because while I have not seen you like this, I have definitely seen all the components."

He had his hands on his hips. He oozed confidence and it was turning me on.

"Just give it a moment, you'll see it."

What I was seeing was that he was getting harder the longer I stared at him, and that was pulling my focus as I studied his naked form. Then my gaze snagged on it.

Nestled deep in the crease of his hip bone.

"Is that the Sweet Nothing bakery sign?"

I had spent a lot of time doodling what I wanted my bakery sign to look like. I thought if I had the logo, then it would make everything more real, and I would work harder to make it a reality. One day, I drew a large cookie with cupcakes for chunks and I knew that I had found it. When Liam had finished his hockey practice that day, he had met me by the car, and I'd shoved it in his face. I told him to get used to the design because he was gonna see it in Westchester one day. He told me he didn't doubt it and then drove us to get dinner.

And he had that very logo tattooed on him. Six years before it would have any importance.

"Why is the Sweet Nothing bakery sign tattooed that close to your dick?" I watched his now fully hard dick twitch.

"I did it on a whim but put enough thought into it to remember that I still knew Teddy. If it was somewhere that he could see it, he would never let me hear the end of it. You just don't look in the general direction of people's junk in the locker room, so it felt like the safest bet."

"And no one you had sex with questioned why there was a cookie that close to it? Didn't make a weird joke? Mel didn't clock that the sign for the bakery she visited quite often was also tattooed in an intimate place on your body?"

"Yes, some girls questioned it. Yes, a couple made a cookie joke. Mel commented on it, but she never asked if it had anything to do with you. I'm not saying she didn't think it, but she never asked. Which was probably for the best because I have no idea how I would have explained without making it sound like I was half in love with you. Any more questions?"

"Did you get hard while it was being done?"

"Seriously, that is your question?" He leant down and pulled his shorts back up, trapping his erection in the waistband, before he sat back on the bed.

"I just think pain might turn you on a little bit, so yeah, I am more interested to know if having a cookie tattooed in that particular area caused the same situation you're rocking right now. Rather than talking about all the other women who have seen it." I ran a finger up his length. He moaned softly.

"Yeah, I got a little hard. The guy doing it told me that it wasn't an abnormal reaction."

"You busy today?" I asked, aware that I was changing the subject, but a thought had just occurred to me.

As always, Liam didn't bat an eyelid at the change of direction. "Not unless you're busy today."

"You wanna find out what perks come with being the Coach's daughter?"

"What perks are we talking here?"

"It's a game day, right?"

"For some people, yeah. I don't know if you remember, but I retired this year."

"And you don't miss the arena at all?" I would always think he made the right choice, but that didn't mean I couldn't appreciate that the right choice was sometimes the hardest.

"I don't miss this particular game of the season; it was always a bit rough. If we're talking big picture then yeah, I miss it sometimes, but mostly I miss the energy of the arena the moment my skates hit the ice for the first time."

"I can give you clean ice. No crowds, but clean ice, I think." I had to talk to my dad first, but I was pretty sure he would say yes. I was his favourite daughter, after all.

Liam was oddly silent.

"We don't have to go. I just thought—"

He reached out his hand and laced his fingers through mine, squeezing them gently.

"No, I do want to. If Rob says yes, then I want to go. Just…" I waited. "How much like game day do you want this to be?"

"This a superstition thing?" I knew Liam had a few. I never knew all of them, but I knew that his game day mornings had to go a certain way, or he was convinced the world was going to end.

He nodded.

"I used to have to jerk off pre-game, and then before the first game of my professional career, your wonderful father called me in the middle of it. I shouldn't have answered it, but it was your dad, and he was instrumental in me even thinking I could get on the ice professionally, so I didn't want to ignore him."

I laughed. "Was he aware you had your hand around your dick just before you answered that call?"

"I doubt it. Anyway, that phone call took up the rest of my time before I had to leave. So, I went without release. We won that game. The next game I carried out my ritual as usual; we lost."

Heat was settling low in my core.

"Therefore, you had to start edging yourself before every game?"

"Correct."

"So, what does this have to do with today?"

"Don't ask questions you already know the answer to," he said, his voice was huskier now. I squeezed my thighs together.

"Okay, when did you let yourself come then?"

"Whenever I got back into my own bed."

"Wait your *own* bed? What about away games?"

"I mean, it went soft eventually, so it was fine. Made coming back home a little bit sweeter, though."

"What would be the rules here then?" We were in New York for a few more days.

"The main thing about it is that I needed to feel at home. There is nowhere I feel more at home than when I'm around you, Alana."

Oh.

"Right, well." This was going to be fun. "Go have a shower and get close. It's game day, baby!" I pressed a kiss to his cheek and got out of bed.

"I love you. You know that, right?" Liam said just as I got to the door. I turned back to look at him, the words on the tip of my tongue.

"I know," I said instead. He smiled and I went to ask my dad a favour.

Thirty Five

ALANA

I had the keys in my hand and the high school ice rink literally had my surname on it, but as I turned on the lights, I still felt like we were doing something that we shouldn't.

"Fuck," Liam whispered from behind me.

"What?" I turned to look at him as he looked around the empty rink that used to be his third home.

"Just really weird being back where it all started."

"Yeah? Bringing back all the good, the bad, and the ugly memories?"

"Something like that. Where exactly did you get these skates from?" He tugged at the pair draped over his right shoulder, his were over his left.

"When I asked if we could use the rink, Dad remembered that he saw them in the garage not too long ago and gave them the all-clear to skate on." I slid them off his shoulder, sat down on a nearby bench and started unzipping my boots to put them on. Liam knelt in front of me and took over.

"Thank you for this. For today. And for the last week or so," he said quietly as he loosened the laces on the skates.

"All I did was agree to be your fake girlfriend so your

parents could change the broken record. Oh, does your dad know you're here?" I don't why I was bringing him up, but it seemed like the kind of thing he would have an opinion on, and I wanted to be prepared, just in case I had to fight him on this issue at all.

"You didn't have to agree to anything. I'm not questioning a good thing too much because calling you my girlfriend is the best way to round out my year, but you definitely didn't have to agree to anything. And no, I haven't spoken to him today." He carefully lifted one of my feet and put one of my skates on.

"I'm sorry that I didn't give you the chance to round out your year in the best possible way years ago."

Liam paused and looked up at me, his green-blue eyes wide.

"I know you are," he said simply, before resuming putting my skates on.

"Not one bit of you is annoyed at me for denying us the last twelve years? I'm just forgiven?"

He looked up at me again. "I forgave you years ago. No, I didn't like it, but I forgave you for it by the time I was drafted for the NHL. Things happen for a reason, you know? This week has shown me that we both lived the lives we were supposed to live, and we came back to each other when the timing was right. There is no guarantee we would have made it long-term back then. I might not have been drafted when I was and for who I was. You might not have found the best place to open a business. I might have wanted to move teams more while you were looking to make roots in a city, and that could have added tension.

"There are a thousand different ways that our relationship could have fallen apart because we didn't know who we were or what we wanted. We were also incapable of really communicating with one another because we were kids. Maybe the fact that we were eighteen and didn't quite know how to cope with the big feelings, which led to us avoiding them, was a blessing. The last twelve years have been good. They've made us who we are and now we can move forward together, knowing we're capable of the big stuff." He looked back down and moved to my second skate.

"I hadn't thought of it like that, actually. I've spent a lot of this week thinking I could have spent the last twelve years feeling like I was flying and I'm an idiot for denying us that."

He secured my skate and then tapped them twice as he looked back at me with a loose grin on his face. "I make you feel like you can fly?"

"Yeah, sometimes you do. But you're right, it's only because we lived our lives and made our choices that this feels so right now. Like maybe this could be a forever thing."

I stood up and made my way to the ice, stopping just before I put my blade down to look down at Liam.

"You wanna break in this ice first?" His eyes dragged up from my skates to my eyes, his gaze was darker now.

"Nah, babe, it's all yours."

"It does it for you, doesn't it?" I teased.

"What, seeing you on the ice? Yeah, it's hot."

My eyes flicked down to his crotch; the line of his erection was visible against his sweatpants.

"I might make every day game day," I said before I slid onto the ice.

I was starting to find Liam's erection distracting. How he was skating with it, I didn't know, but he wasn't showing any signs of slowing down, so I wasn't going to suggest we call it a day just yet. We still had half an hour before Dad was coming by to clean the ice.

I, however, was exhausted, so I was sitting on the edge of

the rink, reading while Liam sped around the ice when my screen went black and then Kai's face popped up.

Kai hadn't been in touch enough since we broke up for me to bother blocking his number, so I hadn't. But I had forgotten that it was still in my contacts list. Out of sheer curiosity, I answered.

"Hey," I said, injecting my voice with fake cheer. Kai's eyebrows were drawn together in a way that told me he was annoyed. It wasn't too dissimilar to how he looked when he realised I wasn't saying yes to his proposal.

"Hey yourself. How are you?"

The formalities felt forced, and it made me itch.

"Eating, drinking, and baking. Losing at board games, you? How's Aspen?"

"It's beautiful. Hey, so a bit of a random question, but do you know Liam Mulligan?"

The itchy feeling morphed into something else. Liam skidded to a dead stop opposite me at the sound of his name.

"Uhhh, yeah I do, why?"

"I think it's interesting that you personally know one of my favourite sportspeople and failed to mention it in the eight years we were together," he said angrily.

I took a deep breath. "Well, we weren't exactly friends while you and I were together. So, I don't know why I would have brought it up."

"How long have you known him?" he snapped.

"We were friends throughout our childhood, but I went to Michigan, and he went to Harvard, and we stopped speaking until recently."

"Right about the time you broke up with me. Are you doing this to spite me?"

That caught me off guard and I physically recoiled at the suggestion. "Am I doing *what* to spite you?"

"Dating my favourite hockey player."

"Did you not say he went down in your estimations when he retired earlier this year?" Liam was now next to me, close enough that I could feel his body heat, but far enough that not even his shadow was on my screen.

"I said that in the heat of the moment when the announcement came. The team could actually do with him this season. I forgot how key he was to some plays and Teddy could do with the support."

"Sure, if you say so."

I heard Liam try to stifle his laughter at just how little I knew about his former team. Why would I? Any update I received about them came mostly because someone wanted to tell me how Liam was doing. If he wasn't on the ice anymore, what use were those updates to me?

"Do you even like hockey? How can you be with a man like that when you don't like hockey?"

"The same way I can have a father who's a hockey coach and not like it. It's not their entire lives so they know how to talk about other things. Besides, Liam's always known I'm indifferent to the sport, so it's not a problem."

Kai flinched at the mention of just how long I had known Liam. "How did you even reconnect with him?"

"We bumped into each other at the airport."

"And you're already all over each other?" The distaste was thick in his tone. I hadn't looked up the pictures of us that had ended up online, but I was pretty sure that none of them would display *that* much, if any, of us being all over each other. There would be hand-holding at most.

"He's not a stranger. We were friends for fourteen years and it picked up where we left off. Whatever narrative you have concocted in your head isn't true."

"It all seems very convenient," he spat. Liam scoffed and when I turned to look at him, I could see how annoyed he was.

"Kai, I wasn't holding out on you. We didn't talk for years

and now we do. That's it. I'm sorry that you couldn't use me to get a meeting with the Golden Boy, but it was physically impossible until about a week ago, and you and I are no longer in contact with one another." Or at least we weren't until this call.

"Seems like you're doing a lot more than talking," he sneered. A noise that sounded an awful lot like a growl came from the man standing next to me.

"Yeah, we're dating. Now, do you need anything else or did you just call to express your annoyance about who my boyfriend is?"

"Boyfriend? That quick?" Now he looked horrified. It took him nearly six months before he started calling me his girlfriend.

"So that's a no on needing anything else then? Well, this has been fun Kai, but Muller might pop a blood vessel if he has to listen to anything else, and I'd rather he didn't go out on the ice, no matter how much other people wanted him to."

Liam skated so he was in front of me, but behind my phone, his hands cupping my calves before they ran up to my thighs. His thumbs settled in the crease of my hips, and I felt a low pulse in my core. He smirked at me, and with my free hand, I cupped his erection, knocking the smirk right off his face.

"His nickname is Gunner," Kai said. I'd forgotten he was still on the phone.

"To hockey people, yeah sure. But he's Muller to me."

Something hit me then. He wasn't always called Gunner. His first ever hockey team when we were in elementary school called him Muller and I'd told him that it was dumb and would never catch on. Until one day in our freshman year of high school, I had used it as a joke and realised it wasn't quite as dumb as I'd previously thought, so I started using it full-time.

And the hockey team called him Gunner from then onwards.

"Look, Kai, not that this conversation hasn't been thrilling, but I'm gonna go because I have Liam Mulligan on an ice rink and that is much more interesting than this." I hung up before he could respond and then clicked on his contact and blocked the number.

"He seems nice," Liam said, his thumbs sweeping up and down my hip crease.

"You can park the sarcasm. He was a good boyfriend. I guess his ego is feeling a little bruised because I went from him to his favourite hockey player. Hey, how come everyone stopped calling you Muller?" I asked.

"How come you always tell people that your name is Alana when they try giving you a nickname? Or when they follow my lead and try to call you Lenny?" he countered.

"Because my name *is* Alana." And I hated nicknames. My name wasn't that long to say in full.

"Don't know if you've noticed Len, but I hardly call you that."

Of course I'd noticed. I hadn't been called Lenny for over a decade and I would have told anyone who would listen that I didn't miss it. But I did. Because it was *his* name for me.

Liam paused the movement of his thumbs. "It's yours," he started. "The first time you called me Muller, I knew I would never let anyone else use it again. I made up some story about how I felt like it was messing up my game and well, you know how us sportspeople are."

"Superstitious little fucks," I huffed. "Well, same here. My name is Alana unless you happen to be my brother. Or you," I finished quietly. He pressed a kiss to my forehead and the movement shifted his cock harder into the hand I still had hovering over the area. "It's cold in here, how are you still this hard? You didn't play like this, did you?"

"No, it calmed itself down and the cup did a lot of the work. This right here is all your fault. Your ass in these leggings when you're skating is the best visual. I didn't get to fully appreciate it the other day." His hands moved around to cup the top of my ass.

"We should get out of here. You good to go?" I squeezed my hand around him once more for good measure, and he groaned in my ear.

"Yeah, let's go home."

LIAM

"How much like a pre-game ritual do you want here?" I asked as I turned onto our street.

"Why, do you do something weird?"

"Not weird as such and I think you'll like it, but I need you to give me five minutes when we get in."

I pulled into the Fitzpatrick's driveway.

"Fine, I'll give you twenty and make pasta dough so we can have fresh stuff for dinner. Might as well get yourself close again while you're at it," she replied, reaching over and giving my cock a firm stroke before getting out of the car.

I leant my head back against the seat and groaned.

No matter where I went, I always packed a dress shirt and suit pants, just in case. It never occurred to me that one day my 'just in case' would be putting it on for the sole purpose of edging myself in front of my girlfriend.

When I got back to our room, I changed out of my sweatpants into the suit pants, leaving the zip open and perfectly framing my leaking cock in my boxers. Then I pulled on my dress shirt, leaving it unbuttoned, and rolled the sleeves up to the elbows.

Mostly dressed again, I picked up the cock ring and the lube and lay back on the bed, tugging my boxers down to rest under my balls.

I started with slow, teasing touches that made the tip leak and my lower abdomen tense almost painfully. It didn't take long before I felt like I was ready to explode, which was when I released my cock and took a few deep breaths. There was only so much teasing I could take before I came and I wanted, *needed,* Lenny to get back before the twenty minutes were up.

She'd made cookies in less time, surely pasta dough was easier.

When I felt like I could touch my dick again without erupting all over my stomach, I grabbed the lube and the cock ring, applying an almost excessive amount of lube to both my dick and the toy, before securing it at the base of my dick. I pulled my boxers back up to cover me, and the damp cotton almost stung against my over-sensitive flesh.

I couldn't remember the last time I was so desperate to come. I closed my eyes and focused on my breathing.

Twenty-four minutes after we got home, the bedroom door opened. I opened my eyes to see Alana close the door behind her.

"Are you fucking kidding me?" she said, leaning back against the door.

"I said I thought you'd like it." My voice sounded wrecked. It matched how I felt, still so close and yet so far from the release my body so desperately needed.

"Can I ask how this particular pre-game ritual came to be? For some reason, that was all I could think about while making pasta. I had to start it again." She was twisting the ring on her thumb, something she mostly did when she was nervous. Her fingers had found it a lot earlier in the week, but she had been playing with it less since we went skating. There was a chance that she was nervous at this moment, but she had control of this situation, which led me to believe that she was playing with it now for a different reason. She also played with that ring when she was thinking.

I was probably about to find myself in a whole world of pain. And I'd thank her for it when she was done with me.

"Sure. Look out your window."

Her eyes tore themselves away from me and to her window.

"I'm looking at your bedroom." When she looked back at me, my cock twitched, and I took one more steadying breath.

"We were sixteen, and I was getting ready to go to a game when you came back into your room wearing a towel. You walked past the window and then threw your towel across the room. I saw it fly past the window and I couldn't stop thinking about the fact that you were naked, just out of sight. I'd never thought about you like that until then, and I thought maybe it was just a passing thought, but I couldn't stop wondering about what shade of brown your nipples were or what the curve of your waist into your hip would feel like under my hands. Before I knew what I was doing, I was stroking myself, thinking about you, and I promised myself that once I came, I wouldn't do it again, that I wouldn't think of you like that."

"Except you won," she interjected, her voice breathless, her body still.

"We won," I whispered.

"So, did you think of me every time, or just pre-game?"

She stepped away from the door towards the bed, her movements slow.

"Pre-game."

"That makes sense, I guess, what with it being embedded in a superstition. When did it stop?"

"Consistently? When I started in college. But you made a guest appearance every now and then and I always seemed to play better on those days." I always won on those days. Every time. Without fail. It became a superstition within a superstition by my junior year of college.

She nodded, then pulled her sweater off and dropped it on the floor. She reached behind her back, undid the clasp of her bra, and let that join her sweater on the floor before she climbed on the bed, her nipples already puckering.

"You can look, but not touch. Unless you're touching yourself, which you should definitely start doing."

I groaned.

"If I do that, I'm gonna come. The last however many minutes have been a real exercise of my endurance."

She smirked as she reached for the waistband of my boxers and pulled them down, tucking it under my balls. She gasped.

"You're wearing the cock ring."

"Yeah," I said, my voice barely above a desperate whisper as she ran a finger along the silicone, the barest of brushes against my length.

"I remember you telling me that it vibrates." Her fingers brushed against my swollen balls, and I twitched. I then felt the press of something cool in my hand. "Do me a favour, baby, and get that wet with your mouth. Try not to bite down on it."

The second part of her sentence only made sense when she waited for me to suck the tip of her vibrator into my mouth and then turned on the cock ring. My hips bucked off the bed and the worst of my moans were muffled by the vibrator in my mouth. When I looked at her, she looked positively gleeful.

"Good boy. Now, turn that on." She pointed to the vibrator as I pulled it out of my mouth. I clicked it on. "Good, click through to setting three." I did, the pattern was just random enough that it didn't feel like you'd ever quite get the pressure you needed to come.

Her finger circled my frenulum. "Hold that right here."

"I'm gonna come," I warned her as I dropped the point of the vibrator down to where she asked. Her hand covered my mouth and muffled the noise I made. Every muscle in my body was screaming at me to find release.

"Give me two minutes, then I'll let you," she said, removing her hand and pressing a brief kiss to my lips before getting off the bed and disappearing into her closet.

I started counting to 120 in my head to distract myself from the dual vibrations.

"I knew you could last." I opened my eyes to find Lenny at the end of the bed, a wide smile on her face, and wearing a jersey for our high school hockey team. She turned around slowly and there on the back was Mulligan, 17. I almost lost it.

"When the fuck did you get that?"

She turned back around. "Our junior year at high school. I was going to start wearing it to games but then I got all in my head about what that meant, and so I never did. You can turn the vibrators off."

I clicked the vibe against my cock off and reached down to turn the ring off. If I thought I felt close to coming before, it was nothing compared to now. I'd been on edge for hours and my cock felt full, my balls heavy, and the woman that I loved more than anything was wearing my high school jersey.

"If I take this ring off, I'm gonna come, so it might be best if you have the honours."

She climbed on the bed and straddled my lower thighs, her hands rested close to the crease of my hips.

"How do you want to come? Dealer's choice?"

I quirked an eyebrow. "Pun intended?"

"Only a little bit. Your answer?"

"I'm too fragile to fuck you the way I want, so you do your thing."

"What makes you think I have a thing?" Her hand wrapped around my cock loosely, barely enough pressure for me to even register that she was holding me.

I whined before I managed to find my words.

"You keep looking at it."

"What, your cock? Yeah, it looks huge. And *so* red. It won't stop leaking. And this vein, fuck, I want to tease this vein for hours." My cock twitched under her touch along said vein. I didn't doubt that she would enjoy just how sensitive that particular line was when given half the chance.

"Not what I'm talking about, and you know it. *Please,* Alana, I'm so close. Please let me come."

"Since you asked so nicely." She leant down and took the tip in her mouth. The wet heat of her made me buck upwards, but her weight on my legs kept me pinned down. She moved the ring up my shaft and when it was off, she held me tightly. All the nerve endings in my body felt like livewires and all of them were begging for one thing.

And Lenny gave it to me. She loosened her grip until she was holding me just right and it took three more strokes before I came. I bit down on the collar of my shirt, trying to muffle the roar that ripped out of me at the first wave of release. Lenny's grip on my cock didn't let up and she milked my orgasm out of me, her other hand rolling my balls.

Just as I was about to veer into over-stimulated territory, she let me go. She waited until I was mostly back in the room before she made her next move, which had the power to get me hard again, despite my dick's protest that it stayed exactly where it was to recover.

She brought the hand coated in my release to her mouth and started licking it off, making a show of hollowing her cheeks as she cleaned off her fingers. Once her hand was clean, she looked down at the mess on my stomach, most of it covering my tattoo. She smeared it around with her finger and then, careful to avoid my rallying dick, she cleaned that up with her tongue too.

When it looked clean enough and I felt like I had proper control of my limbs again, I pulled her up and sealed my mouth over hers. I could taste myself on her tongue and I deepened the kiss until she went lax against me.

My hands settled on her ass, and I discovered that she wasn't wearing any underwear. I broke the kiss and took a deep breath. Lenny started kissing along my jaw. The kissing turned into sucking, and I realised that she was darkening the deep pink of the birthmark on my neck.

"Someone seems to like the thought of me marking them." I could feel her smile against my neck as she pressed her leg down on my cock, already almost back at full hardness.

"It's a combination of that and this naked pussy lying close to it while you're wearing *my* jersey."

She pulled back and looked back at me. "You still want to fuck me?" Her voice dripped into my ear as she ground her pussy against me.

"There is so much I want to do, but yes, I still want to fuck you. I just can't decide if I want you naked so I can see all of you when I make you come, or if I want you to keep wearing that so I can see my number on your back while I fuck you."

She rolled her hips against me before she reached over to the bedside drawer and pulled out a handful of condoms, throwing them on the bed.

"Say this is the last time we have sex—which it won't be, before you start freaking out that I'm going to slip out in the middle of the night—which one would you want to be your lasting memory?"

I lightly slapped her ass. "Get on your hands and knees."

"On one condition." I nodded. "Don't take the suit off."

"Done."

LIAM

Despite the steady movement of her ribcage against me, I could tell that Lenny wasn't asleep. If she hadn't removed her ring earlier, mid-handjob, when I told her the coolness of the silver against my heated skin was too much, I knew it would be spinning faster than the speed of light now.

I waited.

"You said you wanted a hockey team once," she eventually whispered.

My hand stilled where it was rubbing circles on her naked thigh. "Huh?"

"You said you wanted enough kids to field a full squad once."

"Oh, that. Weren't we like twelve when I said that?"

"Well, I was twelve when I said that I didn't want them and I haven't changed my mind, so who's to say that you haven't?"

It was a fair point.

"Yeah, I stopped wanting a hockey team a long time ago."

"But...?"

"There is no but. I'm indifferent to the whole thing,

which is probably a sign that I don't want kids. So I'm not going to wake up one day and feel like I was deprived of something because I fell in love with a woman who has made it abundantly clear for almost the entire time that I've known her that she doesn't want them. We have friends. I'm sure some of them will have kids. We'll be that aunt and uncle who have a mysterious amount of money and do fun things."

"Liam, you were on a multi-million-dollar contract for nearly a decade. There is nothing mysterious about the amount of money you have." She poked me in the side.

"Fair, but the rest of my point still stands. We can fly in, spoil them, leave, and then sleep through the night. Or at least I will sleep through the night, you will do whatever it is you do with your sleep schedule."

"We've shared a bed for the past week, you know I sleep." She poked me again. "Now is probably also a good time to establish that being with me means you can't give up condoms because I've not met a birth control that suits me and I'm not going on it again."

"I was never going to ask you to do that. I have no issues with using condoms. I'll live. Although there is an option that has nothing to do with you and everything to do with me," I tacked on.

"I'm not asking you to do that," she mumbled.

"I know you're not. I'm just saying I'd do it. Once we get out of the honeymoon phase, I can get the snip and then we are free to go at it like nobody's business."

She rose up onto her elbow and looked down at me. "Do you have a breeding kink that I need to worry about?"

"Do you mean do I get turned on by the idea of your body being swollen with our child? Not at all. You'd be miserable and then at the end of the whole thing, there would be a legit person that we would have to raise. So really, at what cost? Also, I just don't think you'd take me seriously if, in the throes of passion, I referred to filling you up with my seed and putting a baby in you."

She laughed. "A sure-fire way to make me drier than the Sahara. You're serious about this, aren't you?"

"Yeah. We don't have to keep talking about this right now. But I'll do it, one day. I'd say I might not tell you when it happens, but there are seven days with no sex at all, so you'd probably notice. While we're kind of on the subject, I also won't revoke your face-sitting access if you don't get your hair yanked out of your body every six weeks by a ball of sugar paste." I realised, as I finished, that I had shown my hand, and that hand was that this was not just a passing thought I'd had at this very moment, but was something that I had actively looked into in the last week or so.

"Which did you Google first, vasectomy procedures or sugaring?"

Before I could answer, a phone started vibrating on the bedside table. She twisted around to grab her phone, and I nipped at the skin on the side of her breast.

"Hey Max," she said, excitement in her voice.

"Hey yourself," the voice of my former nutritionist came through the phone. I had questions about how Maxxy knew Lenny.

"To what do I owe the pleasure of this call?"

"Need to talk to you about this party."

"Shit! Give me a second," Lenny muted the call and looked at me with an apology already swimming in her eyes. "So, I have literally just remembered that I'm supposed to be going back to Detroit tomorrow."

"Because you're having a party?" She rolled her eyes at my obvious confusion over the whole sentence.

"Yeah, I didn't plan it. Kai was, I guess rightfully, a bit presumptuous and thought that he would combine an engagement party with New Year's Eve. So he sent out all these invites, which I forgot about until my final week at work when Maxxy mentioned she was going to have to deal with the setup because I was here, not in Detroit."

"How do you even know the nutritionist of the Panthers?"

"Oh, Maxxy was my freshman roommate, and we clicked. She's my best friend and the reason your entire team can eat countless baked goods. I tweak the recipes of their favourites so they fit in with their meal plans, which I get from good ol' Maxine."

"You do that?" Just when I thought I couldn't love her more.

"Yeah, it's not that big a deal. That team keeps me in business. Don't worry, your birthday brownies were full of all the good shit."

"Wait, when did he propose?"

"September," she replied, reluctantly. I knew why.

"He didn't?"

"Technically, no. My birthday was on the Sunday, he proposed on the Saturday."

"You spent your thirty-first birthday alone?"

"No, I spent it with Max," she unmuted the call. "Sorry about that. What about this party?"

"Well, I am looking at all the decorations and they are very..."

"Engagement heavy?"

"Yeah, so unless you're marrying number seventeen after ten days, the decorations are non-existent. What do you wanna do?"

"Are even the balloons contaminated?"

"There are a lot and the ones that don't have some engagement reference on them are gold, which doesn't really fit your overall vibe. But don't think I didn't notice just now that you avoided acknowledging my comment on number seventeen.

Which, let's be real, is the real reason I called, because I can deal with the decorations. Can we circle back to who you are dating? When and how did you meet the man who broke a thousand hearts?"

Lenny looked at me, her eyebrows pinched together. "Is that a thing?"

It was. I tried to avoid it, but it followed me around, and Teddy liked to rib me for it when he thought I was enjoying retirement a little bit too much. Which was often.

"You're avoiding the question once again," Maxxy said. Lenny rolled her eyes.

"Short answer, we met at the airport when we both flew home for Christmas."

"No, that is not going to cut it because I know you, and there is no way you would have done half the things I've seen splashed over the internet with a person you had known mere days. So, long answer, please."

I smiled because I'd always liked Maxxy, but I liked her even more now knowing just how well she knew my girl.

"Remember I told you about that guy in high school..." she trailed off and let Maxxy fill in the blanks. Maxxy didn't take long to piece it together.

"Of course, your 'the one that got away' is Liam fucking Mulligan. It should be illegal for the two of you to be together. Too much beauty in one place, the cheekbones alone."

"Yeah, I get it, he's very attractive. Can we get back to the party? Do you feel like bracing the store for decorations that will make the bakery look less like, well a bakery?"

"Is that jealousy I detect in your tone there, Alana?" Maxxy teased.

I heard it too. It was less obvious than it had been with Chantelle, but it was still there just under the surface. I pressed a kiss to her temple.

"No. Maybe. I don't think so. Are you going to answer my question?" she huffed.

"I already said I would. The decorations really were just a cover for me to get the gossip on you and Liam. Wait, will he be coming to this party?"

"Yeah Maxxy, I will see you there," I answered, setting off a string of semi-muffled curses.

"Were you ever going to tell me that he could hear this conversation?" she asked when she had stopped swearing at us.

"I didn't think it would matter; we're only talking about a party. Sorry, I should have said it was on speakerphone."

"It would have prevented me from banging on about how hot your boyfriend was. To your boyfriend."

"I wouldn't say you were banging on. You just mentioned it a couple of times. Besides, unfortunately for us all, he knows he is good-looking, so no harm done really."

"Careful there, Len, I think that was almost a compliment." I pressed a series of kisses along the line of her neck.

"Did he just call you Len? A nickname? I swear to God, Alana, when you get back to Detroit, we are having a full debrief on this. I want all the details. Starting from high school."

"It goes back to us being toddlers, but fine, I will give you a full debrief on me and Muller."

"And now she's out here calling him Muller like that's his name," Maxxy started mumbling to herself. "I've been low-key annoyed at you for dumping this task on me because you went back home, but knowing that in leaving, you reconnected with the literal love of your life, I can't be annoyed at you anymore. But I'm serious, Alana. Full. Debrief." Maxxy hung up and Lenny threw her phone back on the bedside table.

"So, you're coming back to Detroit for New Year's," she said to me.

"You really think I'm going to deprive you of your first

New Year's with the one that got away?" I pulled her in closer, she settled against my side.

"I hate that you heard that. I can't even say that it's a lie, but it is going to make you insufferable." Her words were muffled against my neck.

"You're mine too. The one that got away, that is. And I can't wait to get all your New Year midnights now."

I felt her eye roll against my skin before she lifted her head and pressed her lips to mine.

Thirty Seven

LIAM

I hadn't fully appreciated how little time I had spent with my parents over the last ten days until I was sitting at a table with them, eating spaghetti.

"I'm going back to Detroit early," I said to fill the weird silence we had found ourselves in.

"Oh, I thought you were staying through until the New Year?" Mom asked, sounding sad.

"Yeah, I was, but Len is throwing a New Year's party, so I'm going to go to that."

"Did you know about it before you came back?" Dad asked, derision thick in his voice.

"I want to spend New Year with her, so I am going to fly back the day after tomorrow. She goes back tomorrow." That worked as an answer that didn't also expose that no, I hadn't known about it before I came back because we'd lied about the timeline of our relationship. Although Lenny had barely remembered it was happening, so there was no way I could have known earlier anyway.

"It will be nice to spend the day with you tomorrow," Mom said, a soft smile on her face.

"Maybe we can get out on the ice," Dad chimed in. I regretted mentioning how I spent the other day at the Fitzpatrick Arena. It had given him more hope than ever.

"I don't think so," I said calmly.

"You went with Alana," he replied. There was a bite to the way he said her name. It made my nerves bad.

"Yeah, because it's fun with her and it doesn't mean anything when we're on the ice together. I haven't legitimately been on the ice in a way that would be beneficial to a hockey career since I retired. In April."

"Don't you miss it?"

"How many times do I have to tell you that I don't? I made the best decision for me at the time, and I stand by that decision."

"It's not too late. Don't you want Alana to see you out there on the ice professionally?" Now he said her name like it was the answer to all his prayers. If only he knew.

I pulled out my phone to call Lenny, putting her on speaker.

"Baby, it's barely been two hours since you last saw me, you can't possibly miss me that much," she answered immediately.

"Yeah, I miss you terribly," I deadpanned. Although I did a bit. "Anyway, quick question, babe, remind me how you feel about the fact that I am now a retired athlete?"

There was a long pause before she answered.

"Are you still on this? Do you need me to get it tattooed on my forehead that I don't care? Should I make it one of your daily affirmations, 'Lenny doesn't care that I don't play hockey anymore'? If you want, I can wear your jersey and cheer you on while you make dinner or something."

"When did I say I was making you dinner?" I ignored the part about her wearing my jersey. It was best that any and all thoughts of that image stayed in the very back of my mind while I was sitting at a dinner table with my parents.

"You didn't, but I go back to work in five days so I'm saying in about six days, you're going to be in my kitchen making pasta or roasting a chicken so you know I've eaten something."

"Ah, so that's why you don't care that I stopped playing, you get a new chef and don't have to think about what you want for dinner every day," I joked.

"Liam, I am only going to say this one more time and then if you ask me again, I will cover you in flour and set a hose on you. When you injured your shoulder the first time, you thought your life was over. The only thing that got you through that rehab process was the promise of getting back out onto that ice with your blades on and a stick in your hand. That was what you *wanted*. I'm guessing that was what you wanted the second time it took you out and the third time. If, at the *fourth time* of asking, you didn't think the world would end if you didn't get back on the ice, then you made the right choice. Fuck what you are supposed to do because you're thirty, and in theory, still have some good years left. Screw the people who insist on having an opinion about it, like they know your body better than you do. It's not up to PTs and doctors and random fans on the internet, it's up to *you*. If you didn't want it, then you didn't want it. You had a good career, some might even say that it was great, and that was enough for you. That's all that matters."

I took the phone off speaker and brought it to my ear.

"Would you ever have said that to my face?"

"Of course not. I would get all distracted by your stupid face trying not to look smug while I was being nice to you and lose my train of thought. Besides, I don't think you were the one who needed to hear it." I smiled to myself at just how well she knew me. "So you're welcome. Are you coming back here tonight?"

"Of course I am."

"Good. All right, I'll leave you to your dinner. I gotta go take some cookies out of the oven."

"You're eating an actual meal though, right?"

"See, this is why I have you making dinners for me in the not-so-distant future. Yes, I am. Dad is finishing it up now. But seriously, I have to go and deal with these cookies, and I need both hands."

"Save me at least one."

"Always. I love you," she said as she hung up. It figured that the first time Lenny threw those three words at me, it would be over the phone with no time for me to say it back. I put my phone back in my pocket and picked up my fork.

"As you heard, Alana doesn't care," I said, shovelling more pasta into my mouth. I didn't care about the silence as much now.

Thirty Eight

ALANA

I was staring at my phone like it had just grown legs and started walking.

I'd just told Liam I loved him. Not the casual 'love' that I said to people I knew well, but the weightier version. I. Love. You. And I'd told him over the phone. I had planned on saying it to his face the first time, but every time I went to say it, I chickened out. My brain was too conditioned to refrain from blurting it out to him and it hadn't quite caught up with the fact that it was fine now.

Except, I guess, if I was on the phone with him trying to, once again, get his dad off his back about hockey and I wanted him to know that I was there for him. Then I could say it easily. Maybe he didn't notice. Maybe he'd been focused on something else, like a shooting star, and hadn't heard the way I signed off the call.

"Did you just tell Liam you loved him for the first time?"

Oh yeah, I was in the kitchen with my parents and Aaron around the table, pretending not to listen to me talk to Liam.

My dad had asked the question. Gently, like he was worried he was going to startle me.

"Uh, yeah, I kind of did. How could you tell?" I picked up a tea towel and took my tray of cookies out of the oven. Aaron had been bugging me since he got home to make peanut butter cookies. Now that it was my final night, I'd finally made them. They'd turned out perfect.

"Just the general air of alarm around you when you hung the phone up. Everything okay?" Mom asked.

"Yeah, everything is fine. Just not what I planned."

"And did he say it back?" Mom sounded wary. I laughed softly.

"Oh, he's already said it. A few times, actually. I just... couldn't, I guess."

"Why do you think that was?"

"Because I'm still that eighteen-year-old girl who can't admit her feelings for him, and so she won't let thirty-one-year-old me say it. Unless he's next door and there are several walls between us and I don't have to look directly at him, I guess," I joked.

"He already knew. It's probably why he wasn't feeling insecure about the fact that you hadn't said it back, which by the sound of things, he wasn't. You've always been good at showing him that you love him. I've seen it, we've all seen it. You might have lied about the timeline of your reunion, but you can't fake the kind of love that you two have for each other. We're glad that you both managed to find your way back to each other," Mom said.

My brain snagged on the word 'fake'.

"What do you mean, lied?"

I looked at Aaron. He wouldn't have told her, and I definitely hadn't. The slight shake of his head confirmed that he had said nothing. Yet my parents were looking at me like they were in on the joke. Dad took a deep breath before he started speaking.

"Alana, we weren't born yesterday. You didn't mention that Liam had been to the bakery between the birthday party and you getting back here. You went into great detail about how annoying you found it when he transferred to Detroit because you were so sure that you were going to see him, so not mentioning when it happened didn't seem like you. That and, I don't know if you've noticed, but photos of you two keep popping up on the internet. Now I know you don't go outside much, but to be dating him for six weeks in the city that he retired in, and for there to be no sign of you in the background of a picture didn't make sense. Not when you've been so clearly in them over the last ten days. I'm sorry that you felt like coming home was going to be so bad that you felt like you needed something to deflect from that. We care about you, that's all. We want to know that you're happy, not put you under an interrogation process."

The three of them waited for me to say something.

"It wasn't just to get you off my back. I mean I didn't know what I was walking into because we'd only talked about it on the phone, and I figured maybe you'd want to talk about it more when we were face to face and I didn't want that. It was kind of a big deal but everything I told you over the phone was all that I really had to say about it. I thought I wanted to marry Kai, but he asked, and I hesitated and, in my hesitation, I saw the answer and the answer was no.

"I mostly did it for him. He gave up his job. A job that was, in a lot of ways, also his life. And he gave it up for very valid reasons, but in doing so, he lost his girlfriend and whatever version of his future he thought he had with her. Then he was going to come home to a dad who did not agree with the career choice his son made. So, when he suggested we give them something else to talk about it, felt like the easiest yes I could give. And it was only really a lie for about two days because, in the lie, we found the truth. And the truth is that I love him. I've always loved him, and he loves me, and it feels *good to* be loved by him. He said something the other day about how we lived the lives we were meant to live and those lives let us back to each other and that's that."

There was silence for a moment.

"Alana, we had no intention of bringing Kai up again. I know it's easy to say that now, but it's the truth. Sometimes the answer just can't be yes, and it is what it is. However, I can't say that I am not thrilled about the development," Mom said.

"Yeah, yeah, I know you've been wishing us together since we could write whole sentences or some shit like that," I said teasingly.

"Yes, I can acknowledge that a small part of me had always hoped that you two would fall in love and live great, big lives by each other's sides, but more than that, I just wanted you happy. And you were always happy with him. He was always your calm, and I think you might have been his. I understand why you ran away from your feelings for him when they changed. Big feelings can be terrifying, especially when they are about someone who is such a huge part of your life. So, I don't think you made a bad choice when you went to Michigan. It made you happy at the time. And Kai made you happy. In different ways, he made you happy and that was good. We're proud of you for knowing that marrying him wouldn't keep making you happy. We know that it can't have been easy, but when you know, you know.

"And you've been happy since you got back home. The kind of happy you were when you were younger. Except it's different this time because you're much more open to the idea of being *in* love with him and it's everything we could want for you," Mom continued.

"It feels good. It feels right," I admitted. I couldn't help but smile as I said it.

"Can he still get us tickets to games if he's out of it?" Aaron, who had been surprisingly quiet throughout this, asked. I laughed.

"He mentioned something about one of the perks of dating him was getting access to tickets to hockey games, so yeah, probably."

Although even if that wasn't the case, Liam would still try to find a way to get Aaron tickets to whatever game he wanted because he loved Aaron like he was his own brother and always wanted him to get what he wanted.

"Amazing. Keep him. I want forever access to games."

"I haven't even confirmed if it's possible yet and you're already planning your future games."

"Ally, everyone in this room knows that if you ask Liam for something, he will move heaven and earth to get it for you. So yeah, I like my odds with this one. I don't want to go to Detroit a lot though because of work, so if he could get me tickets for games in and around this state, that would be great."

"Enough, Aaron. Don't get so ahead of yourself." Mom playfully slapped Aaron's shoulder and all conversation of Liam died down while we sat down for dinner.

In the quiet of my room after dinner, while reading a book with the hot chocolate that Dad had made, I remembered that I told Liam I loved him, and immediate panic rushed over me.

I knew without a shadow of a doubt that he would bring it up. I wouldn't blame him, either. But I still needed to buy myself a little bit of time before he made me confront my feelings face to face.

I quickly stripped off my leggings and sweater and slipped on his jersey. I didn't know how much time it would give me, but it would be enough.

I took off my underwear as well, for good measure.

LIAM

When I went back next door, I was greeted by Rob and Stassie having one last cup of tea. I stopped to have a quick chat with them before going to find Lenny.

I wondered if she had even noticed that she had told me she loved me before she hung up on me. When I got to her partially open bedroom door and saw her sitting on her bed with a book in one hand and the other cradled around a mug while wearing my number, I knew that she knew exactly what she had done.

I leant against the door and looked at her. The long line of her legs stretched out in front of her. The curve of her thigh before it disappeared underneath the dark grey jersey. The way her bottom lip was drawn in between her teeth as her eyes moved across the pages of her book. The way her curls fell across her face from the pineapple on top of her head.

"You're being weird, you know that?" she said, not looking up from her book.

"What's weird about me admiring you?" I asked as I closed the door behind me.

"You were doing it in a very brooding fashion from the doorway." She closed the book around her finger.

"That's where the best vantage point is."

"Right, you need a good vantage point of me reading a book and drinking hot chocolate spiked with whiskey."

"Yes, it's a very nice sight. It might be topped by you baking, but it's definitely making my top three sights of you."

"Most people would say they like to see someone naked, not covered in flour."

"You naked is number three. And I think you're underestimating what it does to me to see you in your element. Or with my number on you." I took the fabric of her sleeve between my fingers and pulled her closer to me.

"You want to tell me how you have a Panthers jersey with my name on it in your possession? And why is this the first time I am seeing you in it?"

"Aaron thought it was a funny gift. He gave it to me secretly while you were arguing about something in Catan. I have no idea how he got one in his possession, but he said I might have more use for it than him." She shrugged as she slotted her bookmark into place. "How was the rest of your dinner?"

"Fine. Dad dropped the hockey thing, although I somehow doubt that is the last I will hear of it. He may go on about it until I reach the age he thinks I should have retired at."

"What, forty?"

"Yeah, probably. I did want to talk to you about something, though."

Lenny took a long sip of her hot chocolate.

"Wait, I have something as well. Turns out my parents knew we were lying about dating. They let us have it because it became apparent very quickly that we were definitely into each other."

I nodded. It didn't surprise me that they had figured it out. "That kind of makes sense. This is good; means I don't have to worry about slipping up one day."

Lenny would not have been the one to slip, she would never have forgotten our fake origin story.

"Back to my thing though," I said. I wouldn't let her get out of it this time.

"Yeah, what?" she said quietly before taking another sip.

A dab of cream caught on the corner of her mouth and her tongue peeked out to catch it, putting me at risk of getting us off topic. I shook my head and cleared my thoughts.

"You know you said the wildest thing on the phone earlier?"

"What, that you made the right choice to retire before you went ahead and actually damaged yourself further? We calling that wild? I thought that it was common sense," she said quickly, her fingers tracing the edge of her thumb ring.

"No, there was something else." I moved to sit in between her legs and settled my feet on either side of her hips.

"Are you putting in a formal complaint about the way I signed you up for cooking duties indefinitely? Because I will consider it, but I can't guarantee that the outcome will change."

"No, I'll cook your every meal forever if you want me to," I replied with zero hesitation.

"Then I have no idea what you're referring to." She was fighting off a smile behind the rim of her mug. I cupped her thighs and squeezed, making her shiver.

"Just say it once when you look me in the eyes and then you never have to say it again to my face if you don't want to."

"Yeah, right," she scoffed, blowing more cream onto her face, which she wiped away with her fingers.

"I'm serious, Alana. I know you'll say it enough over the phone or text or any time that doesn't require being soft in plain sight. I know you'll show it in your actions. I know I'll feel it in the quiet moments and the loud ones. I know you well enough to know that, so just give me one. Look me in the eyes and say it once."

She took another long sip from her mug before setting her shoulders back.

"I love you."

I leant forward and pressed my lips against hers. She tasted like chocolate, cream, and the barest hint of whiskey. I removed her mug from her hand and pulled her in closer. Her hands threaded through my hair.

She shifted into my lap, and I felt the wet heat of her core against me.

"Are you not wearing underwear?" I asked in between kisses.

"I was hoping to distract you with that before you made me confront my feelings face to face, but you just went straight to it."

"No, but...the door was open," I said.

"And given that you only just noticed when you've been sitting this close to me for the last ten minutes, I think it's safe to say that this jersey did a great job of covering me."

I wrapped my arm around her waist and fell back onto the bed, bringing her with me.

"Get up here," I said as I nipped at her bottom lip.

"Absolutely not."

"Why not? And if either of your reasons are you're worried you'll crush me or something to do with body hair then skip them and just get up here. I told you that you had unlimited face-sitting privileges and I meant that. Starting now."

"I wasn't going to say either of those things," she shot back.

"Then what were you going to say?"

"Okay fine, I was going to say something about that being hella exposing but I guess I'll just settle on saying I love you and moving on up."

I warmed at hearing the words again as she scooched up the bed until her knees were on either side of my head. My hands settled on her thighs, and I guided her down onto my face.

My tongue swiped along her and dipped inside before moving up to her clit. I swirled around it, adding suction now and again. I could feel her inner thigh muscles starting to quake as I drove her closer to release. Her hands pulled at my hair as she tried to ground herself.

"You've got to be kidding me," her words were said in a breathy whisper as her hips started grinding down against me. I focused solely on her clit. Lenny's body bowed forward as she came, muttering a steady stream of curses as she rode out her orgasm. As the aftershocks ran through her, she lifted herself off my face and lay next to me.

"I don't understand how that's possible," she said in between deep breaths.

"What?"

"The speed with which you can get me to come is alarming and confusing. I mean great, but confusing."

"It's because you feel safe. You know I'm not lying there secretly thinking about all the ways that you've let yourself go or just ticking a box to look good before we get back to me. Which means you do fun things like come on my face in two minutes."

Her hand slipped under the waistband of my sweatpants and covered my hard cock. I groaned at the touch.

"You know you make me look like an asshole, right?" she said as she applied pressure, making my hips buck up.

"Oh yeah, how?"

"You're so open about feelings and shit and then you say

things like 'you only have to say it once to my face' about the words 'I love you', like they don't hold meaning. You are all about my orgasms and I would honestly quite happily just leave you on edge all day—"

"You can do that if you want." I cut in. It would be torture, but the best kind. "Besides, no one's gonna know any of the other shit because it's none of their business. You've said it twice now to my face so maybe your brain will finally cotton on to the fact that it's fine to say it and I am not going to say, 'Ah, that's nice, but no thanks, let's just be friends.'"

Lenny laughed as she sat back up.

"I'll be nice to you today and let you come within a reasonable timeframe."

I didn't have a chance to reply before I was drawn into the wet heat of her mouth.

Forty

ALANA

Detroit felt cold.

It wasn't necessarily colder than New York, but it felt that way. The whole journey back had felt different. It wasn't the first time I'd landed in this airport alone. It wouldn't be the first time I walked into an empty apartment. It definitely wasn't the first time I had been in this city on my own, yet while I sat on the plane and waited for the seatbelt sign to go off, I felt off. Unsettled.

It wasn't until I was waiting for my suitcase to arrive that I realised what I was feeling.

Homesick. Which made no sense because I was home.

Except I wasn't. As I waited for my suitcase to come, I pulled out my phone and opened my messages to Liam.

Landed! X

His reply was immediate.

Yay! Quick q do you think your parents would let me sleep in your bed if you're not here?

Aw, you worried you won't be able to sleep in your own bed? ;)

Yes. Plus your mattress has already moulded to my body.

You want me to sleep on a lumpy mattress and sleep poorly? Spoiler alert, I am no better on minimal sleep than I was as a teenager. You want me to fly home to you grumpy?

The ache in my chest was already easing as I pulled my case off the carousel and started heading to the taxi bay.

I always liked it when you were grumpy. You have a great pout. It's cute.

Don't think you've ever called me cute before.

I probably hadn't. Not to his face, anyway. He'd been 'this cute boy' in many a story I told about him back in college. 'Cute' lets you get away with a lot of things. People were fine with 'cute'. But you were playing with fire the moment you called a guy 'hot' in a conversation. People then wanted details on the hot guy, and I didn't want to give people details about Liam. The details were mine.

Well you are. And my parents will be fine with it. At least one of us should have a good night's sleep tonight.

Aw, you worried you won't be able to sleep in your bed now you've gotten used to the one you grew up with? ;)

I wanted to say that I missed him, but only a few hours had passed since he dropped me off at the airport and saying that I missed him already sounded ridiculous. Then I realised ridiculous didn't exist with Liam. He wanted it all. He loved it all.

Not quite. My bed is fine, it's more the lack of you and your radiator tendencies. I am worried that I won't fall asleep at all without it. You could almost say that I'm worried I might miss you...

Oh I forgot we were texting and so you would be more prone to being sweet. In that case, I'm not worried about my lumpy mattress, I slept in that bed a couple of months ago, it was fine. Your bed smells like you and I don't know how I'm supposed to sleep without being surrounded by the smell of vanilla and silk brushing my cheek.

I just about managed to stop myself from 'awwing' out loud as another message came in.

Yes, you left your pillowcase here. Yes, I will bring it with me.

Thanks

"You're making a face at your phone that can only be described as sickening," I heard a familiar voice say as soon as I got outside. It was one that I wasn't expecting to hear this soon, but welcomed, nonetheless.

"Hello to you too, Maxine," I said, turning to look at Maxxy as she came to stand next to me. I sent a final text to Liam, letting him know I was with Maxxy and would probably be quiet for the rest of the day, before putting my phone in my coat pocket.

"Hello, Len?" Her eyebrows drew together as she tried the name out.

"Don't," I said, although I knew she was going to ask for an explanation. She tried for so long to give me a nickname and I vetoed every single one.

"I just find it interesting that in all our years of friendship, you never once mentioned that you had one of the most attractive men I have ever seen tucked away in your brain as a former best friend who had his own little nickname for you."

"If you remember correctly, when we met, I was trying to get over someone. Why would I give you that much detail? You would have used it against me or worse, used logic as to why I should give it a go. Especially when said man moved to our city."

"And I may never forgive you for not telling me the person you were trying to get over was Liam. Mulligan. Even at a college level, he was touted as one of the best in the sport. It's not like I would have told anyone. I also probably wouldn't have told you to give it a go back in college. Athletes don't have the best of reputations, and I wouldn't have wanted you to be heartbroken by him twice. But you're right. The moment he moved to Detroit, I would have made it my mission to get you two together."

I shook my head. "Which would have been a disaster."

"I'm not mad at you. I understand why you did it. But I now know, so come on, give me *something*. How come he gets to give you a nickname and no one else does?"

"Aaron calls me Ally," I pointed out. He did it because he knew I hated nicknames and wanted to be annoying. It was a source of great annoyance for *him* when it stopped bugging me but by that point, he was out of the habit of using my full name and still hasn't managed to give it up.

"Doesn't count, he's your brother. Siblings get away with murder."

A fair point.

"So do people who have known you since you were four. I don't know how it started; I think he misheard my name when we met. I didn't hate it, so he has always gotten away with it. I need to stress it is *only* him who gets away with it. Don't think you've got a fun new name to call me. My name is still Alana."

"Fine, I won't. But please explain what the hell has happened in the last two weeks that means you've got an old nickname back?" she asked as she started leading us out of the airport.

"Honestly? He bumped into me at the airport and made a wild suggestion that we pretend we had started dating so that my parents wouldn't ask me any questions about Kai. And his parents, mostly his dad, wouldn't keep asking him about his career or lack thereof or his relationship ending."

"If it was pretend, then what happened? Seems like you're in it now."

"What happened, Maxine, is that we dated. He took me on dates and bought me hot chocolate. He kept taking my hand and not letting go. He made sure I slept and fuck, I slept so well in his arms. Then there was the sex." I could hear that I sounded wistful. Over sex, of all things. The thing that up until recently, I didn't think could be better than a warm chocolate chip cookie.

"Oh, are we talking about your sex life now?" Maxxy teased. I had always been tight-lipped about my sex life, mostly because there wasn't ever anything to write home about.

"Not really. But it is more satisfying than it was. Enough about me, though. How was your Christmas?"

Maxxy fell quiet. The kind of quiet that was very out of character for her.

"Max?" I asked as she unlocked her car.

"I was in Boston."

"Did you travel with the team?" That was unusual for Maxxy; she didn't need to be with the team during away games. Especially not an away game that fell over the holidays where her advice was basically 'have fun'.

"Kind of?"

"I thought you were going to your sister's. How did you end up in Boston?"

"Jo got a stomach bug on the twenty-third, so I didn't go. So, I went to Sweet Nothing to drown myself in panettone, you nailed that recipe this year, by the way, and Teddy came in. He overheard me complaining about the fact that I was going to have to spend Christmas alone and he—"

"Invited you to spend Christmas with him. In Boston?"

"Yeah, kind of." She shrugged.

"It's either yes or no."

"Then yes, I spent Christmas with Teddy. And his family."

Now it was my turn to be speechless.

"And...how was that?" I eventually said.

"Really nice, actually. His family is cool. Super welcoming and they are all so proud of him, which was nice to be around."

"Yeah, the Carters are great. They can be a bit over-whelming at times, especially because Teddy in isolation really doesn't give you an idea of what the whole family is like." I laughed. I knew the Carters well and spending even an hour with them taught me everything I needed to know about where Teddy got his patience from. And his ruthlessness on the ice. He needed to get it out somehow.

"Of course, this is why you have always been buddy buddy with Teddy. If you knew Liam, then you also knew Teddy because they played together in high school. I could never figure that one out and I didn't want to ask in case you said something wild like you used to hook up." I noticed that there was a tone to her voice, it sounded like jealousy.

"Funny how that worked for them though," she contin-ued. "Besties who dominated together in their youth finishing it out together."

"Not quite together. Teddy still plays." I pointed out. Maxxy was quiet again. Only this time, she was acting shifty.

"What do you know?" I asked. Liam hadn't mentioned anything about Teddy retiring.

"It started when those pictures of you and Liam walking around the city ended up in some articles. Have I said to your face that you two make a cute couple? And when I say cute, I mean very attractive and very tall and it's cute that you share clothes." She flicked her gaze to me briefly.

I smiled.

"It's his sweater," I said. I could see the confusion flicker across her face.

"But *you've* had it for years?"

"Yeah, I stole it from him. It wasn't intentional. Or maybe it was, I don't know. But it was his first."

"And he took it back?"

He hadn't. It was in my suitcase. Liam had made a huge show of putting it in there, talking about how he was doing me a massive favour by giving up his favourite sweater once again. Like I wasn't very aware that it made him quietly feral seeing me in his clothes.

"Not exactly," I said. I smiled again.

"Oh no. I've seen you in love before, but I don't think I've ever seen you *in love* like this," Maxxy said.

I laughed. "What are you talking about?"

"Just the way you love Liam is very different to the way you loved Kai. You seem lighter. Happier. The kind of happy that has you smiling at your phone and basking in memories that make you look like you're glowing. It's nice. I'm happy for you."

"You were saying something about Teddy?" I prompted, keen to stop talking about myself.

"Oh yeah, he saw those photos of you two and it got him thinking. Liam sounded really happy when Teddy talked to him, and he looked it too. And if he hadn't had the time to go home for Christmas this year, then he wouldn't have bumped into you and you two wouldn't be together, being all happy and shit. And he only had the time to do that because he retired. I couldn't help but think when I saw the photos that if he hadn't been there, you wouldn't have left your parents' house for nearly a fortnight."

"I would have gone outside. Why does everyone think I never want to leave the house?" I asked incredulously.

"You wouldn't have gone ice skating. Or gone to see the lights in the city. Or held hands while you walked around. You wouldn't have passively engaged with Christmas in New York, which is such a New Yorker way of doing things, but I guess that sums you up. I think Liam made you *engage*. So, you may have gone outside but you wouldn't have gone *outside*."

I hated that she had a point.

"What does this have to do with Teddy?"

"I think it made him a bit sad. This is the first season he's played knowing Liam isn't ever coming back. Even when they were on different teams, they still had that shared thing that meant they were both still on the ice and doing what they did best. When Liam joined Detroit, it was like no time had passed and they fell straight back in with each other, it was impressive. But Liam's gone now and getting to fuck around and fall in love over Christmas like he's in some kind of Hallmark movie—" Maxxy cut herself off by bursting into laughter. I let her cackle herself back to normality.

"Sorry, I just tried to imagine you in a Hallmark movie, full of pep and cheer trying to get your small-town lover to fall in love with the magic of Christmas or some shit and couldn't do it. It really should work because you're a baker; they love bakers in those things, but you are just not the pep and cheer kind of girl. How you managed to fake it as a cheerleader for so long might remain one of life's great mysteries."

"Liam would be the one full of pep and cheer, trying to get the grumpy baker to believe in the magic she sells in the form of candy cane shaped cookies and gingerbread houses," I said, which prompted more laughter from Maxxy.

"Have you been thinking about this a lot? That came way too easily for you. And highlighted that you have clearly seen a side to Liam Mulligan that no one else has because pep and cheer are not words I would associate with him either."

"I haven't thought about it at all until this very moment, but some things just make sense when you think about them. And if we're talking Hallmark pep and cheer then no, that doesn't exist within him, but he is the more likely of the two of us to find it within himself. My already limited reserves of the stuff were poured into being a cheerleader, that's how I did it for so long. Now, back to Teddy."

"There isn't much else to say about him. I think he misses his friend out on the ice and it's hitting him that he is closer to the end of his career than the beginning of it."

"And is that all that happened while you were in Boston?" It still felt like there was something that she wasn't telling me.

"Yeah, it is. Ate a lot of food and now I'm back here with you to pull together the best end-of-year sendoff we can."

"Alright, let's go to mine and hash out a proper plan of action."

Maxxy cheered as she continued the drive back home.

Forty One

LIAM

Adult men didn't pout when their mom didn't drive them to the airport.

That's what I had to tell myself when I walked into my house and found Dad waiting for me instead of Mom. I ran through the whole conversation I'd had with her the day before and in hindsight, she never said that *she* would drive me to the airport, just that one of them would and I had hoped that it would be her.

But of course, this was being used as an opportunity.

And so, I didn't pout when Dad waved the keys in front of him with a half-smile and a clap on my right shoulder, but it was a close call.

I did, however, send Lenny a message as I pushed the seat back and settled in the car.

Dad's driving me to the airport...

I'll remind you once more, you made the right call. Imagine how annoying I would be about your shoulder if you were still getting slammed into boards ;)

No bookcases :(

Actually you might get off lucky, I would feel like I would

have to do all the work to avoid undue stress on it, can you imagine how tired I would be?

I do like you on top ;)

I need to remind you that are in the car with your dad, please do not be thinking such things, you're easily excitable

What does it say about me that I think I would rather you do your utmost to excite me while I'm in a car with him than talk to him?

It says that your dad has been less than supportive of your choices now that you're off the ice and maybe you need to let him know that and then fly away from the aftermath

I hate it when you're right

You must hate me often...

Never as much as I love you

There was a pause before she replied, and I smiled to myself at the image of her debating just how to respond.

I'd say that I love you more but I think you might be more interested to hear that I stole your shirt from that suit you wore the other day and wore it to work...

I'm also hoping that your brain has short circuited with the image so much that you don't call me out on the fact that I'm working this morning. Good luck! See you later XX

"That Alana?" Dad's voice cut through my bubble, and I locked my phone, trying not to think about anything that Lenny had just sent me, even if she had said she loved me more.

"Yeah, she's just letting me know that she is at work now," I replied.

"High demand for baked goods at this time of year?"

"Well, yeah, it's the holiday season. There is a lot more demand for baked goods at this time of year," I replied, trying to keep the sarcasm out of my voice and failing miserably.

"And yet she took the time off?"

"Is she not entitled to take a vacation? She runs a

successful business; they can run things without her there. So yes, she took time off for the first time in years. I imagine she's only working now because everyone she hangs out with loves her bakery and she didn't want to just sit around when she could be helping out."

Teddy and the team were back in Detroit and there was no way he wasn't getting a trip to Sweet Nothing in the moment he could. He was probably also desperate for a debrief from Lenny's perspective.

"She's got a good work ethic," he said. It sounded… pointed.

"She does, but she might not have a good balance," I said, calmly.

"You qualified to comment on that?" He scoffed.

I shifted my body to face him. "Meaning?"

"You went from one extreme to the next, are you sure that you can comment on balance?"

"I didn't say that I could. But I notice you had no issue with one extreme but seem to take issue with the other."

His hands tightened around the steering wheel. I took a deep breath and braced for impact.

"You worked so hard for your career and then you gave it all up for a nothing injury. How can you be so okay with that?" He sounded almost pained, like the injury and the retirement, my entire career, had been *his* to lose.

"It wasn't a nothing injury though, Dad. It was a direct hit on an injury that has been with me for half my life. It was weeks of rehab on a body that was already tired after giving a physical sport so much of me. It was having to, once again, modify the way I handle a stick to try and protect my shoulder. It was knowing deep down that I was lucky to not have had worse happen to me and realising that by that point, I was tempting fate to take me out in a worse way, which would have ended my career anyway. It was the chance to leave the sport that I love and that has given me so much on *my* terms. Why is that so hard for you to accept?"

There was a pause. A silence that seemed to go on for minutes rather than seconds.

"Because it doesn't seem like you. This time last year, you were talking about all the things that you had left to achieve with your career. You were so excited, and then five months later, you just gave it up? That doesn't make any sense."

I nodded my head once and pressed my lips together knowing that I was probably going to regret my next question, but Lenny had been right about one thing. I needed to let him know how his attitude since April had been making me feel and this was the way into it.

"Why don't you just ask the question that you actually want to ask?"

"Fine. Did Alana ask you to retire? She was never overly happy about you playing hockey and she left because of it. Was it a condition of this out-of-the-blue relationship of yours?"

It was my turn to scoff now. I didn't quite know what to think about the fact that my dad thought Lenny had that much power over me, and that I was incapable of retiring simply because it was best for me, but that wasn't the real issue here. Had he always disliked Alana that much? He had seemed happy that she wasn't my prom date and wasn't the most sympathetic to how I felt in the days after she left. In fact, more than once, he told me it was probably for the best. It didn't feel like it was at the time, but I'd meant what I said to Lenny. We had lived the lives we were supposed to live, and we were better off for it.

"Firstly, we hadn't even reconnected by April, so she had no input on *my* decision. Secondly, Alana was fine with me playing hockey, what she wasn't happy with was me putting all my eggs in that basket. But she did ice time with me, she came to the games that she could, she sat in that ice rink and waited for me on days she didn't have after-school clubs. So, she was supportive of my potential career path and if she hadn't left, I am certain she would have continued to be supportive. Thirdly, you've got a lot of nerve telling me that this relationship is out of the blue when she was pretty much the only thing I made time for outside of hockey and school when we were teenagers."

"You became more focused when she left."

I rolled my eyes.

"Because she left! It was because of *her* that I even still had hockey. She was the one who supported me through the bulk of the emotional turmoil of rehab when I tore my rotator cuff. She was the one who consistently reminded me that I was still a person if I wasn't a hockey player. She was the reason I took my time with the whole thing and got back on that ice stronger than ever. So when she left, I became more focused on it because I had two things in high school and they were my hockey team and her.

"And let's not pretend that even if I was the most focused person in the world, luck played a big part in everything as well. I was lucky that I managed to transfer my college ability to the big leagues. I was lucky that I got to play for the teams I played for. I was lucky to make the Olympic team. I was even lucky enough to win the Stanley Cup. I gave it everything I had for eight years, and I ran out of steam. And here's something I don't think you want to hear, even though it has no bearing on your life, Alana would never have asked me to quit while I still loved it, but if she came back into my life while I was still playing, I probably would have given it all up anyway. Because if I had her, after all this time, I wouldn't have wanted to spend weeks on the road when I could have been with her."

I took a deep breath and tried to calm myself down.

"You were managing to make it work with Mel," he started

quietly, a tremor of anger still present in his voice. "Why would Alana have been any different? Why would you have given it all up for that girl?"

My jaw clenched at the way he referred to Lenny, but I took a deep breath and let it go.

"I think deep down I always knew that Mel loved me because I was a hockey player. She loved what came with that. The galas, the money, the travel. She loved the glam and the status of it all. The moment she caught onto the fact that I was going to give that all up, she wanted out. I don't blame her for it. I just wish maybe I'd been stronger and ended it before it got to that point. And retiring isn't giving up Dad, it's ending a career on my terms. Now I have Alana to support me while I continue to figure out what the hell I want to do next."

"Which is what? Wait on her hand and foot," he scoffed.

"Dad, you can be mean and try to belittle my career choices all you want. You hold that grudge against me for all that it's worth, I don't care anymore. But what you will not do is disrespect Alana. If she needs someone to sometimes take care of her and the life admin parts of her day because she is busy running a very successful business, for which she is the head baker, then I am happy to do that for her. You can also stop making sly remarks about the fact that she left because you know what? Eighteen-year-olds make all kinds of decisions that are sometimes bad and are sometimes great. Neither of us would be the people that we are if she hadn't left, and I think we both like the people that we are now. So even though it sucked and took me the better part of my freshman year to get over, I think she made the right decision. I forgive her and we now get to venture down a road not taken. If that road means I have to support her by making her fucking dinner, then I will because you know who supported me when it looked like my hockey career might have been over before it began? Alana."

He turned into the drop-off area of the airport and brought the car to a stop.

"Your mother and I supported you then as well."

"Yeah, Mom did. But you pushed for me to get back on the ice then as well. You made me feel like I was going crazy for choosing to respect the rehab process in its entirety. It has always felt like you wanted to live vicariously through me, which I've never really understood because you didn't even play sports."

"I never had the talent for it. The moment you stepped on the ice, it was clear that you were made for it. I just wanted you to reach your full potential."

"I did, and I'm done now. If you can't accept that, then we have nothing left to say to each other because my professional career is over and I'm moving on. Thanks for the lift."

I unlocked my car door and got out, walking around to the trunk and getting my bag out. I didn't turn around once as I walked into the airport.

I did, however, look at my phone, and waiting for me was a photo of Lenny who, sure enough, was wearing my shirt, which looked crisper against her brown skin. It was tucked into a pair of jeans as she leant against a counter, the Sweet Nothing logo a neon purple blaze behind her.

T-minus four hours until I saw her again.

Forty Two

LIAM

By the time I landed in Detroit, I was over it. The talk with my dad had exhausted me and then I had ended up cramped in a middle seat between two people who spoke to each other the whole time, but inexplicably, did not want to switch with me. Now I was faced with the fact that I was going to have to battle someone for a taxi out of here so I could get back to my girlfriend.

I took a moment to collect myself and pulled my phone out to message Lenny.

"Liam?" The voice that called my name sounded familiar but not familiar enough for me to look up from my phone.

Liam was a common name. The person probably wasn't talking to me.

"Liam?" The voice was closer this time. Close enough that whoever it was, was actually speaking to me. I turned my head to the right.

Blonde hair, blue eyes, and a long black coat that I would recognise anywhere—because it was hung up next to mine for many years—greeted me.

"Melanie?"

"How have you been?" she asked, a gentle smile on her face.

"Uh, yeah. I've been really good, thanks. You?"

"Not too bad. You went away for Christmas?" She pointed at my duffle bag.

"I went to Westchester, yeah."

"How are your mom and dad? They must have liked having you back."

"Yeah, they're not too bad. It was nice being back there. Things are a bit rocky with Dad, but it was nice to see them for longer than two days. Where have you been?" I nodded to her large pink suitcase. Not something she had when we were together.

Once upon a time, we had a wealth of things to talk about. We never got tired of talking to each other. I realised in the dying days of our relationship that we had stopped talking about anything remotely important. If it wasn't hockey-related or linked to an event that we were supposed to go to, we didn't talk about it.

Now, we were reduced to small talk at an airport about our holidays.

"I spent a few days with Asher. The team played an away game the other day, so they were in Boston," she said, sounding sheepish. Asher was my replacement. He had been on the team for a couple of seasons and played when I wasn't at my best. He'd played the final three games of last season and every time he stepped out onto the ice, he played like he had a point to prove. He wanted my spot. He wanted it more than I did, and in the end, I was more than happy to give it to him.

"And how is Asher and the rest of the team?" I knew how most of them were given that I talked to Teddy after their win, but I still knew Mel well enough to know that she wanted reassurance that she hadn't done something wrong. She wanted to know that I didn't hate her for replacing me with the same person that the team did.

Given that I had firmly moved on, I didn't care what she did with her life. Romantically or otherwise.

"They're good. They got the win, which improved the mood," she said, sounding more confident now we had moved into familiar territory.

"Yeah, Teddy told me about the win. Asher played well, apparently. I didn't get to see it. Alana doesn't really watch hockey, and she'd made plans for us when it was on." Mel didn't know that those plans were completely rewiring my association with a certain superstition and then not leaving her bed for most of the afternoon.

Mel pursed her lips for a moment before speaking. "Alana. That's who was with you in those pictures? She really doesn't like hockey?"

"That's her. It's not that she doesn't like it, more that she typically has other things she would rather do. It used to be studying or cheering for one of the other sports teams. Now it's baking or seeing if she can read a whole book in the time it takes to play a whole match."

Or seeing how many times I can come in a six-hour period. We reached four, but I know she wants to try and go for five. I'm already excited for her attempt.

"She's the one, isn't she?"

I shook my head to clear it of thoughts of that afternoon. "The one who?"

"I'm not an idiot, Liam. That well-hidden tattoo matches the sign of that bakery all the Panthers are obsessed with. The place where I got your birthday cakes from, Sweet Nothing. The problem is, four different people work there, and I could never figure out which one was connected to you because two are from New York and one is from Boston. But it's her, I've seen her. Rarely, because she's almost always in the kitchen, but sometimes she would come out and say hi. I met her boyfriend a couple of times as well. He seemed like an interesting guy. I guess he's an ex too, now."

"Let me guess, you talked hockey with him?"

She laughed softly. "Yeah, we did. What's the story there?"

"Between me and Alana?" She nodded. "We lived next door to each other and were in each other's pockets all the time. She's been my best friend since I was four."

"What happened?" She sounded almost sad.

"She left before high school graduation because she thought I would break her heart and she wanted to get ahead of the game," I answered truthfully. It was nice to be able to have an answer for it now.

"Is she why you wanted to move here? I did think it was an odd choice when you could have gone back to New York."

"I didn't want to go to New York because my parents live there and I love them, but my dad coming to my games frequently and having lots of opinions face to face was not something that I wanted for myself. But hey, if I moved to New York, I would probably still be playing because I wouldn't have wanted to disappoint him."

"But why Detroit? There were other teams interested in you that would have kept you from your dad."

"You don't have to believe me, but I didn't choose Detroit because it was where Alana lived. I wouldn't have done that to you. Alana and I hadn't spoken until about two weeks ago when we bumped into each other in this very airport. I came to Detroit because Teddy was here, and I was twenty-six and distinctly aware that I was closer to the end of my career than the beginning of it. And while I still could, I wanted to play with him. It was the best choice for me.

"Just like retiring at the end of last season was. I guess you ending our relationship might have also been for the best because I think we might both be better for it. You look good,

Mel. I might see you around if you keep hanging out with the team because I told Teddy that I would help with the kids outreach program in the new year, but I've gotta go."

She nodded her head.

"It was good to see you too, Liam," she said softly before she turned and walked away.

When she had disappeared from view, I walked out of the airport.

The moment I stepped outside, a long, checked coat that looked vaguely familiar caught my eye. I stopped and turned towards it.

"Alright there, Muller?" Lenny said, leaning against a car.

"Len?"

"Your eyes are not deceiving you. I am here. In the flesh. You're welcome." She smiled as I walked over to her.

"Where did you get a car?"

"It's Max's. Pretty sure she only let me drive it because I said I wanted it to pick you up."

"You didn't have to come get me," I said as I wrapped an arm around her waist and pulled her closer to me.

"I know, that's what makes me so nice," she said before she pressed her lips against mine. The kiss started chaste and just as I was about to pull away, she looped her arms around my shoulders and pulled me closer, sweeping her tongue into my mouth and deepening the kiss. I sunk into it.

She pulled away first, breathless.

"Well, that's quite the welcome home," I teased.

"Don't get used to it. The glasses, sweatpants combo you have going on short-circuited my brain for a moment."

"You know you shouldn't have told me that, right?" I pulled her in for another kiss, my hand cupping the back of her neck. She deepened it instantly.

I was the one to pull away this time. Lenny cast her eyes down and noticed the hardness pressed against my sweatpants.

She dropped a hand down against it and squeezed, my hips stuttered into her grip before she released me.

"That's quite enough of that." She winked. "Come on, Max is at mine. She's cooking, and she keeps texting with threats of using my brownie ingredients to make them herself because I'm taking too long to get back. She might call my bluff and actually do it, which we need to prevent because Max is not a baker."

"You were gonna make me brownies?"

"Yeah, I am making you brownies."

"Lucky me. Give me the car keys." I held out one of my hands as I readjusted myself with the other.

"I can drive back," she countered, although her eyes were looking downwards.

"Yeah, but you don't have to."

She looked back up and our eyes locked. She smiled and dropped the keys in my hand.

"You better start thinking unsexy things now because Max will notice that thing if it's still standing to attention when we get back. And I have welcome home plans for you that do not involve you coming any time soon," she said, as she climbed in the car.

I got in on the driver's side. "What do your plans entail?"

"You'll find out," she teased, brushing her lips against mine once more before I turned the car on and drove out of the airport.

Forty Three

ALANA

Sweet Nothing's New Year's Eve party had been in full swing for nearly three hours, and I had yet to make an appearance. Liam had gone down early to greet people, and I had procrastinated in every way imaginable to avoid showing up. I knew there was a high chance of bumping into someone who was going to want to talk to me about Kai. It was a toss-up whether they would ask for the gossip, or if they would plead his case.

Either scenario was less than ideal. The likely combination of both, even more so.

When I had truly run out of things to do and started to feel bad about leaving Liam on his own, I headed downstairs.

"Alana."

For a brief moment, I thought I was making him up, but Kai always had a very specific way of saying my name that even my memory couldn't replicate exactly. Of course, he would be the first person I see upon entering what should have been our engagement party.

It was too late for me to turn around now.

"Kai," I replied, false pep making me sound high-pitched.

"Happy New Year's Eve." Kai raised a glass at me, which would have worked better if I had one to clink against his. As it was, my hands were hovering in the air, and I wished I had picked a dress with pockets. But no, I had to wear a dress that I knew would fuck with my boyfriend.

"And to you. Wasn't expecting to see you here?"

"I was invited, wasn't I?"

"Technically, sure. I guess, I thought you would...it doesn't matter," I said.

"We still share friends, Alana. They said they were coming, and I didn't want to spend New Year's alone."

I nodded. I really had no clue what to say to him anymore.

"Where's your—"

Liam was not a small man. No one would ever say that they hadn't noticed him if he was in a room and yet, as I felt a hand come around my waist and pull me ever so slightly backwards as a drink came into my line of vision, I realised that I hadn't seen him coming. I knew he was out in the party somewhere, but I hadn't had a chance to look for him. Clearly, he had seen me. I took the drink, a whiskey neat, and laced the fingers of my other hand through the one on my waist. *That* was where my hands should be.

"You must be Kai," Liam said. I doubted Kai even noticed the edge in his voice.

"Holy shit, it's you," Kai near squealed. I refrained from laughing out loud at his excitement. It dawned on me then why he had still showed up. He could have talked his friends out of coming here if he really wanted to; they weren't that attached to me. We hadn't spoken since the break-up. But he thought a 'chance' encounter with his favourite NHL player might happen. Kai was probably getting more than he bargained for, actually. The Panthers had a home game this week, and Teddy had caught wind of the party, so he was planning to drag as much of the team to the bakery as possible.

"Yeah, it is," Liam said, his voice softer now, morphing into the version of himself I saw every time he was approached by a fan. Muller had been buried. He was all Gunner now.

I zoned out and let Kai have his moment with Liam. I could feel the rumble of Liam's voice against my back. I was pleasantly swimming in the sea salt scent of him. My fingers had unlaced from his and were aimlessly tracing the veins of his exposed forearm. The warm weight of his hand splayed against me was a grounding force.

"You okay?" Liam's voice in my ear brought me fully back into the room from where I had zoned out looking at Teddy and Maxxy by the counter. Kai was no longer in front of us.

"Yeah. I thought that would be worse," I admitted.

"He's smaller than I thought he would be."

"You mean he's smaller than me? Almost everyone is. Even you barely beat me." I had almost put on heels to come downstairs tonight but ultimately just threw on a pair of Converse because the dress was doing most of the work, and that was the most important part.

"That he was fine with, but sex toys were too far for him?" I turned around and both of his hands settled on my lower back.

"You're going to have to let that one go eventually, you know that right?"

"I just cannot comprehend how he could know what you look like when you come and not want to do everything in his power to make you look like that as much as possible." His hand squeezed my ass, and my thigh slotted in between his.

I rolled my eyes. "Looking past that, that wasn't too bad, was it?"

"No different to any other fan interaction I've had. He really knew my stats."

"And used them to try and convince you to go back to the game?"

"Yeah, like I said, it was no different to any fan interaction. You ready to join this party?"

I sighed. "No. Yes. Don't know. Sorry."

"Why are you apologising?"

"This is my party, and I have left you to deal with it. I don't think I have it in me to pretend I want to be here at the moment."

"You haven't left me to do anything. I'm good at schmoozing. Always have been, so you don't have to be if you don't want to. So, I'll ask you again, are you ready to join this party?" He squeezed my ass and dropped a kiss on my shoulder.

I paused and really thought about my answer. In the end, I didn't have to answer out loud.

"Okay, look, go back upstairs and finish a book or something. I will be up at five to twelve. Can I just make one small request?"

"Don't see why not."

"Can you leave this dress on? Or at least be in it again by the time I come upstairs?"

His pupils were blown, and I could feel him getting hard against my leg, which meant, as I suspected, the dress was doing its job.

"I think that can be arranged, Muller," I replied, smiling as I pressed a quick kiss to his lips and went back upstairs to my apartment.

Forty Four

LIAM

"What are you still doing down here?" Maxxy was leaning against the makeshift bar, the straw of her drink resting in the corner of her mouth.

"Enjoying a party?"

"Yeah, but you've been doing that for hours. Why are you still doing it when your girlfriend is upstairs? Gosh, can't believe I'm saying that. My best friend is your girlfriend."

"She was my best friend first," I teased.

"Yeah, and now she is your girlfriend. Your very hot and capable girlfriend who is upstairs. Even though I only saw her for all of a minute from afar, she's looking like hot shit. Why are you not ringing in the new year by her side?"

"I told her I would be upstairs at five to."

"So you're ten minutes early, give her a taste of her own medicine."

"You good to wrap this thing up, then? I doubt I'm coming back down."

"Gosh, if you came back downstairs, I think I'd lose it. Or maybe think that you had lost it. I'll be fine closing things down. I'll rope Teddy into it. I would have followed that woman upstairs the moment she went."

"You're not factoring in the fact that she needs to process some things alone, like that her current boyfriend held a civil conversation with her ex-boyfriend and instead of making her come to her own party, the current boyfriend told her to go back upstairs and read whatever book she is desperate to finish."

Maxxy smiled broadly.

"Which would have sent her into a tailspin because the ex-boyfriend would have carried her around like a trophy for a while. And he wouldn't have given her hours to brace herself for a party entry, either. Not when she was one of the hosts. You make me sick, Liam."

I laughed. "Why is that?"

"You really love her. And you understand her as well, and I want that. I've never been jealous of people in relationships, but you're making me feel sad and alone with your cute little love."

"Not to be that person, but it will come when you least expect it. I didn't know at the beginning of this month that I would be ending the year like this, and yet, here I am."

"I'll let you be that person because you make *my* best friend happy. Happy New Year, Liam." She raised her near-empty glass at me, I did the same.

"Happy New Year, Maxxy," I replied, kissing her on the cheek and then going upstairs.

It smelled like bread when I walked into the apartment.

"Len?" I called as I locked the door.

"Kitchen," she called back. When I walked into the

kitchen, she was leaning against one of the counters, holding a book in one hand and a timer in the other.

"Are you baking bread?" I asked just as the timer went off. She closed the book around her finger as she switched the timer for a tea towel and opened the oven, pulling out a bread tin and setting it on a cooling rack.

"No, I've baked some bread. Rosemary and olive," she said proudly.

"And you did that in this dress?" The idea of it was hotter than I was expecting.

"No, I've only just put the dress back on. I had a feeling you'd make your reappearance before five to, so I wanted to be prepared. I made the bread in my underwear."

I groaned.

"You told me that on purpose, didn't you?"

"Of course I did, Muller. How was the party when you left it?"

"It looked like everyone was bracing for the ringing in of a new year. They all seemed like they were having fun. I would say that your party is a success."

"How was Maxxy?" she asked casually, but with a hint of suspicion.

"She seemed fine just now."

"She's been spending more time with Teddy the last couple of weeks. Did he tell you that she spent Christmas with him and the family?"

I raised my eyebrow. "No, he did not. That's an interesting development."

"It is, right? She's being cagey about the details, but I'm thinking it will all work out in the end."

"I may have said something similar. Only I didn't realise that I was suggesting that it might all work out with Teddy. I think they'd be good together, though."

Lenny walked over to me and draped her arms over my shoulders, one hand still holding her book.

"You look beautiful, by the way. I didn't tell you earlier. But I am starting to think that I might be the only person who will ever see you in this dress." It was the one I bought on Christmas Eve Eve.

"This dress and your jerseys. What a range of 'for your eyes only' outfits I am acquiring. You're looking very dapper, yourself. Black dress shirts are definitely your thing." Her fingers traced around the collar.

"Len, I'm going to need you to put that book down in a safe place and then wrap your legs around my waist. And don't you dare tell me you can't because of my shoulder. I'm walking you to bed, not up a mountain."

Lenny huffed a breath before she closed the book and set it on a counter. She jumped and I assisted her in settling around my waist. I could feel the wet heat of her against my shirt.

"Are you bare under this dress, Alana?"

Her eyes sparkled under the kitchen lights.

"Do you want to know what else I have been doing while you've been downstairs being a sociable person?"

I buried my head in the crook of her neck and nipped at the skin there.

"I don't think I do, but go on, tell me."

"I have spent the last however many hours getting myself right to the edge and then stopping. I still don't know how you managed to play like that. I feel like my skin is on fire. Anyway, underwear became uncomfortable, so I took them off just after I put that bread in the oven."

I groaned.

"Yeah, I was right, I didn't want to know. I've been schmoozing downstairs, and you've been playing with your pretty pussy and getting it all wet and ready for me. I would have immediately followed you upstairs if I knew that was what your evening was going to entail."

Although something tells me if I had, it would have been me on the receiving end of the edging because Lenny was mean like that.

"Nah, this evening went exactly the way it was supposed to go. There is a button pressed against my clit right now that might get me over the edge if I shift even a little bit. So, dealer's choice, how do you want me?"

"Do you think you can come more than once?"

"I think I might just have one really good one in me tonight."

"In that case, I wanna feel you come around my cock." I clung to her thighs tighter.

Lenny reached down and grabbed my cock through my trousers, squeezing me, and laughed when I shuddered under the touch.

"Someone is happy to be here," she said.

"I'm happy whenever you are around, Len."

"You are such a fucking sap. Now be a good boy and rail me into a new year."

I laughed. "Is that what getting all your New Year midnights means from now on? Railing you into new years?"

"What could be better, Muller?" She squeezed me again. Distantly, I heard a countdown start from ten.

"Absolutely nothing, Lenny."

Five, four, three, two, one.

"Happy New Year, Liam."

"Happy New Year, Al—"

She cut me off with a kiss, which I didn't break until I laid her on her bed and gave her exactly what she asked for.

Forty Five

LIAM

"This isn't as bad as I thought it would be," Lenny said as she took in the aftermath of the party.

It looked like Maxxy had started the cleanup. Although balloons sagged from the ceiling and bottles were strewn everywhere, bunting and streamers were piled in two corners of the room. There were half-empty black bags filled with empty cups and any leftover food had already been removed.

"We're going to have to get Max a thank-you gift for starting the cleanup. I imagine there are better things she could have been doing in the early hours of a new year," she said, picking up a black bag and ramming a pile of streamers into it.

"You might need to get Teddy one as well. She mentioned that she might rope him into helping her."

Lenny stopped halfway through throwing more streamers away and threw me a look.

"Well, find out if he helped and I will add him to the list. Just need to figure out what says, 'Thanks for throwing food out at midnight so my bakery doesn't get rats because I was riding my boyfriend into oblivion.'"

I snorted. "I'm sure you'll think of something. You've always been good at giving people gifts," I said as I picked up a bag of my own and collected bottles.

"Wolf keychains not included," she joked.

I pulled my keys out of my pocket and waved the keychain about. I'd added it immediately. It was the only keychain I had on my keys.

"I happen to love wolf keychains."

Lenny studied my keys.

"It looks good, I'll give you that. Why do you have four sets of keys?"

I should have figured that she would notice that. Lenny noticed everything.

"I was going to wait a couple more days before talking about this, but I can't tell you why I have four sets of keys without playing my hand, so…One set is for my house here, one set is for my parents' house, and the other is for your parents' house."

She expected those three, though.

"And the fourth?" she prompted.

I took a deep breath.

"You told me I should get used to seeing that very logo," I pointed to the back wall behind her where it was printed in a coffee brown, "around Westchester once upon a time. You also have had your heart set on a very particular shop front for at least half of your life. The fourth set are the keys to that."

Her fingers started playing with her thumb ring. "Why the hell do you have them?"

I was only ninety per cent certain that she wouldn't run. She might give me shit. Or shut down for a moment. She might leave me to clean up the rest of the carcass from this party and go for a walk, but I was pretty sure she wouldn't run if I told her the truth.

"I have them because I am the landlord," I said quietly.

"And how long have you been the landlord?" she asked, her voice cracking, and I noticed her eyes were glossy.

"I went home for a week the summer I turned pro, and it was for sale. I had just received my signing bonus and, well, on the day my blades touched the ice for the first time professionally, I also became the owner of that particular space."

"You would have been—"

"Twenty-two. I've owned it for nearly nine years. Ten months in, there was interest in renting it out, but Rob mentioned when I was home that you were staying in Detroit to make your bakery dreams come true there, so I rented it out. That business moved out just after I retired and someone else showed interest almost immediately, once it was vacated, but something told me to hold out just a little while longer. So I did. Then I bumped into you at the airport."

She was quiet for a while. But she wasn't running, which was a good sign.

"You bought me a fucking shop?" A tear ran down her cheek.

"If you want it. Then yes, it's yours."

"But what about here? What about you?"

"This brings me to the second thing I wanted to talk to you about. Your dad offered me a job. Assistant coach, starting next season. So, that's an option for me. But I am in a very fortunate position where I am not under any huge pressure to figure out my next steps. Suspicious amount of money, remember?"

She laughed, wetly. "Do you want to do that? Coach?"

This wasn't about me.

"Can you run two bakeries in different cities?"

"Well, yeah it's always been the dream, but it's a lot of work and I've never been able to figure out the costs or the logistics."

I dropped my bin bag and walked over to her, placing my hands on her shoulders.

"If you sat down and figured it out, you could make it work, right? You don't need a location anymore. I know a guy who can give you a really good rate on a unit."

She laughed again.

"Opening a bakery next to Westchester Bakes is career-ending. It will die before it even gets off the ground."

"I remember someone telling me that their bakery would offer different things to Bakes, which is why it would work. Westchester would have *all* its baked goods needs met if you rocked up too."

She smiled. I wiped the tears off her cheeks and cupped her face in my hands.

"You didn't answer my question. Do you want to coach? I'm not hypothetically moving to Westchester if there's nothing for you there."

"You'd be there. I go where you go. If you wanna stay here, then we'll stay here. If you wanna open a new site back home, we'll go there. I go where you go, Alana. So where do you want to go?"

Epilogue

ALANA

18 MONTHS LATER

Frankly, it was obscene.

And deeply unnecessary.

I had been staring off into space while my coffee brewed, thinking about all the things that could possibly go wrong tonight when he had joined me in the kitchen.

Wearing only his boxers and, for reasons unknown, his skates over one of his shoulders. He looked indecent. All sleep soft with pillow creases embedded into his cheekbones, his hair an artful mess. Forever thick thighs and strong arms. The skates on his shoulder were a reminder that he could still be lethal if he got onto that ice in a competitive manner, which was making him even sexier.

I watched him out of the corner of my eye while I dumped my V60 in the sink and picked up my coffee. He was pulling things together for his breakfast like it was normal to just roll out of bed and throw a pair of skates over your shoulder.

"What the fuck are you doing?" I asked once I had taken a sip of my coffee.

"There she is," he laughed.

My eyebrows drew together. "There who is?"

"You. You were all in your head and I needed something that would drag you out of it. Come on, let's hear it," he said as he gestured down at his body.

"You look ridiculous."

He smiled. "What else?"

"And you look like Mr. December."

"Oh, now there is an idea. You know, I might give you a calendar that is nothing but me for Christmas. Then you can always stare at me."

"We live together. I can stare at you all I want already," I pointed out.

"You could if you actually came home." He pouted and became even sexier. I hated him.

"I've been sleeping above the bakery for barely two weeks and besides, you've been here, there, and everywhere with your hockey stuff so it's not like we would have been seeing much of each other anyway."

Liam did everything he could to make the new site mirror the set-up in Detroit, which included an apartment over the bakery. Mostly because he didn't like me walking home late at night, even though our house was less than fifteen minutes away. If he was home though, he would make that walk all the time.

"Hockey stuff. Just inspiring the next generation of ice hockey players. No big deal."

"Getting a lot of mothers interested in hockey as well, I bet," I half muttered.

"They are interested for all of five minutes, and then they either get over it or notice my left hand."

He waved his left hand around, showing off a silver band nestled on his ring finger, like I wasn't aware that it was there. We weren't married. When we had a conversation about marriage, it became abundantly clear that we were both stubborn about the whole getting married to each other thing. Being told it was inevitable from a young age made us both determined to never do it. We could be in love and live together and all that shit, but we couldn't get married.

However, Liam learned something that I had known for a while—a ring got people off your back a lot quicker than just saying that you had a partner. So, he started wearing one.

Liam took his skates off and hung them over the island chairs.

"I didn't risk cutting a nipple off for you to go back into your head. What do you need?"

I put my coffee on the island and wrapped my arms around him. His arms held me tightly and I sunk into his warmth.

"This is a good start," I mumbled against his skin.

"It's gonna be fine. This is a soft launch full of people who love you, and then on Monday, when you open to the public, they will flock to it just like they did in Detroit. We've got hockey teams here too. They can keep you in business."

"No one can keep me in business in the way that Teddy can," I joked.

"He'll be there today. I'll try to stop him from buying up everything. But back to you, today is going to be fine. You picked this location because you knew it would work. You have great products and the best damn brownies in the world. You're gonna be fine. And if it goes to shit, which it won't, there will be other opportunities."

"Can you put the skates back on over your shoulder and go to the launch party looking like that? I think that would help." I felt the rumble of his laugh through his chest.

"That is for your eyes only. And the eyes of the people who get my calendar."

"You're not serious about the calendar, are you?" If he was, there would be no other eyes but mine that see it.

"You did all the extra photography for the yearbook, right? You're good with a camera. Can you imagine how much fun we could have with some underwear, sexy positions, and body oil?"

Suddenly I had an idea. "You got anything to do today before tonight?"

"No, I'm here for you."

I teased a finger across the hem of the back of his boxers.

"It's technically game day, right?"

I felt him start to stiffen against me.

"It can be game day if you want." His voice was deeper than normal. That rich, honey drip that made my whole body tingle.

I smiled to myself as I slipped both hands under his boxers and palmed his ass. He moaned.

"It's game day, baby. Can you go get on the bed? Keep the underwear on. And don't worry, I'll probably let you come before we leave."

"Are you telling me that there is a chance you are going to keep me on edge for hours and still not let me come?" He sounded both pained and excited.

"It's a small chance, but yeah, a chance."

I was going to let him come. Probably more than once. I was so sure we could get him to five. I could already feel the stress of tonight melt away as he handed power over to me.

"I'm gonna get my own back for this, at a time when you have a little less on and I'm not going to summer hockey camps every other week. I just want you to know that."

I pressed a quick kiss to his lips.

"I look forward to you trying," I whispered before I let him go and do what I asked.

Sweet Nothing: Westchester had a line out the door on the first Monday that we opened.

Bonus Scene

Want to read Alana making Liam's locker room fantasy (sort of) come true?

Get the bonus scene here:

Acknowledgments

No joke, it feels like the first thing I should thank here is *The Kiss Quotient* by Helen Hoang for being the thing that made it abundantly clear that the writer I am is, in fact, a romance one. The signs have always been there but that book really unlocked something in me.

Second, go me for actually doing this. This book was a random idea that wouldn't leave me alone and became a safe haven for me while I lived in query limbo, a place that battered my self esteem. When I floated the idea of self-publishing this book at the beginning of the year, I didn't actually think I would go through with it. I didn't tell anyone I was even thinking about it so that no one could hold me accountable. But the fact that you are at the acknowledgments section of this book means I did. And I am terrible at acknowledging when I actually achieve things and so I am proud of myself for this.

This would, however, not have been possible without Laura, who is the greatest cheerleader/editor to have in my corner. Really didn't see the biggest point of contention being whether or not I could get away with using the word 'knickers'. And I still think about that brownie falling to the floor often. It's still so sad!

Emilie, an equally great cheerleader (and for a hot minute one of the only people that I could go off with headcanons about the way these two would intertwine Twilight into their everyday conversations).

Thanks to Sam for creating the actual cover of my dreams.

It was that image that started it all and to see it come to life so beautifully is everything and more.

Almost every word of this book was drafted, edited, and edited again (and again) in a *London Writer's Salon* Writers Hour session. Fifty focused minutes alone but somehow together is a kind of alchemy I will never quite understand but will be eternally grateful for. This book (and future ones) would not exist without those sessions.

Social media gets a bad rep (in a lot of ways, rightfully so, it is WILD in those streets) but it did give me a bunch of people who are in my orbit from their own little corners of the internet and that has made this thing a lot less lonely. Especially on the days when I just want to call the whole thing off.

To the Glinda to my Elphaba (aka, my person) I truly have been changed for the better because I know you and I am having the time of my life fighting dragons with you. Thanks for appearing next to me out of nowhere (from across the classroom of a lesson that we had shared for...I want to say a year by that point) all those years ago, and thanks for answering all my random creative questions with no hesitation.

To my parents, for putting a book in my hands when I was young and then always putting them in my hands until I could do it myself (and wow, have I filled the house with books). I would never have even thought of being a writer if I wasn't a reader first. And finally, to my brother, for saying 'when' and not 'if'.

About the Author

Sophie Thomas is a Londoner, writer and reader.

She breaks the rules of grammar far too often for someone with an English degree.

When she's not coming up with ideas on her hot girl walks or sitting in a theatre watching a musical she enjoys getting people to fall in love and kiss each other (and get secret tattoos for one another).

Also by Sophie Thomas

Detroit Panthers

Looks Real Good Now

Marry Me A Little

The Love You Want

Summer of Love

Change My Mind

Road to the Olympics Series

Play the Game